SHADOW
OF A
HERO

SHADOW OF A HERO

PETER DICKINSON

Delacorte  **Press**

Published by
Delacorte Press
Bantam Doubleday Dell Publishing Group, Inc.
1540 Broadway
New York, New York 10036

This work was first published in Great Britain in 1994 by Victor Gollancz Ltd.

The trademark Delacorte Press® is registered in
the U.S. Patent and Trademark Office.

Book design by Joseph Rutt

Library of Congress Cataloging in Publication Data

Dickinson, Peter
    Shadow of a hero / by Peter Dickinson.
        p.   cm.
    Summary: In 1989, Letta, an English teenager, learns of her heritage from her
grandfather, great-grandson of the legendary hero of Varina, as he becomes
involved in the nationalistic political struggles in Eastern Europe.
    ISBN 0-385-32110-4
    [1. Grandfathers—Fiction.   2. Europe, Eastern—History—Fiction.
3. Nationalism—Fiction.]   I. Title.
PZ7.D562Sh   1994
[Fic]—dc20   94-8667   CIP   AC

Manufactured in the United States of America

November 1994

10 9 8 7 6 5 4 3 2 1

BVG

SHADOW
OF A
HERO

LEGEND

Naming the Hero

In the days when the Turks ruled Varina there was a farmer of Talosh who had one son and one daughter. Then a second son was born, and when this child was four months old the farmer and his wife left their elder children in the care of an aunt and set out for Potok, so that the child might be brought good fortune by being given his name by the Bishop Supreme in the Cathedral of St. Joseph on the Feast of St. Valia.

As they passed over the shoulder of Mount Athur a great storm arose and they were forced to take shelter in a cave, where came also for refuge a young priest, a bandit,[1] and a scholar. The storm did not abate, so they saw they would all have to spend the night where they were. The farmer's wife, being a prudent woman, had packed good stores and was able to cook them a meal, but there was an old feud between the clans of the bandit and the scholar and when they had drunk a little wine these two began to quarrel. The scholar's tongue was very sharp, and there might well have been murder done if the priest had not threatened both men with an implacable curse if they failed to hold their peace. When the time came to sleep he lay down between them, so that neither should harm the other.

Next morning the storm raged still more fiercely, and the farmer and his wife wept at the knowledge that it was now the Feast of St. Valia and they would miss the naming mass, and the child lose his fortune. But the priest said, "I will name the boy. My name is Father Pango, and before he is a grown man I myself will be Bishop Supreme. Moreover this mountain is the heart of Varina, as much as any cathedral. All that is done in Potok is done with the will and consent of the Turks, but here on the mountain we are a free people. So let these two gentlemen stand sponsor, for neither a scholar nor a bandit calls any man master. And the child's fortune shall be this, that he shall live to see Varina a free nation."

So it was agreed, and while the mountain shook with the storm they named the child Restaur Vax.

After that, the woman cooked the naming feast and they ate and drank in fellowship, and fell to wondering what life the child might have, since his elder brother would inherit the father's farm.

"He has a good forehead," said the scholar. "I think he will lead a life of writing and study."

"He has sturdy arms," said the bandit. "He will lead a life of valor and of battle."

"I see wisdom in his eyes," said the priest. "I think he will serve his people and his God."

So to settle the matter the scholar took his seal ring and the bandit took a silver buckle from his coat and the priest took an amber bead from his rosary and they tied them over the blanket where the child lay, to see which he should choose. But when the child saw them glinting in the firelight he laughed with pleasure, and with one sure movement put up his hands and grasped all three.

======

1. *In both Formal and Field Varinian the word* bandit *has a range of meanings, from armed highway robber to patriotic rebel. Since one man might well be both robber and rebel, this reflects the historical facts.*

When Letta was born she was much the youngest in the family. Her two brothers were already grown up, and she had a nephew who was three months older than she was. At least now she had a niece, Donna, who was only two and a half.

Letta's brothers had been born far away in Varina, but she was born in England, in the Royal Hampshire County Hospital at the top of the hill in Romsey Road, Winchester. She knew it well, because Momma drove past it every Saturday morning on her way to Sainsbury's, the supermarket, so when she was small she used to imagine that Varina was another place like the Royal, a huge, muddled brick building with old parts and new parts, a place for babies to get born into and sometimes go back to be measured and tested and be given horrible injections and lied to about how brave they were, but mostly to wait, and wait, and wait.

Even when she was older and understood that Varina was a

whole piece of country (though to confuse things it was also pieces of three other countries) about the size of Hampshire, parts of the hospital picture still popped up in her picture of it. She knew there were real mountains in Varina, with snow on them half the year round, and blazing hot summers, and brown-faced women in black dresses driving donkeys with huge baskets of maize on either side, and things like that, very very foreign, but then the blanks spaces would fill up with doctors in white coats, and nurses with syringes, and waiting rooms where you sat for hours, and the ordinary people had worried, unhappy looks on their faces, and nobody told you what was happening.

One morning, later still—she must have been twelve—she told her grandfather about this, because she thought it might amuse him, and also waste a little of the Formal Varinian lesson he gave her on Sundays, after breakfast. He put the tips of his fingers together. Two of them were missing on his left hand, but you could almost see their ghosts where they pressed against their right-hand opposites. He looked at her over his fingertips and wrinkled up his forehead.

"You saw more truly than you know," he said.

"What do you mean?"

"Varina is like that these days. Ah well, let us get on. Where were we? Conditional optatives, I think."

There were two Varinian languages, Field and Formal. Letta had talked Field for as long as she'd talked English. She'd never had to think about it. That was what it was for, talking, and writing letters and so on. Letta was talking Field with Grandad now. Formal was for poems, and important speeches, and serious books. It had words in it which nobody ever said except at times like funerals, and weird grammar too. Who needs the negative passive conditional optative, for heaven's sake?

Grandad seemed to hear the question in her sigh.

"How I used to hate these," he said. "My desk was by the window, and I could see the hillside above my father's farm. We were beaten for every mistake. I had many beatings that year. You are a far better scholar than ever I was, my darling."

"I mean, what are they for?" said Letta. "If ever I get to Varina I'm not going to go to the supermarket and—hang on while I work it out—when I get to the checkout with all this stuff in my basket and then I find I've left my purse at home, I'm not going to say 'Would that my purse had not been left behind!' Am I?"

"You would not find a supermarket in Varina, and if there were one you would find almost nothing on the shelves to fill your basket."

"Really? But . . . Anyway, just suppose . . ."

"First you must express the wish for me in Formal."

"Oh, hell. *Fayaletu bijon?*"

"*Fayo* is a weak irregular deponent, remember. And you must modify the noun."

"Hell and hell! Let's see . . . *Gefayaleto* . . . no, *Gefayalento bijoñ?*"

"Well done. You had bad luck choosing *fayo*. We used to call it the pig verb. Now, suppose you found this supermarket and suppose you were able to fill your basket and suppose there were any chance of your having the money to pay for what you had bought, and suppose you then said to the checkout clerk—if such a creature were conceivable in Varina—*Gefayalento bijoñ*, why, she would certainly burst out laughing."

"What's the point, then?"

"The point is not to bury a great treasure beyond human reach. For instance, my great-grandfather, your great-great-great-grandfather, when he was in exile in Rome, wrote a poem retelling one of our stories about a feud between two families over a piece of mountain pasture. At the end of it a father finds the bodies of his three sons, killed in an ambush. He stands on the mountain track and thinks about the disputed field. He sees it in his mind, after the snow melts, the swathes of bright mountain flowers with the sweet new grass springing between. The last line of the poem is a single word. *Anastrondaitu.* Can you tell me what that means?"

"Is it *strondu* with the twiddly bits?"

"Yes."

" 'If only it had not been remembered,' then?"

"Yes, and no. Yes, because that is what it literally means. No, because as a single word, complex but exact, coming after the simple words describing the pasture, it pierces right to the heart with its loss and grief. My darling, I would never force you to learn Formal. It is no use unless you genuinely want to."

"But I do!"

This was old stuff. The family had argued it through and through. Momma had been against the idea, because she said it was a waste of time when Letta should be doing English schoolwork, and Letta—partly to please Grandad, partly because she thought it might be interesting, but mainly to get her own way with Momma about something—had insisted she did want to learn Formal, and Poppa, who usually kept out of arguments between his wife and his father-in-law, had this time taken Letta's side. It would be difficult for her to back out now. Besides, whatever he said, Grandad would have been desperately hurt. Again, he seemed to read her thought.

"It is not for you or for me," he said. "It is somehow for all mankind. If there is nobody left in the world whom the single word *anastrondaitu* can pierce to the heart, then a great treasure will have become buried beyond human reach. Well now, enough of that. No, one thing more. It is for you too. It is more than a treasure. It is life itself. I have survived experiences which, if it had not been for this thing"—and he tapped the worn old grammar book with the two fingers of his left hand—"would either have killed me or driven me mad. Oh, may you never have the same need, my darling! Now we must get on."

Letta was too astonished to work well. Grandad never spoke about what had been done to him. If anyone asked what had happened to his hand he would glance at it and say "Frostbite" and change the subject. Occasionally strangers came to visit him. They talked to him in his room, and after they'd gone he usually seemed a bit depressed. Once Letta had asked who they were and he'd said they'd been policemen, just checking that he still wasn't plotting to assassinate the Queen. That had been one of his unsmiling jokes, of course, but it had also a way of telling her he didn't want to be asked.

What did she know about him, really? Not much, though she felt closer to him than anyone else in the family, and he seemed to feel the same. "We arrived together," he used to say, meaning that in the same week she'd been born he'd been allowed out of Varina to join his daughter in England. And they were the two who were mostly at home. Poppa was a road engineer, always flying around the world to advise on tricky bits of highway building, and Momma worked for IBM outside Winchester and often didn't get home till late.

But there was more to their closeness than that. Letta was pretty well certain that she'd been born by accident. After all,

Momma had been getting on forty, with a really good job, and a grandchild on the way, when she'd got pregnant. And it was the same with Grandad. Nobody'd ever really expected the Communists would let him out, though there'd been a terrific campaign, and Momma must have been really happy when it happened, still, now she'd got this old man to think about as well as the baby . . . Momma was a perfectly good mother. She did everything she was supposed to, and took trouble over it, but somehow there was a sort of barrier between her and Letta. They didn't touch or hug much, or talk about things that mattered. Letta felt closer to her eldest brother, Steff, whom she saw only four or five times a year, than she did to Momma. And Poppa was away too much for her to get to know him well, either, if you could. She wasn't sure about that either. So Grandad was the person who mattered most in her life. They shared a sort of outsidishness, accidentalness, not-quite-fittingness as members of the family. They didn't talk about any of this, but Letta was pretty sure that Grandad knew about it and felt it too.

But what else? Last birthday he'd been eighty-one. And years before that, when he was still almost a young man, he'd been Prime Minister of Varina for a fortnight "because I had the same name as my great-grandfather." Another of his jokes. He never said any more about it than that. Then the Communists had taken over and put him in prison, and he'd stayed there over thirty years. He never talked about that either. Today was the first time Letta had heard him even hint at it.

About twenty minutes later he sighed and closed the grammar.

"Neither of us is paying attention," he said.

"I'm sorry, but . . ."

"We are both thinking of other things. It's my fault. I

should not have talked about the past. What shall we do
instead?"

"Well, there's the goat boy book. We never finished that."
Grandad made a face.

"I think we can spare ourselves that," he said.

Letta had done her first lessons from the book, which was
even more battered than the grammar, simple stories written
years and years ago for children to start learning Formal, but
whoever had written it—she was called Anya Orestes,
Grandad said, though the title page was missing—didn't
seem to have had much idea what children are interested in, so
the stories were the worst kind of soppy-pretty, and boring
with it.

"Couldn't you read me the poem about the blood feud? I'm
sure I'd understand some of it."

"Not enough, and that would spoil it for both of us. Let's
try one of these. They're still a bit beyond you. I was keeping
them for later."

"What are they?"

"The Legends. A collection of folk tales about the War of
Independence. We Varinians are great storytellers, you know,
but for us the story is far more important than the truth. Years
ago, before the war, I was walking in the mountains and an
old shepherd told me a story about a bandit, or hero—the
word he used means both things—who was trapped in a cave
by his enemies—the shepherd showed me the cave—and because they were afraid to fight him in the dark, with the light
behind them, they had built a great fire at the cave entrance to
suffocate him. But rather than die like that he had charged
out through the flames and with his clothing all on fire had
fallen on his enemies and slain them and then died himself."

"How horrible."

"Stories of heroism tend to be horrible as soon as you think about them. Well, I slept that night at a village in the valley. A traveling film show was set up, showing a Western of some sort, silent, which ended in exactly the way my friend had described."

"You mean he was lying?"

"Not exactly. He had seen the film and been struck by the episode, so he had made it part of his landscape. Now for him it was true. Well, these legends are of that nature. There are varying levels of—ah, let's call it creativity in them. But there are also notes pointing out some of the more outrageous falsehoods. I find the language rather stilted, even by Formal standards, but I think you will find the stories amusing."

"Are there any about Restaur Vax? Not you, I mean—the old one. Steff used to tell me them, but I don't really remember."

"That is what they are. Legends are about heroes and heroines and villains, so this is the history of the War of Independence as if almost the only people who fought in it were Restaur Vax and Lash the Golden and Selim Pasha. Let's see . . . ah, yes, I'm afraid the first one is missing. See what you make of this."

Letta took the book. It was almost falling to bits, and the paper was the color of brown bread, covered with small, cramped print. At the top of the left-hand page was the end of a sentence, something to do with a baby laughing, followed by an almost unreadably tiny footnote. A new story started opposite. *Restaur Vax and . . .*

"What's *opiscu?*" she said.

"Drop the *o* and turn the *c* into a *zh.*"

"Oh, yes, of course. 'Restaur Vax and the Bishop.' Is that Bishop Pango?"

"In the Legends all bishops are Bishop Pango, all heroes are Restaur or Lash the Golden, all enemies are Turks, and all traitors are Greeks, Serbs, Romanians, or Bulgars. The world is a simple place, in legends."

LEGEND

RESTAUR VAX AND THE BISHOP: I

Bishop Pango[1] was a proud, proud man. On his left hand he wore three rings, and on his right five. He knew more Latin than the Pope and more Greek than the Patriarch.[2] When he came to the seminary the young men who were studying to be priests were brought before him, one by one, so that he could test them and know their worth.

Last of all Restaur Vax stood before him, and the Bishop tested him with a hard question. Restaur Vax answered him perfectly.

"Good," said the Bishop. "We will make you a priest."

"I would sooner fight the Turks," said Restaur Vax.

The Bishop frowned, and tested him with a harder question. Again Restaur Vax answered him perfectly.

"Good," said the Bishop. "When you have done being a priest, we will make you a bishop."

"I would sooner fight the Turks," said Restaur Vax.

The Bishop frowned and bit his lip and tested him with the

hardest question he knew. For the third time Restaur Vax answered perfectly.

"Good," said the Bishop. "When I myself am taken hence you will sit on my throne."

"I would sooner fight the Turks," said Restaur Vax.

"How can you fight the Turks?" said the Bishop. "Seven hundred years they have been our masters. You have neither sword nor gun nor horse. You had far best be a priest."

"Without sword or horse or gun I will fight the Turks," said Restaur Vax.

The Bishop took a ring from his left hand.

"With this you may buy yourself a sword," he said.

He took two rings from his left hand.

"With these you may buy yourself a gun," he said.

He took four rings—all but his great bishop's ring—from his right hand.

"With these you may buy yourself the best horse in the mountains," he said. "Now I have nothing to give you but my blessing. Go and fight the Turks."

———

1. *Pango XIV (1766–1850), Bishop Supreme of Varina from 1818 and Prince-Bishop from 1829. During the period leading up to the War of Independence he was more than once arrested by the Turkish authorities on suspicion of support for nationalist leaders, but released because of popular unrest and international pressure. The nature of his support for nationalist ideals remains unclear. He may well have examined the young Restaur Vax for the priesthood.*
2. *The National Church of Varina was, and remains, unique. At the Great Schism of 1054 it announced its allegiance to both Rome and Byzantium, accepting Pope and Patriarch as equal spiritual*

heads. Both major Churches pronounced the Varinian compromise heretical, but with characteristic obstinacy the Church of Varina still insists that it accepts only the joint authority. The authority is theoretical. In practice it goes its own way.

AUTUMN 1989

It must have been high summer when they started reading the Legends, the summer before the demo outside the Romanian Embassy. Their house was halfway up the hill, and Grandad's room was at the top, at the back, so from his window you could see right down over Winchester, with the green tops of the trees poking up between the rain-washed slates, and the squat tower of the cathedral dim in the valley.

Letta remembered that because Grandad had talked about staring out of his schoolroom window at the hillside above his father's farm, and she had imagined its sun-baked brown harshness and the difference from what she was actually seeing had struck her. Then there had been the summer holidays, and then things had begun to change.

It started with several visits, three at least, from the men Grandad called "the policemen." She knew because he was tired, and told her it was from having to talk English. His English was fluent, but with a thick, gravelly accent and a quaint way of twisting sentences inside out. After one of the visits he said, "I find the American accent particularly hard to attend to."

Another time Momma told Letta to be sure to take her key to school as Grandad would be out when she got home. She happened to be at the window and saw the car drive up. A very tall blond young man got out and opened the passenger door for Grandad and helped him up the front steps. Letta met them at the door. Grandad said, "This is my granddaughter, Letta," and the man gave a quick smile that didn't mean anything and said, "Hi, Letta. Then you're in good hands, sir," and ran down the steps.

Letta made a pot of tea, but when she took it up she found Grandad in bed, in his shirtsleeves, making notes on a clipboard. He thanked her and stopped work to drink and nod and smile while she chatted, mostly about her friend Angel's latest absurdities. When he gave her the cup back he said, "When Momma comes home, would you ask her if she can spare me a few minutes?"

Letta did, but the few minutes was still going on an hour later. Part of Momma's way of proving to herself that she wasn't sacrificing her family to her job was to see that there was a proper cooked supper. Even if it was just her and Letta, because Poppa was away and Grandad was tired and only wanted a snack in his room, there'd be at least two courses and sometimes three, hot and ready at eight o'clock, but that evening Letta realized it wasn't going to happen so she made scrambled eggs and took a tray up. Momma and Grandad hadn't been having one of their fights, she realized as soon as she went in. It was too serious for that.

Momma looked vaguely at the scrambled eggs, then pulled herself together and said, "Oh, thank you, Letta. Well done.

Got something for yourself? Be a saint and put the stuff in my basket in the fridge, will you?"

Grandad just raised a hand and smiled tiredly at her as she left. Letta didn't mind. It meant she could read while she ate, and she had a mountain of homework still to do.

Next afternoon she got home and found men putting a telephone into Grandad's room, which meant he had to come downstairs for tea and she did the crumpets in the toaster, instead of the proper way on a toasting fork in front of his gas fire. (Grandad used to say, "When all England's triumphs and mistakes are forgotten, mankind will still owe her four price-less gifts—bread sauce to go with turkey, steak-and-kidney pudding, marmalade, and hot buttered crumpets.")

"What's going on?" said Letta. "I mean, a telephone! You hate telephones, and anyway you get about three calls a year."

"The world is falling apart. This is a minor symptom of its collapse."

"The world's been falling apart ever since I can remember. At least once a month. Then they have a summit . . ."

"No more summits," said Grandad. "It takes two equal world powers to compose a summit . . ."

"They must have forgotten to tell Mount Everest."

"No doubt that is why Mount Everest is still there. But soon the U.S.S.R. will cease to exist. China is permanently contemplating the chaos in its own navel. With whom can the U.S. President hold a summit?"

"Do you mean he's going to start calling you up instead? Is it a hot line? Can I have a go? There are a lot of things I'm aching to tell him."

"Fortunately for his peace of mind it is not a hot line. If you would be kind enough to stuff your mouth with crumpet so that you can't interrupt, I will tell you what is going on. The

Eastern Bloc is falling apart. It seemed like a great unshakable slab of stone, but it is cracking into separate pieces. At the moment everybody in the West is very happy about this. They think they have won the Cold War, and soon instead of the dreadful old Communist enemy there are going to be a lot of nice friendly democratic nations to trade with. But, my darling, they are going to be disappointed. First, because democracy takes a lot of practice, and there isn't time for that. Second, because there is no money, and soon there will be no food. And third, because the crumbling of the great bloc is not going to stop when the nations you see in your atlas have separated from each other. You see, most of those nations are not nations at all, but are themselves composed of a number of smaller nations . . ."

"Like Varina?"

"We are smaller than most, but still we are a nation. Small nations have long memories. There are three things, my darling, which bind people into a nation—the place they live, though they may share it with others; the language they speak, though they may also speak the language of their rulers; and their memories, which are theirs alone.

"What do they remember? They remember their victories and their wrongs, but not of course their defeats and the wrongs that they themselves have done. In effect they remember chiefly their enemies. Sometimes those enemies are big and distant conquerors, like the Turks in the Legends or the Germans in my own lifetime, but mostly their ancient enemies are other small nations, just across the border, with whom there have been cattle raids and blood feuds and wife snatchings for generation after generation back and forth.

"Now these small nations are going to bring their memories out and patch and repair and renew them and parade them up and down, all their victories which tell them they can conquer, all their wrongs which tell them to trust none but themselves. Czechoslovakia will fall apart, Yugoslavia will fall apart, the U.S.S.R. will fall into twenty fragments, and the Eastern Bloc, that great slab, will have become not the pieces of shaped stone which the West was hoping to use, but a heap of pebbles. Discontented pebbles, because after all the upheavals they will have nothing that they want, not wealth, not comfort, not peace, not plenty, nothing. Nothing but their nationhood. Think. A heap of infuriated pebbles. That is the future of Eastern Europe."

"Us too? Varina?"

"Ah, we are the center of the universe, of course."

"We're the center of *our* universe. I mean, everyone is, to themselves, I think . . . Oh! Are they giving you a telephone because they want you to do something? They aren't going to make you go back! Please don't. I'll be miserable without you. I suppose I shouldn't say that, if you want to, but it's true!"

"And I should be miserable without you, my darling. Between us we will do our best to resist their idiot demands."

"Can't you tell them you're too old? I mean, you're terrific for eighty-one, but . . ."

"Of course I am far, far too old. In practical terms the idea is ridiculous. But it is not me they want, it is my name. If a waxwork dummy were called Restaur Vax, that would suit them as well. Better, perhaps. Even at eighty-one there is a danger that I may have ideas of my own."

"Of course you have."

"Occasionally, but I suppress them."

He shook his head, as if at somebody else's stupidity, and fell silent.

"Go on," she said. "If you want to, I mean. I'm really interested."

"I promised your mother I would not involve you in my political affairs."

"You aren't involving me. I'll involve myself if I want to, but I don't see how unless I know what's what."

"I suppose that is reasonable. Where were we?"

"Names. And suppressing ideas."

"Yes. A name, you see, has no ideas, and for most of my life I have been not myself but my name. Suppose your name were not Letta Ozolins but, say, Florence Nightingale or Margaret Thatcher or . . ."

"Kylie Minoghe?"

"A singer?"

"Sort of."

"Then people would think of you differently, wouldn't they? They'd expect you to sing, or to order people about, or to want to be a nurse. In my case they expected me to be a hero. My grandfather, you see, was both a rogue and a fool. He used the fact that he was Restaur Vax's son to make himself rich, and thus wasted his real inheritance, which was the family's name and honor. He then squandered what he had got, and had nothing to leave his son but one farm. My father named me Restaur Vax in the feeble hope that I would somehow restore the family honor. Already at school my name was a burden. People expected great things of me. I would have none of it, and chose to become a schoolmaster. I thought I had found a way to be myself.

"When the Germans invaded Yugoslavia to crush the Serbs, I was teaching at Virnu, in our western province—part of Yugoslavia, as you know. Being Varinians, we resisted the Germans, as we have always resisted invaders, though we had

no fondness for the Serbs. Whatever my name, I think I too
would have joined the Resistance, but before I could make up
my mind, men came to me saying 'We need you to lead us.'
Me? What did I know about fighting? But of course it wasn't
me they needed. It was my name. That is how I became a
Resistance leader.

"Before long our northern and southern provinces, in
Romania and Hungary, had joined us. Romania joined the
war on the German side and tried to conscript our men into
their army, to go and fight in Russia, but the men just ran
away into the hills and joined the Resistance. So soon we had
German troops in all three provinces, trying to control us.

"Varinians aren't easy to lead. Our national sport is the
blood feud. There were a dozen groups in the mountains,
often as eager to fight each other as the Germans. The only
name under which they would sometimes consent to cooperate
was that of Restaur Vax. So, nominally at least, I was accepted
as leader of the Resistance, and when peace came it was I
whom the Varinians expected to go to the victorious Allies
and tell them what we had done to ensure their victory, and in
their gratitude they would make us a separate nation again, all
three hundred thousand of us, as we used to be under the
Prince-bishopric, and had always been in our own minds. No
longer would we be ruled from Sofia and Belgrade and Bucharest. We would rule ourselves, from Potok.

"I knew roughly what was going to happen, though it was
far worse than even I had feared, but because of my name I
was forced to go. The Russians provided us with a safe conduct and an escort, but before we had gone a hundred miles
our escort was replaced. The new escort then arrested us. My
companions were shot, without trial, massacred beside the
road and buried in a clay pit, but because of my name, which

might possibly still be used to bargain with, I was kept alive. Eighteen years I spent in camps in Siberia . . ."

"Was that where you lost your fingers?"

"Yes, but not in fact from frostbite. There was a misunderstanding. It is not important. Where was I?"

"Eighteen years in Siberia. You don't have to tell me if you don't want to."

"I would like you to understand. Well, then, for reasons I still know nothing about I was sent back to Bulgaria and spent another twelve years in prison . . ."

"But it was better than Siberia?"

"Prison is prison. Physically it was, I suppose, better, but there was a spirit in the camps in Siberia, among the inmates, I mean—not all of them, of course—a sort of sullen undefeatability. I didn't find that in sleazy, deceitful Bulgaria. There! You see, in spite of all I know I am speaking and thinking like a Varinian peasant. Hatred and contempt for Bulgaria is in my bloodstream. Ah, well. At last my name came to my rescue. Very few people outside Varina have heard of Restaur Vax, though he was not merely our national hero but one of the great European poets. I mean that, my darling. This is not mere patriotism. He is fit to rank with Goethe and Byron and Victor Hugo, except that he wrote in a language known by only three hundred thousand people . . ."

"And anyway they speak Field most of the time."

"That too. Still, even the ignorant can respond to the notion of a hero-poet. Now his great-grandson, bearing the same name, once a fighter against Hitler, elected leader of his people, thirty years a prisoner of the Communists, etcetera, etcetera . . . My case was an easier cause to publicize than many just as deserving. I was in the end released as part of a trade deal, the British government of the time wishing to be able to

reply to critics who rightly said that they should not be having commercial dealings with the unspeakable Bulgarian regime. I was a bit of icing on the cake of commerce, allowing
them to claim that they had insisted on an increase in human
rights being part of the deal. About a dozen political prisoners
were released. Several thousand remained in prison. But because of my name I was one of those dozen. So, as with everything else in my life, it was my name that sent me to prison,
having saved me from being massacred by the roadside, and
my name that thirty years later released me again."

"And they want you to take it back to Varina now? Hey!
You could change it by deed poll. Angel's dad changed his
name because he wanted to be double-barreled."

Grandad smiled and shook his head.

"It is my name. I have grown to the shape of it," he said.
"Anyway, it has not yet come to that. Part of the deal under
which I was released was that the British government guaran-
teed the Bulgarians that I would not take part in political
activities."

"Is that what the policemen keep coming to see you
about?"

"Approximately."

"And they've changed their minds? Is this a different lot?
You said there was an American the other day."

"There are always people interested in fishing in troubled
waters. But what is mainly happening at the moment is that
the people I call the policemen have realized that none of the
three regimes which control Varina can last, and that many
Varinians will believe that the time has come to try once more
for independence. Inevitably, because of my name, and whatever the British government may have promised, they will
come to me, so the policemen have decided that they will have

more control of events if I am acting under their protection. I am seen as a moderating influence—a ridiculous concept in Varinian terms. We are not a moderate people. So they have allowed the main organization of Varinians in exile to provide me with a telephone—which the policemen will no doubt tap —and a part-time secretary."

"Wow! A beautiful spy!"

"May I be so fortunate. I was talking all this over with your momma last night."

"What did she say?"

"She didn't like it, of course. She has quite reasonably de- cided that her future is to forget her own roots and transplant herself here and grow fresh roots and become an English- woman. Still, in the end she said what Varinian women have had to say to their men for the past twelve centuries—'If you must go, you must go.' "

"Well, don't forget you've got to get my permission too."

"Of course."

"And I'm not going to give it."

"You forbid me to take part in any political activities?"

"Oh, no. That's all right. I'm talking about going. I'm not one of those stupid women who say 'If you must go, you must go.' "

"Go where?"

"Varina, of course. You can't go back and start politicking in Varina unless I can come too. All right?"

"I hear and obey."

Letta stuck out her chin and glared at him like all the tyrants who have ever sat on thrones.

"Good!" she said.

LEGEND

The Woman at the Avar Bridge

Restaur Vax came to the bridge over the Avar, and found it guarded by three *bazouks*[1] who took tolls from all who passed. This oppression had lasted many years.

"Little priestling, you must pay the toll," said the corporal of *bazouks*.

"This bridge was built by Count Axur,"[2] said Restaur Vax, "and he decreed it free for all to pass. That is the law."

"Count Axur is dead seven hundred years," said the corporal of *bazouks*. "Among the living, the law is our law."

"Not so," said Restaur Vax. "For I am going to send you to where you may beg an audience of Count Axur, and be instructed in matters of law by him."

He held his staff before him and the corporal of *bazouks* rushed forward and smote at him with his scimitar. But Restaur Vax parried the blow and with the afterstroke drove the butt of his staff into the *bazouk*'s stomach, and smote him with his knee as he fell forward, and thus stunned him. The other two *bazouks* then rushed at Restaur Vax but he ran to meet them on the crown of the bridge, where the passage was wide enough for only one, and the first one he smote with the butt of his staff and with his knee, as before, stunning him also, and when the second turned to run he followed him and felled him with a blow to the head. Then he picked up the three bodies and tossed them into the river, which carried them away. And he threw their weapons after them.

Then the woman who kept the inn by the bridge came to her door and said, "Why have you done this to me? You have slain three Turks at my door. I can run with my daughters to the hills, but the Turks will come and burn my roof in vengeance."

Restaur Vax, knowing she spoke the truth, said in his heart, "Somewhere I shall find myself a sword." He took from his wallet the first ring that the Bishop had given him, a ring of fine silver set with opals and garnets, and gave it to the woman, saying, "Take your goods and your daughters and hide in the mountains. Return when the Turks have gone, and sell this ring and buy timber and hire labor, and build your roof anew."

At that the woman blessed him and brought out bread and peaches and wine, and while he ate she said, "You are too fine a man to be a priest, and moreover my husband was an old man, and he died, so I am a widow.[3] I have three good fields on the mountain, and a sound hut, and twenty-seven sheep. You could do worse."

Restaur Vax looked her over. She was a handsome woman.

"It is a fair offer," he said. "One day I may return. But first I must go to fight the Turks."

"If you must go, you must go," said the woman.

She went into the house and brought out a sword which she had kept hidden among her roof beams.

"This was my husband's sword," she said. "It was his father's, and his father's before him. But my husband gave me only daughters, and it will be long before either of them bears a son, and longer still before he will wear it. Take it with my blessing, and fight the Turks."

Restaur Vax tested the sword, bending it across his knee, and it sprang singing back to straightness. So he put it through his belt, beneath his priest's gown, and thanked the woman and went on his way.

===

1. Bashi-bazouks *were Turkish irregulars, often indistinguishable from brigands. In Varinian,* bazouk *denoted any Turkish soldier of low rank.*

2. *Count Axur was the largely legendary last count of Varina, who is said to have resisted the Turkish conquest until his death in battle.*

3. *Like Orthodox priests, those of the Church of Varina are permitted to marry, but presumably as an attempt to compromise with Roman Catholic doctrines of celibacy, they may only marry widows.*

AUTUMN 1989

T he secretary turned out not to be beautiful, but he still could have been a spy, Letta thought. He was a plump, twitchy little man with clever dark eyes, about thirty-something, she guessed. His name was Mr. Jaunis (pronounced Jones, roughly, because that is how Varinian works) but he at once told Letta to call him Teddy. She decided not to make up her mind right away as to whether she liked him. It wasn't that his smiling brightness seemed forced, but it didn't tell you anything. It was like the twinkle on a sheet of water, which might hide anything below the surface, or nothing.

Dutifully Letta called him Teddy. He came by train from London and walked up the hill from the station. One of his afternoons was Tuesday, when Letta was late home from school because of Choral Soc, so it was only Fridays that the three of them had tea together. The first time he was horrified by crumpets, though they were Sainsbury's best, and insisted on reading the list of ingredients on the package. When he'd decided they wouldn't kill him, he consented to try a corner of Letta's but wouldn't allow her to butter it, though melted butter is at least half the point of having crumpets at all. Letta noticed Grandad watching the byplay over his spectacles with a look of sharp amusement, but when she began to act up herself, coaxing and teasing, he gave a tiny shake of his head, and she stopped.

"You will have to be more cautious," he said after Mr. Jaunis had left.

"I don't think he realized."

"I think perhaps he did. He is a clever and ambitious young man."

"I wouldn't have thought being a secretary was all that ambitious."

"It is only two afternoons a week, and for the moment he is not going to let some rival have the chance. The position has its possibilities, apart from the simple one of knowing what I am up to. I am an old man, he may think, and I prefer not to be over-wearied with work. No doubt I would welcome a trusted assistant who could speak for me at times, using my name . . ."

"You aren't going to let him!"

"He has just discovered that. This afternoon he brought me papers to sign—an appeal to various world leaders, a statement to the press, a memorandum to the British Foreign Office and another to the American State Department, and so on. We had settled the texts last Tuesday, but I found both memoranda now contained an extra paragraph, not very significant but on a delicate point. I told him to take them away and bring them back next Tuesday without it."

"You mean he was trying to make you say things you didn't agree with!"

"That would have been stupid, and he is far from stupid. I might well have agreed to the addition if he had suggested it while we were settling the text. He knew that, and was just testing my reactions."

"Anyway what is there to disagree about? Don't we all just want Varina to be a proper country on its own, like it used to be?"

"That is the romantic view, and since we are a romantic people that is what practically every Varinian would vote for, if it came to a vote. But the historical argument is not strong. Since the mythical days of Count Axur we were a precariously separate country for just over two years, more than a hundred and fifty years ago, from the expulsion of the Pashas until the Treaty of Milan. Then for the next eighty years we were a quasi-autonomous Prince-bishopric, first under the hegemony of the Turks and then under the Austrians."

"Yes, I know all that, but it doesn't make any difference. We know what we are and where we belong, don't we?"

"We know it only too well. That is part of the difficulty. It makes it harder for us to share the knowledge with our neighbors. Remember there are areas in all three provinces in which there are more Serbs, or more Romanians, or more Bulgarians than there are Varinians. And then, my darling, what are we to say to the realists who ask us how a country of three hundred thousand people, landlocked, with barely a town larger than an English village, apart from Potok, how could such a country survive economically in the modern world?"

"I don't know. There are lots of tiny countries . . . I mean how big's Luxembourg? Oh, come off it, Grandad! I know how you'd vote, and so do you!"

"Yes, of course. Whether it would work or not, we would have to prove to ourselves, and not leave it to the rest of the world to tell us it wouldn't. But that is not the real argument. The real argument comes in three parts. First, what is the best that we can hope for? Second, what should we demand, as a bargaining position, in order to achieve that best? And third, what promises or threats, what tools or weapons, do we have to bargain with?"

"Weapons? Do you mean actual weapons?"

"Some of us do. Some of us want nothing less than everything and would do nothing less than everything to get it."

"What do you mean? Hijacking? Murder? Like the IRA?"

"I will tell you a story. During the war some of my people ambushed a German patrol. Lives were lost on both sides in the gun battle. My people thought that a fair price. But the Germans came to the nearest village and burned it to the ground and shot all the men and the older boys and took the women and children to camps where many of them died also. My people were outraged, but it merely hardened our resolve. We immediately raided down into territory which the Germans thought they held securely, so as to show them that we were prepared to pay for our freedom not only with our own lives but also with the lives of those we loved."

"That's horrible. But it's different, isn't it? I mean it was war."

"The IRA will tell you they are fighting a war against an invading power."

"But it isn't true."

"It is in their eyes. And with us it is certainly true in the case of the Romanian province. Even by the standards of Eastern Europe the Romanian regime is peculiarly disgusting. They have a policy of trying to turn all their people into robots, all the same as each other and all worshiping their abominable dictator, Ceauşescu. To this end the army is sweeping peasants out of their ancestral villages, and bulldozing the houses and settling the people into dreary identical concrete towns, far from their own fields and farms. The English papers have other things to write about, but Mr. Jaunis has reliable information that the process has now reached Varina. There has been fighting between the Romanian army and some of our own people in the Lower Olta valley."

"But that's different. They've got to fight, haven't they? I mean if people come to smash your home and drive you away."

"Yes, in the end you must fight, though you know that it will only mean the army returning in greater force, with greater ferocity. It has happened before. I told you, small nations have long memories. There were never fewer than nine thousand Germans, well trained and heavily armed, trying to control our western province in the war, and they still did not succeed."

"Isn't there anything we can do? Us, here? Shall I write to our MP? Oh, there must be a Romanian Embassy. Why aren't we chaining ourselves to the railings, or something?"

"By all means write to your MP."

"I'll get Biddie and Angel to write too. I'll tell them what to say. What about the Embassy?"

"A vigil is being organized for next week."

"Magic! Can I go? Next week's half term, and Momma's said I can go to London and meet Mollie and Nigel and go Christmas shopping. That won't take all day."

Grandad started to say something, and stopped and did his trick with the invisible fingers instead. Then he said, "We have got away from the subject. I was trying to explain that there are perfectly honorable Varinian patriots who would argue that the only effective form of protest would be not a vigil but a car bomb."

"They can't! That would be absolutely criminal!"

"Worse than a crime, a mistake, as Napoleon said."

"Did he? He was a jerk anyway. What about the vigil? Is it all right if I go? If we time it right I could take my sleeping bag and vigil all night and join up with Mollie and Nigel next day."

"No," said Grandad sharply, but then shook his head, not at Letta but at himself.

"It's all right," she said. "There isn't an earthly Momma would let me. I'll do exactly what you tell me. Things must be quite tricky enough for you already, without me butting in."

"Listen, my darling. I am pleased—oh, far more than pleased—that you should want to learn Formal, and listen to boring lectures about the politics of my country. One day I hope you will be able to go there, to see where you come from. But it is not your country, despite your name, and despite your talking Field as easily as a native. You are an English girl. You will live your life in this country, marry an Englishman, bear English children. That is your future."

He spoke urgently, but sounded grim and tired. Letta looked at him, and saw that for the moment he really seemed to be eighty-something.

"Did Momma make you say that?" she said.

He hesitated, shrugged, and then said, "It was one of the things we agreed. I am not to involve you actively in Varinian politics."

"Momma's much Englisher than I'll ever be. You can't tell

me what I'm going to be, not even you, Grandad. I'm going to choose for myself. Poppa isn't English, really."

"No, but nor is he Varinian any longer. He is an exile, a citizen of Exilia. There is no country he can ever call home. Perhaps women are more sensible about such things than men."

"You aren't allowed to talk like that anymore. The gender police will come after you. Do you know about the gender police? It was something Angel saw in a sketch on the telly. They hang around in plainclothes and pick you up for making sexist remarks."

"I will plead senility. Listen, my darling. This is important. Not for what I agreed with your momma, but for your sake and mine. I want you to be very cautious, now that this sort of thing is starting to happen, about how you involve yourself in Varinian affairs. All exile communities are full of factions and troublemakers, and ours is no exception. Because you are my granddaughter, and the great-great-great-granddaughter of Restaur Vax, my namesake, there will always be people trying to use you for their own ends and purposes. I will not have you so used. Do you understand?"

"Sort of."

"Which is about as much understanding as can be hoped for in affairs of this sort."

"Are you going to the vigil?"

"I am booked to inaugurate it by handing in a protest at the Embassy, or at least attempting to, as they will certainly refuse to accept it."

"If I fix Momma can I come with you? I won't tell anyone you're my grandad. I'll just mingle and vigil for a bit."

"You must make it clear to your momma that I did my best to dissuade you."

"She won't know you had anything to do with it."

"How will you achieve that? It seems highly implausible."

"Tsk, tsk, Grandad. You're not supposed to know anything about it. Just give me Mr. Jaunis's phone number. It's okay, I'm not going to call him myself."

She grinned teasingly at him as she wrote it down, then loaded the tray and took it downstairs. Momma would be at least half an hour before she got home, so she called up her nephew, Nigel—the one who was three months older than she —and chatted for a bit, then asked if Steff was home.

Steff was Nigel's father, the older of her two brothers. Although he'd been grown up when she was born he'd always, ever since she could remember, been her chief ally in the family, especially when it came to getting around Momma about something. She started to explain about the vigil.

"Oh, yes," he said. "They sent me a leaflet. I actually thought of going. I'm having the day off anyway to look after Donna while Mollie takes you two shopping, but I decided it wouldn't be much fun for her. Well, what about it?"

She told him. He laughed.

"I'll put it to Mollie," he said. "It sounds just her line of business. What's the betting she'll have taken the whole show over by the time Grandad gets there?"

LEGEND

LASH THE GOLDEN

When Restaur Vax came to Talosh an old woman met him by the gate and knew him. She cast dust on her head and said to him, "Your father is dead. The Pasha of Potok came with his *bazouks* and slew him. Your brother and sister they have taken away. Your rooftree they have burned. Your walls they have cast down. Your fields they have plowed with salt. You have no more place among us."

"Why have they done this thing?" said Restaur Vax.

"The son of the Pasha was hunting and saw your sister and would have taken her, but your father smote him with his staff and drove him away."

Restaur Vax stood silent. Then he said, "I will not ask you to give me bread, lest the Turks should do the same to you."

The woman put her hand into her basket and brought out a fresh-baked loaf and broke it in two and gave him half.

"I and your grandmother drew water at the same well," she said. "What are the Turks to me?"

Then Restaur Vax climbed the hill and saw the ruin of his father's farm and wept.[1] When he had wept an hour he paced distances this way and that, and then loosed the earth with his sword and uncovered a great stone, but he could not move it with his hands. As he was levering at the stone with a hoe handle which the Turks had broken, a stranger came down the hill, a man of the old blood[2] with yellow hair and beard. He stood two handsbreadths taller than ordinary men. Though all but *bazouks* were forbidden to bear weapons he carried a musket at his back and two fine pistols in his belt. He saw Restaur Vax levering at the stone.

"What is it you do?" he said.

"That is my business," said Restaur Vax.

"Well, I will help you," said the man, and with his bare hands he lifted the stone aside as if it had been thin timber. Below it in a pit lay a clay pot.

"So you dug for treasure," said the stranger. "Well, since we have found it together, we will now share it."

"It is my inheritance," said Restaur Vax.

"What need has a priest of an inheritance?" said the stranger.

"Great need," said Restaur Vax, "if I am to fight the Turks."

"First you will have to fight me for my share of the treasure," said the stranger.

"Not so," said Restaur Vax. "For you are going to come with me and fight the Turks. What use is it to me to break your bones?"

The stranger laughed and said, "You are a better priest than most I have met. Very well, we will not fight each other, but we will have a contest. If I am to trust you as a comrade against the Turks, then you must show me you can use a gun.

We will shoot in turn, once with each of my pistols and once with my musket. If I win, I shall take my half of the treasure and go, and if you win I shall come with you to fight the Turks."

Restaur Vax saw the man's thought. How should a priest shoot better than a bandit? But his father had kept a gun in among his rafters, and had taught him its use, so he agreed to the contest.

The first target was two peaches set upon a rock. With his shot the stranger knocked one peach off the rock, but with his Restaur Vax shot the stone out of the other peach, leaving the fruit where it was.

"That was a lucky shot," said the stranger.

They reloaded and exchanged pistols.

The second target was two pigeons that chanced to fly past. With his shot the stranger knocked three tail feathers away, but the bird flew on. With his Restaur Vax shot the bird through the head, and it dropped like a stone.

"That was a lucky shot," said the stranger.

Now, as they were choosing a target for the musket, the son of the Pasha of Potok came along the road with some of his household on the way to their hunting ground. Hearing shots where by their law none should carry weapons they turned aside and saw two Varinians, one of them loading a musket. The Pasha's son sent five *bazouks* to arrest them, but the stranger raised his musket and shot the leading *bazouk* in the shoulder and he fell down, and the others took cover and fired back, and Restaur Vax and the stranger sheltered behind a broken wall while the stranger reloaded.

Now the Pasha of Potok's son rode up to find the cause of the delay, and Restaur Vax saw him and knew him. He took the musket from the stranger, saying, "Now it is my turn."

When he stood up, the Turks all fired at him but he did not flinch. He took steady aim and shot the Pasha of Potok's son through the heart, so that he dropped from his horse, dead. And all the Turks ran away, rather than face such shooting.

"That was more than a lucky shot," said the stranger. "You have won our contest, and I will fight the Turks at your side. There is no help for it, since we have killed the Pasha of Potok's son, and now there will be a price of many gold pieces on our heads. My name is Lash.[3] Some call me the Golden, for I am of the old blood."

Now, he was a famous bandit, who had killed many men.

"My name is Restaur Vax," said Restaur Vax.

"You may keep my musket," said Lash the Golden, "for you have won it fairly and you cannot fight the Turks without a gun."

"A gift for a gift," said Restaur Vax, and gave him the two rings which the Bishop had given for the purchase of a gun. One was of silver, set with a ruby, and one was of pure gold.

So they vowed everlasting brotherhood, and gathered up Restaur Vax's inheritance, and left.

———

1. *This incident is described by Vax himself in* Homecoming (Collected Works of Restaur Vax, *Rome, 1868).*

2. *It is popularly believed that Varina derives its name from the Varingian Guard, the famous regiment of Norsemen who served the Emperors in Byzantium. The occasional appearance of blond hair among the normally dark Varinians is regarded as evidence of this. A colony of veterans is supposed to have been established on the Danube sometime around the ninth century* A.D.*, though there is no documentary or archaeological evidence of this being so.*

3. *Alexo Lash (1785?–1826), chief lieutenant to Restaur Vax in*

the struggle for independence. A flamboyant figure, to whom legends concerning earlier folk heroes naturally attached themselves. Throughout the whole period of Turkish domination there were always both groups and individuals who refused to accept it, and fought and raided from inaccessible refuges among the mountains.

WINTER 1989

"Hi, Auntie," said Nigel.

"Good morning, nephew," said Letta. "I trust you are behaving yourself and getting good marks for your schoolwork."

It was their standard greeting. A car had come for Grandad and she'd driven up with him, but she'd got the driver to stop at the top of the road and walked down by herself, so as not to be seen arriving with the great man. It was a bright November morning. The road was a wide avenue of plane trees, with a big park and some sort of palace on the left and huge solemn houses on the right. Most of the houses seemed to be embassies or something now, with flags and coats of arms over the porches. Some of them had a policeman on guard. She found the Romanian Embassy about halfway down the hill with about thirty people standing around while Grandad shook hands with them. There were barriers on the pavement to keep the small crowd in order. Nigel had seen her coming and had walked a little way up to meet her.

"What's up?" she said.

"Mum's taken over, of course."

"Already?"

"She called the man you said, and the man knew our name and asked if she'd got anything to do with Grandad and she said yes. And she told him she knew about protests and he was keen to have her along. Dad says it's because she isn't bothered by policemen and anyone who's had to live in Varina can't help being."

"At least the cocoa will be hot. Where is she?"

"Over there, by the gate."

Letta turned and saw her sister-in-law, with Mr. Jaunis and another man, arguing about something with the policeman who guarded the Embassy. Mollie was a bit older than Steff. She was a square, cheerful woman who loved taking problems on, stray dogs, charity appeals, protests about pedestrian crossings, Nigel's school friends when they had troubles they didn't want to talk to their parents about. She was easy to like, but your first thought about having her to help you was "Um?," because she gave an impression of having just too much energy, like an Old English sheepdog pup which is full of goodwill but liable to knock tables over and trample the flower beds. In fact she was terrifically organized, and she always took the trouble to know her stuff. She'd once done an interview on local radio with some kind of junior government minister about a school closure, and he'd tried to get away with waffling at her, and she'd wiped the floor with him and left him without a waffle to his name. Nigel had sent Letta a tape with a note saying "Boadicea rides again."

Letta had been pretty certain Mollie wouldn't mind coming

to the vigil for a bit, though she was English, and the family talked English at home. (Nigel could only just about get along in Field.) Steff wasn't like Momma. He thought and talked about Varina, though he'd left there before he was six. Anyway, Mollie, being Mollie, would have known all about Ceauşescu, and how disgusting he was and what he was up to. Still, Letta hadn't expected her to be quite so in the thick of things yet.

It was interesting to watch her in action. Letta had mainly heard about her through Nigel, who of course regarded her as rather a joke, which is one of the important things good parents are for, Letta thought. (The chief problem with Poppa was that he wasn't there enough for jokes about him to build up properly.) Mollie, she saw, wasn't all Boadicea. She couldn't actually hear what the people at the gate were saying —the policeman, Mollie, Mr. Jaunis, and a slightly creepy-looking skinny bald man in a fur hat—but she could see from the way they held themselves that all three men were a bit unsure of themselves and Mollie wasn't, and they found that soothing. She was using a portable telephone which the skinny man had handed her. She finished the call and came over just as Grandad reached the end of the line where Letta and Nigel had joined on.

"We're waiting for the bloody press, as usual," she said. "Sorry about this, Grandad. You're early and they're late. Are you warm enough? I've got some cocoa in a thermos. I suppose they wouldn't let the car wait."

"My Marks and Spencer thermal underwear I am wearing," said Grandad, in English. Mollie could hardly speak Field at all.

"Good for you," she said. "Don't you think we look a miserable bunch? Isn't there something we can sing? A national anthem or something?"

"The words nobody will know. Funereal also the tune."

"Well then, a folk song. Steff's always whistling bits of folk song. I bet *you* know some folk songs."

She had turned as she spoke and said this to a couple of what looked like students next along the line. They'd been holding hands and staring with adoring expressions at Grandad. The young man began to stammer.

"What about 'The Two Shepherds'?" said the girl. "Everyone knows that."

"Except me," said Mollie. "What about it, Grandad?"

"Good. But Mr. Jaunis and Mr. Orestes you will consult first?"

"Yes, of course."

She darted across. Letta watched the byplay. Mr. Jaunis pursed his lips, but the skinny man, Mr. Orestes presumably, creased his face into a surprisingly gleeful smile and did a couple of small jig steps. Everybody cheered up. They divided without being organized into two groups on either side of the gateway. Mr. Orestes stood in the middle to conduct.

"The Two Shepherds" was a sort of nursery rhyme with silly words, two young men calling to each other across a valley, boasting about how they've got the best sheep, the best dog, the best crook, the prettiest girl, and so on. It had a cheerful tune, but the main point was the chorus, which was pure nonsense, the Varinian version of "With a folderolderolio" and you sort of yodeled it. Everyone enjoyed themselves. Their voices echoed off the stuccoed walls of the Embassy and up through the branches of the planes into the bright winter sky. The yodeling sounded particularly good. To Letta's surprise

they came to a verse she didn't know. Then another. Listening
carefully, she realized why.

"What was that about?" said Nigel, as the other group
took up the tune.

"It's not the sort of thing an aunt should go telling her
innocent little nephew."

"Oh, come off it!"

"Well, he was saying . . . Hold it, I'll tell you next
time."

It was their turn again, and yet another verse she didn't
know. These words were even more surprising—though there
were some of them she'd never heard before. The woman behind her shoulder had a penetrating clear soprano and sang
with great gusto, but when Letta glanced up and caught her
eye she stopped short.

"You understand?" she whispered in English.

"Most of it," said Letta cheerfully. "I can guess the rest. It
makes much more sense like this, doesn't it?"

The woman was not amused, and kept her mouth firmly
shut during the next verse, so Letta missed most of it, and
then, while they were doing the yodel, which seemed to get
longer and twiddlier with each verse, two photographers
showed up. The singing stopped, but the photographers
wanted them to start again because a singing protest was a bit
of a change. Letta heard Mr. Orestes telling them that "The
Two Shepherds" was a patriotic anthem. A few of the women
were wearing national costume—rather bogus-looking, Letta
thought, with a big head shawl and a wide-brimmed hat
down on one side—so the photographers made them stand in
front and sing, or pretend to in the case of the one nearest
Letta. Like Mollie, she was English and didn't know the
words.

Next Grandad was due to deliver his protest. The photographers wanted him to take the Englishwoman in national dress up the steps with him, because she was prettier than the real Varinians, but he put his foot down. He refused to have any of them.

"Not a charade, this is," he said loudly. "A protest we deliver about those serious and tragic events that in our country are taking place. A deliberate effort by the Romanian regime is being made to destroy our country, our culture, our language, our sense who we are. Those who resist they torture and kill. Let this be truly understood."

He had been waiting in the cold and looked frail but his voice came strongly out. Though he was a small man and his English was peculiar, the moment he spoke you forgot about that and he became the one who mattered, the center of things. Mr. Jaunis handed him an envelope and he turned and walked up the driveway, with Mr. Jaunis a pace or two behind his shoulder.

"Who is this guy, then?" said a man who'd come with the photographers. There was a woman with them too. They both had notepads and pencils.

"He is our last democratic Prime Minister, Restaur Vax," said the woman who'd worried about Letta understanding the words of the song.

"Spelling?" said the reporter, and wrote it down. "How old, anyone know?"

"Over eighty, I believe," said the woman.

"Eighty-one," said Letta.

"Sure, love?" said the reporter patronizingly.

"She's his granddaughter," said Nigel. "And I'm his great-grandson."

Letta could have kicked him. It wasn't his fault not knowing about her pact with Grandad, but even so . . . Luckily, no one took him up on it.

The woman started trying to tell the reporters about Grandad being named after the national hero, but they weren't very interested, and at that point things started to happen at the Embassy door. There was a flight of steps up to the pillared porch, and Grandad had been standing patiently on the doormat while Mr. Jaunis rang the bell. He'd tried short rings and nothing had happened, and he now had his finger steadily pressed on the bell push. The door opened a crack. Grandad had the envelope held out and a hand came through the crack and snatched it from him. Whoever it was just tore the envelope in half, stuffed the pieces back through the crack, and tried to close the door, not realizing that Mr. Jaunis had turned his umbrella upside down and hooked the handle around the bottom, so that it wouldn't quite shut.

This was obviously against the rules, because the policeman made a disapproving face, said, "You just wait here, all of you," and started up the drive.

Whoever it was behind the door made several attempts to heave it shut before they realized what had happened. Then they flung it open and rushed out, two stocky, thuggish-looking men in gray suits. They simply shoved Grandad and Mr. Jaunis out of the way, rushed back in, and slammed the door.

Mr. Jaunis was knocked clean off his feet and sprawled across the doormat, and Grandad, staggering back, tripped over him, teetered for a moment, and was actually falling down the steps when the policeman caught him. At the same moment the whole group of Varinians went rushing up the drive and gathered clamoring furiously on the Embassy steps.

Letta was swept up in the rush but managed to push her

way out and found Grandad sitting on the bottom step with Mollie and Nigel kneeling beside him and the policeman standing over them.

"All right now, then?" said the policeman.

"I don't think he's hurt, just shaken," said Mollie. "Thank you very much, Officer. If you hadn't caught him . . . These bloody people! God!"

"Better get him to a hospital," said the policeman. "Now I've got to sort this little lot out."

He turned and started trying to persuade the infuriated Varinians to get back into the road. Letta sat beside Grandad and put her arm around him. She was weeping. She couldn't help it. If the policeman hadn't caught him he'd have been badly hurt, with his thin old bones crashing down the stone steps.

"You two keep an eye on him for the moment," said Mollie. "I'll send for a taxi."

She strode away. Two more policemen appeared from somewhere, but they didn't know what had happened and seemed to think the Varinians were trying to storm the Embassy out of bloody-mindedness.

"Back in the road now," snapped one of them.

"He's hurt," said Letta. "They pushed him down the steps."

"Back in the road, will you," said the policeman, like a robot.

Letta was going to protest again when Grandad said, "We go now, Officer. Help me up, darlings. Good. That's it. I'm a little dizzy, I think. Now."

Together, with their arms around his waist and his around their shoulders, Nigel and Letta steadied him across the gravel. In the gateway the photographers crouched and tensed, cameras busy. Mollie was beyond them, talking into a mobile telephone she'd commandeered from somewhere. The woman reporter was waiting in front of her, notepad poised. Mollie switched the phone off and waved them over.

"Taxi's coming," she said. "How are you, Grandad?"

"I'll do, I'll do. Thank you, my dear."

"Do you feel up to answering a few questions?" said the reporter.

"She's from the *Independent*," Mollie explained. "Mr. Vax was delivering a peaceful protest at the Romanian Embassy when a couple of thugs charged out and threw him down the steps. He might easily . . ."

It looked as if she was going to take the interview over, but Grandad held up a hand and stopped her. Letta thought she actually felt a surge of strength coming from somewhere inside the trembling body.

"I am Restaur Vax," he said. "I am last democratically elected leader of the Varinian nation."

"He led the Resistance against the Germans," said Nigel, getting his two cents in as usual. "Then the Communists put him in prison for thirty years."

"Details you will find in our press leaflet," said Grandad. "Important now is that my people who live in Romania are by the Ceauşescu regime being savagely oppressed, turned from ancestral land and homes, massacred when they protest. This they do here this morning is in small way typical of how they have contempt for civilized modes. On the British government and the British people we are calling to use all means in their power that they dissuade the dictator Ceauşescu from continuing his aggression."

The wave of energy died and left him trembling worse than before. If Letta and Nigel hadn't been holding him he might have fallen. Letta was concentrating on him, and only vaguely aware of Mollie turning and beckoning, and then a taxi pulling up. They helped him in, and climbed in after him.

"We're taking you to the hospital for a checkup," said Mollie.

"No," murmured Grandad. "Wait, please."

"I really think—"

"No," he said firmly. "We will wait, Mollie."

She didn't like it, but she did what he said. He leaned back on the seat and closed his eyes. The meter ticked. The robot policeman came over, wanting to move them on, but Mollie climbed out and persuaded him not to. It didn't look that difficult. Letta guessed that somebody must have told him what had happened on the Embassy steps. The Varinians were allowing themselves to be shepherded out into the road and back behind the barriers. Mr. Orestes was handing out leaflets to the reporters and anyone else who would take them.

When all the protesters were back in place Grandad climbed out and leaning on Letta's shoulder went down the line, shaking hands with them in turn. Some of them, men as well as women, began to cry. He was moving very feebly and trembling badly by the time she got him back to the taxi, but he still refused to go to the hospital.

"For hours they will make us wait," he said. "Much quicker that I go home."

"Well, you're probably right there," said Mollie. "Can you spot your driver, Letta?"

"I'll get him."

"Sure you can manage? Here's a tenner for the fare, and another for emergencies. And put him to bed as soon as you get in, and get the doctor to come over. No, I'll call Momma at work and tell her to arrange for that. Sure you don't want me to come with you?"

As they drove away she heard the protesters starting to sing again, a folk song, but one she didn't know, not at all like "The Two Shepherds," wild and fierce. They sang it as though they meant it.

LEGEND

THE ENGLISH MILORD

For the death of his son the Pasha of Potok put a price on the head of Restaur Vax, of a hundred and seventy pieces of gold, and seventy also on the head of Lash the Golden, but Lash laughed when they told him the news.

"For these nine years," he said, "I have slept with a price on my head, and my dreams have been all the sweeter."

Now Restaur Vax fell ill of a fever, so Lash carried him to a farm where he could lie concealed. A great storm blew down from the north, and an English Milord,[1] traveling past that way, sent his guide to the door to ask for shelter. This guide was a Greek. The Milord brought with him two horses, a black and a bay, while the Greek rode a pony.

The farmer's wife put food and wine before the Milord and he ate, and that done he settled to playing dice for pastime, left hand against right. Now above all else in life Lash loved three things, a hard fight, a fine woman, and the rattle of dice on the board. Moreover he thought in his heart, "If we are to

fight the Turks we must have horses. There are two here for
the taking, with St. Joseph's aid."[2]

When he made his offer the Milord laughed.

"My horses are worth more than a peach and an olive," he
said. "What will you stake against them?"

Lash laid on the table the first of the Bishop's rings, which
Restaur Vax had given him. The Milord examined it and
accepted it as a fair stake. So they played, and the Milord won,
and won the second ring also in the same manner. Then Lash
climbed to the loft where Restaur Vax lay in his fever and
took from his wallet the four remaining rings, and staked
them.

First he staked a ring of fine gold, set with blue lapis carved
to the shape of a dolphin. That he lost.

Next he staked a ring of fine gold set with chrysoprase.
That he lost.

Third he staked a ring of silver entwined with gold, of
marvelous workmanship. That he lost also.

Last he staked a ring of fine gold set with a ruby and three
diamonds.

"This is worth more than a single horse," he said.

"Then I will stake my guide's pony also," said the Milord.

But Lash desired both the Milord's horses, so he said, "The
pony is no more than a skeleton with a mangy hide."

"Not so," said the Milord. "She is a sturdy mare, not six
years old. Come to the barn and see."

They took the lantern and went out to the barn, where the
horses were stabled, and there they found that the pony was
gone, and its saddle and harness too. The Milord called for his
guide, but the Greek did not answer.

Lash said, "This man saw me and knew who I am, for I am
Lash the Golden and there is a price on my head. He has taken

the pony and ridden to Varni, where there are Turkish *bazouks*. I must take my companion and go, for there is a price on his head also. But first, since the stakes are set, let us throw the dice one more time. Then with St. Joseph's aid we will have horses to ride, for my companion is sick and cannot walk, and without horses I must carry him on my back."

The Milord agreed and they rolled the dice on the floor of the barn, and once again Lash lost.

But as he stood up and prepared to go the Milord said, "Wait. I do not love the Turks, and you have played honorably with me, neither cursing your luck nor accusing me of cheating, as most men would have done after such a run on the dice. Moreover you need at least one horse to carry your companion. I will stake either one against a single hair of your beard."

So the stakes were agreed and they rolled the dice for the last time, and now Lash won.

"Now choose," said the Milord. "The black is the better bred and the better-looking, but he was bred in the plains. The bay was bred among mountains, and has the heart of a lion."

"Then I will take the bay," said Lash.

He fetched Restaur Vax down from the loft and wrapped him well against the storm and put him on the bay horse and took him by goat paths and the paths of the hunter to a cave that he knew of on Athur Mountain. But first he bound the Milord and the farmer and his wife with cords, so that they could tell the Turks that they had been forced into all they did.

When Restaur Vax woke in the cave on Athur Mountain the fever was gone and he knew himself.

"What horse is that?" he said.

"He is yours," said Lash the Golden. "I paid a Milord for
him, with the four rings which the Bishop gave you for that
purpose. He was bred among mountains and has the heart of a
lion."

———

1. *In one version of this legend the Milord is identified as Milord
Biroñ. Byron, though sympathetic to the Varinian cause (cf. letter to
Hobhouse, 19 February 1822), did not in fact at any time visit
Varina.*
2. *St. Joseph is the patron saint of Varina. His bones and a chisel
said to be his are kept as sacred relics in the cathedral at Potok. The
story is that Our Lord was in the workshop one day when Joseph
swore at a knot in the timber on which he was working. At that his
chisel leaped in his hand and cut him to the bone. Then Our Lord,
having rebuked his father for his intemperance, touched the wound
and healed it, and then touched the timber and made the grain
straight. Hence the Varinian belief that to swear by St. Joseph is not
accounted blasphemous.*

WINTER 1989

Grandad stayed in bed for two days. Momma tried to unplug his telephone, but he wouldn't let her.

"I must speak my own words," he said, "or people will put words that were never mine into my mouth."

There were photographs of the vigil in some of the papers, two of Grandad almost falling down the steps and one of him being helped away by Nigel and Letta, and two of the singing. The *Independent* had a six-inch news report as well, and next day the *Guardian* actually mentioned Varina in a leader about the Balkans, saying it was one of the problems to which there weren't any right answers but that didn't excuse the filthy way the Romanians were behaving. Some of the kids at school brought copies of the photographs along, which meant that people who didn't have any special reason to be interested in Varina must have noticed.

On Thursday when Letta took the tea up she heard voices before she reached the top of the stairs, so she knocked and waited till Grandad called to her to come in. It wasn't Mr. Jaunis's day, but he was there and so was Mr. Orestes. Without his fur hat you could see that his head really was absolutely shiny bald, which made him look creepier than ever.

"I'll just get another cup, so there's three," said Letta, assuming that Grandad wouldn't want her to stay. The visitors obviously thought the same, but Grandad said, "We will need two more cups. I cannot expect either Mr. Jaunis or Mr. Orestes to toast my crumpet to your standards. Did you meet Mr. Orestes on Tuesday? No? Hector, this is my granddaughter, Letta."

Mr. Orestes rose and waited while she put the tray down so that he could shake hands with her formally, bowing his head as he did so.

"Orestes like in the goat boy book?" she said. "Anya Orestes?"

"My grandmother," he said, in a slightly whining voice.

"Like us, Hector suffers from the burden of a literary ancestor," said Grandad. "Now my darling, if you would be kind enough to bring two more cups and then toast my crumpet, we will continue to settle the future condition of Europe."

She went and returned, bringing extra hot water as well. She poured the tea, refilled the pot, and settled by the fire. Mr. Orestes accepted a crumpet, which he ate with lashings of butter on it. Letta listened to the discussion and did her best to understand. They were talking about how to follow up on the vigil. In spite of what had happened to Grandad—or rather, because of it—the vigil had made much more of a splash than anyone could have hoped, and people who'd never heard of Varina now knew it was there, and real.

They were talking about some kind of delegation to a minister at the Foreign Office, and who should be on it. The problem for Letta was that she didn't know any of the names, which made it all a bit meaningless, but after a while she noticed that as soon as either Mr. Jaunis or Mr. Orestes suggested somebody the other one would come up with a reason against them. Mr. Jaunis was jolly and giggly about this, and Mr. Orestes was sour and cold, so it was odd that it was something Mr. Jaunis said—the way he said it, more—that suddenly made Letta understand that they were neither of them very interested in the delegation for itself but they both were using it to put the other one down. They needed a British MP to lead the delegation and there were two possible choices. Mr. Jaunis wanted one, so naturally Mr. Orestes wanted the other. Grandad suggested a joint leadership.

Mr. Jaunis giggled and said, "The difficulty about that, I'm afraid, is that the two gentlemen happen to detest each other."

With a slight shudder of shock Letta saw that the two who truly detested each other were Mr. Jaunis and Mr. Orestes. She didn't much like either of them herself, but this was different. It was different even from the sort of feud you get between a couple of kids at school, not speaking to each other, letting everyone know how much they despise each other, being generally mean, but all still as a kind of trying-it-out-to-see-if-it-fits exercise, a nasty little game. The way Mr. Jaunis and Mr. Orestes hated each other was real. It filled the room like a horrible smell. Surely Grandad could smell it too.

Grandad never drank more than one cup of tea, but she took the teapot over to his bed and pretended to offer him a refill. He hadn't finished his first, and he'd only eaten half his crumpet and let the rest go cold. He was sitting up in bed and leaning back against the piled pillows with his head held straight, glancing at each of the visitors in turn as they spoke, making notes on his clipboard. He looked alert enough to anyone who didn't know him well, pretty spry for eighty-one, in fact, but Letta could see he was forcing himself to stay like that, and really he was feeling almost as bad as when she and Nigel had got him into the taxi.

She turned and waited for a pause in the argument, feeling herself going red.

"I'm sorry," she said, too loudly. "Grandad's not feeling well."

Mr. Orestes had just been going to say something. He half turned his head and looked at her like an angry snake. Mr. Jaunis gave a surprised giggle.

"The d-doctor said we mustn't let him get tired," she stammered. "Momma—my mother—she'll be very upset, if . . . I mean . . . and you want him well too, don't you?"

"I'm afraid Letta is right," said Grandad's voice behind her. "I apologize for my feebleness, gentlemen, after you have come all this way, but we had better not risk my daughter's wrath. Since we have reached an impasse over the leadership of the delegation I propose to resolve the matter as follows. I have a list here of the names we have agreed upon for the Varinian delegates, and I will write to Mr. Craigforth and Mr. Weller suggesting a joint delegation. I will do a draft in time to mail it to each of you tomorrow, so that you can telephone me with suggestions, if any—I trust that will not be necessary —in time for Mr. Jaunis to bring me the typed-up letters to sign on Monday. We will give tomorrow a miss, Teddy. I trust that is agreeable to you both, gentlemen?"

It obviously wasn't, but they had to put up with it. Letta thought about Grandad as she took them downstairs. He wasn't anything official. He'd just been Prime Minister of Varina for a fortnight over forty years ago, and even in that fortnight nobody except the Varinians had considered it to be a real country—the others didn't want to know about it. But still, when he told Mr. Jaunis and Mr. Orestes what he'd decided, they knew that was it.

She closed the front door behind them with a sigh of relief, and heard Mr. Orestes' voice, low but venomous, before they reached the garden gate. Mr. Jaunis answered with his infuriating giggle. He did it on purpose, she decided.

When she went to pick up the tray she found Grandad had eased himself down the pillows and was lying with his eyes closed. But he wasn't asleep.

"Thank you, my darling," he said. "You did very well. I would myself have asked them to go before long, but it came better from you than from me."

"Do they really hate each other? I suddenly sort of felt it, and it gave me the shivers."

Grandad sighed.

"Tell me some other time," said Letta. "I didn't mean to stir you up."

"No. I would like to talk for a little to someone I know I can trust. There are centuries-old animosities between the two families. I think I told you that the national sport of Varina is the blood feud."

"They're not going to start massacring each other in the front hall!"

"Unlikely. That time is past. For the moment at least, though if things go badly it could well come back. Mr. Orestes' great-uncle, the brother of the woman who wrote the appalling book, was a lawyer by profession. He wore a top hat and tailcoat and went daily to an office, like other lawyers. He was boringly respectable. One evening, and this was only a few years before I was born, he was set upon and knifed to death in the street outside his house. The police arrested a disgruntled client and extracted some kind of confession from him, but very many people, not only members of the Orestes clan, were convinced that the murder was the work of some of the more primitive members of the Jaunis clan."

"But what's the point?"

"Hatred needs no point, my darling. It needs only an object. Now I think I had better attempt to have a nap, or we will both be in trouble when your momma comes home. Later on will you be good enough to listen to the World Service news for me, and make notes if there is anything that might concern us?"

Letta set her timer and listened at ten o'clock, trying to finish her homework at the same time. There was a lot of stuff about Eastern Europe, where all sorts of things seemed to be just going to happen, terrible old Communists giving up power, enormous demonstrations (eighty thousand on the streets of Leipzig, in East Germany—Letta grinned but felt sad when she thought of the handful of Varinians singing in the cold outside the Romanian Embassy), unrest in Bulgaria . . . aha! Slovenians in Yugoslavia wanting to be a separate country and the Serbs trying to stop them . . . Letta knew about the Serbs. They were the ones nearest to the Yugoslavian bit of Varina, south of the Danube. Quite a lot of Serbs actually lived in Varina. Serbs were always traitors in the Legends, Grandad had said . . . hell, she'd stopped listening . . . a woman was talking about Ceauşescu, so it must be Romania. Yes. Rule of iron, she was saying. No chance of him giving anything up. Continuing his policy of sweeping peasants off into his new horrible towns . . . there was nothing about Varina itself, but the biggest of the three provinces was the one in Romania. That's where Potok was, which used to be the capital.

Oh, I'd love to go to Potok, she thought. One day.

She sorted her notes out and when she'd finished her homework got an atlas and checked where Slovenia was. Right up in the north. Miles from Varina. Still, good luck to them. If they could, so could everyone else.

Grandad was up and dressed next day when she took the tea up, but he was on the telephone, trying to explain to somebody who didn't know much about it—Letta could hear the patience in his voice—that Varina presented special problems because it was in three separate countries, and they'd all have to give up bits of territory which had some of their own people living in them before Varina could be a separate country on its own. She knelt by the fire and started toasting the crumpets.

"Indeed," he was saying. "Particularly difficult it is. The objections of the various governments we understand. Yet it is our very profound desire. A small but genuine nation is Varina. Our own language we have, not a dialect, our own history, our own culture, our own church. One of the great poets of Europe, whose name I bear . . . No, at the moment all we ask is recognition we exist. At least as a problem we exist. You understand? This is urgent. The Bucharest regime is attempting the problem to solve by destroying us, by destroying a whole nation. Abominable! You agree? Excellent. No, it is I who am grateful. For your call, thank you."

He shrugged as he put the telephone down.

"I feel myself to be a drip attempting to wear away the great stone of ignorance," he said. "Journalists have such short, inaccurate memories. Because I was thrown down some steps on Tuesday, they think to consult me on Slovene matters on Friday. By Monday they will have forgotten that I and Varina exist."

"You got my note? I did the best I could. It sounded quite hopeful about Slovenia, didn't it?"

"There was a good report in the *Telegraph* as well, but thank you, my darling. Yes, it is a sliver of hope. The Slovenes are a reasonable people—a rare phenomenon in the Balkans. Tell me some gossip. What has Angel been up to?"

LEGEND

THE KAS KALAZ

The Pasha of Potok pursued hotly after Restaur Vax and Lash the Golden, seeking vengeance for the death of his son.

"Let us cross the mountains," said Lash. "The Pasha of Falje is at odds with the Pasha of Potok. He will not trouble us."

"To cross the mountains, our best road runs through Kalaz, and I would welcome the chance to speak with the Kas Kalaz, for we need his aid," said Restaur Vax. "But is there not a feud between you and Kalaz?"

"Indeed there is such a feud," said Lash, "and many lives have been taken. My own grandfather killed the uncle of the present Kas Kalaz, in fair fight, close by the Iron Gates, and threw him into the river."

"So you cannot go by Kalaz," said Restaur Vax.

"I will go by goat paths and the paths of the hunter, and over the Neck of Ram," said Lash. "And you will go through

Kalaz and speak with the Kas, and we will meet in three days time at the Old Stones of Falje."[1]

So they agreed, but what Lash had not said was that beneath the Neck of Ram lived a shepherd who had a fair daughter. Then Restaur Vax rode over the Eastern Pass and came to Kalaz, where he made himself known to the Kas, and spoke very strongly with him, saying that the time was ripe to drive the Turk from Varina. The Kas was an old man, and wasted with illness so that he could not rise from his chair, but he looked fiercely at Restaur Vax and said, "The word is that you have a bandit as your companion, a man called Lash."

"It is so," said Restaur Vax.

"There is blood yet to be paid between us," said the Kas. "This man's grandfather trapped my uncle by a trick at the Iron Gates, and slew him and threw his body in the river. I would see the debt paid before I die."

"Would you not sooner see the Turk driven from the land?" said Restaur Vax.

"Sooner than all the earth," said the Kas Kalaz.

"While brother slays brother and neighbor lies in wait for neighbor it cannot be done," said Restaur Vax. "The time is ripe, but we must plan with a single mind, endure with a single heart, and smite with a single arm. Let the debt be forgotten."

"Blood can never be forgotten," said the Kas Kalaz. "But it can be frozen for a season. Therefore by the bones of St. Joseph I swear that the Kas Kalaz will seek no vengeance from Lash or the clan of Lash until the Turk is driven from the land."

Then he said to his eldest son, who stood at his side, "You hear this? When you yourself are the Kas Kalaz and Restaur

Vax sends word to you to come, you will leave both your harvest and your hunting, you and all the men of Kalaz, and go with him to fight the Turk and all feuds will be frozen."

"By the bones of St. Joseph I will do it," said the son of Kas Kalaz.

Well pleased, Restaur Vax rode on his way and camped by the Old Stones of Falje. For a day and a night and another morning he waited for Lash the Golden, and when the sun was high in the sky he saw a woman come running down the mountain. She fell at his feet half dead from weariness, but he lifted her up and she said, "Ride swiftly to the shepherd's house below the Neck of Ram, for the son of the Kas Kalaz is there with his men, and he has seized Lash the Golden and put a rope about his neck and vowed that he will hang him at sunset."

"How came the son of the Kas Kalaz there?" said Restaur Vax. "I feasted with him in Kalaz town but two nights past."

"Lash visited me," said the woman, "but my father learned of his coming and went secretly over the mountain to the son of Kas Kalaz and told him where his enemy lay. They came at dawn, while Lash still slept, but I was milking the goats and hid, and heard what was said. Then I ran to find you, for Lash had told me where he was to meet you. Now go, and go swiftly."

"You must come with me, for I do not know the path," said Restaur Vax.

"I am overweary," said the woman. "Who among men could have run as I have run this morning?"

Then Restaur Vax put her on his horse and they went by goat paths and the paths of the hunter over the mountain. Where the way was steep he led the horse by the bridle, and where it was level he ran with his hand in the stirrup. Eleven *kolons*[2] he ran between her coming and the sunset, and the sun was low in the sky when they crossed the Neck of Ram and came down to the shepherd's house. There they found Lash the Golden with the rope about his neck, and the son of the Kas Kalaz making ready to hang him.

"Do not do this," said Restaur Vax. "You have sworn by the bones of St. Joseph that the feud is frozen."

"Not so," said the son of Kas Kalaz. "My oath is still free. It was the Kas Kalaz who swore, and I in my turn swore for the time when my father is dead and I am the Kas Kalaz."

Restaur Vax spoke strongly with him, trying to persuade him, but he would not hear, for the feud was old and very bitter, with many deaths. Then, as the rim of the sun touched the Neck of Ram, a man came running up the mountain and fell at the feet of the son of the Kas Kalaz and wept, and then stood and embraced him and called him by his father's name. By this he knew that his father had died, and he was now the Kas Kalaz, and the oath he had sworn was binding.

So he gave orders, and the rope was taken from the neck of Lash the Golden and the bonds that bound him were loosed, and the Kas Kalaz embraced him and said, "The blood between us is frozen, and we are brothers, until we have driven the Turk from Varina."

But Restaur Vax took Lash aside and said, "Speak with honor of this woman all your days, my friend. I have traveled by the path on which she ran to save you, and by St. Joseph I myself could not have done it."

Then Lash was ashamed.

1. *The Old Stones of Falje. A Bronze Age trilith, unique in the Balkans in its design.*
2. *The* kolon *is not a precise measure. Any considerable distance is traditionally described as seven, eleven, or seventeen* kolons.

WINTER 1989–90

Christmas felt strange that year. Usually the holidays began with Letta and Biddie and Angel mooching around Winchester together on the pretense of helping each other buy presents. In fact Angel was far too impatient not to have bought all hers weeks before, so all she could do was enjoy a good wail about the ghastly mistakes she'd made; while Biddie knew exactly what she wanted and where to find it and could get the whole lot in half a morning, so they normally spent most of their time helping Letta, looking in shop windows, and rotting their teeth with soft drinks.

That year there was none of that. Biddie's parents had bought a cottage in Devon and whisked her off there, while Angel's dad, who'd lost his job in the summer when his firm had folded, took the family up north because he'd had an offer up there and wanted them to see how they felt about moving. Normally Letta would have missed them badly. Being almost an only child, they counted as sisters to her, Biddie particu-

larly. She and Biddie had been born within a few hours of each
other, in the same ward of the Royal but on different days,
Letta late on the twenty-eighth of August and Biddie early on
the twenty-ninth, and though they didn't actually meet again
until primary school when they were seven, they had immediately struck up a friendship; and then, when they had found
out about the birthdays and being born in the same ward they
had felt Oh, yes, of course, so that now it was as if they had
known each other all their lives.

But that Christmas she didn't have time to miss Biddie,
even. All she wanted to do was stay at home with Grandad,
listening to the news coming in about the uprising in
Romania and watching the television reports, the swirling
crowds in the streets of Bucharest, the snipers and tear gas,
the lurch of the picture as the cameraman ducked for cover,
and the exhausted faces of ordinary people tense with excitement or weeping with joy while they stammered in broken
English into the microphones. Poppa, who was in England for
once, would get home, and shout before he was through the
door "What's happening? Anything new?" and Letta would
gabble out the news. Momma, astonishingly, started coming
home before half past six, though usually before Christmas she
was working till all hours to get her desk cleared, and she
didn't stop to shop and sent out for pizzas instead, though
every now and then she would laugh, and shake her head as if
she was shaking away tears and say, "It's nothing to do with
us any longer, you know."

Neither telephone stopped ringing, with old Varinian
friends, unheard of for years, wanting to swap excitements,
and almost everyone in England, it sometimes seemed, reporters and politicians and historians and mysterious people who

seemed to have no connection with Varina at all, anxious to know what Grandad thought.

The rest of the family arrived on Christmas Eve, Mollie and Steff and Nigel and little Donna from St. Albans and Van and his Scottish girlfriend Susan from Glasgow, where they both worked in TV studios. The house throbbed with excitement and tension and the frustration of being so far away. There was so much electricity in the air, Steff said, that if they could have found a way of plugging the stove in to it they could have cooked their Christmas dinner for nothing.

On Christmas Day itself came the news that the Ceauşescus had been caught and executed, and Poppa opened the champagne then and there, and Momma, incredibly, turned on the oven but forgot to put the turkey in, so they didn't have lunch till half past five, and Letta and Nigel tripped Poppa up and held him down with Van's help and wouldn't give him any more champagne until he'd taught them the missing verses of "The Two Shepherds" and they sang it all over the house and made up English versions to tell their friends, and still the telephones were ringing and ringing, Varinians all over the world now wanting to talk to Grandad and wish him a happy Christmas and saying "Next year in Potok."

Then, while the dust of the old year's explosions settled grayly onto the new year, and the days went by, Romania and the surrounding countries dropped out of the news, mostly. The United States had invaded Panama and there was a revolt in Liberia and trouble between Russia and Lithuania and a civil war starting in Azerbaijan, and so on. Still, the people you met, kids at school, even—because Letta had a foreign name and some of them knew that her family came from around there—often talked about Romania, shiny-eyed and romantic. The uprising had been so obviously a Good Thing, because Ceauşescu and his gang had been such horrors. And then the news started coming through about things like the orphanages where all the kids were tied into their cots because there weren't enough people to look after them, and they all had AIDS from transfusions of infected blood, but still people talked as if all that was over, and there was going to be democracy and foreign medicine and emergency aid and everything would be all right. Of course there were terrible problems still, but now that Ceauşescu was gone they could all be sorted out. Letta found this depressing. First, she knew from Grandad it wasn't like that. And second, Varina was one of the problems.

About three weeks into the term she got back from school and found that Grandad had visitors, two men in heavy dark suits. Grandad introduced them as Mr. Kronin and Mr. Dashik. Mr. Dashik said, "How do you do?" in English, with a strong accent, as he shook hands. Letta answered in English so as not to seem rude.

"Letta speaks good Varinian," said Grandad, "so there's no need for you to deploy your linguistic skills. They have come from Potok to see me, my darling. We are all three amazed that such a thing is possible."

"That's wonderful!" said Letta. "My first real Varinians! You must have been there during the uprising? What happened? They never even mentioned Varina on the news over here, not once."

Mr. Dashik smiled and shook his head in a puzzled way.

"Everything happened," he said. "It was like a dream, a dream in which happenings rush at you and are gone and before you know who or where you are another happening is rushing at you and you have no time to remember anything. Like that. At first we were so afraid. The police seemed to know everything. But there were rumors, and in certain places on the mountains one could pick up Italian TV reports, and crowds began to gather in Potok and the police told them to disperse and fired on them when they did not go and killed three men and two women and a child—I was there, and I saw it happen—and we began to throw stones. Then more police came and more crowds, and they chased us through the streets but we gathered again and threw stones. But many of the police were unwilling to shoot. In Varina, you know, everybody is somebody's cousin . . ."

"You mean the police were Varinians!" said Letta.

"Some of them, of course," said Mr. Dashik, surprised that she didn't realize.

"The local Secretary of the Communist Party was my sister's husband's uncle," said Mr. Kronin. "He was a hard-line Ceauşescu supporter and had done very well for himself. Everybody was afraid of him. He came out into the square thinking to quell the uprising with the terror of his presence, but the crowd caught him and hanged him. I was not there, but if he had been I wouldn't have lifted a finger to save him, family or not family."

"And then the people in Belgrade took over the broadcasts and told us that the Ceauşescus had been executed," said Mr. Dashik. "And by now a lot of the police had changed sides, so we had guns and we could shoot back, and Mr. Kronin here led the party that took over the Communist headquarters where they were still trying to destroy all their files. . . ."

"It was a great shock to read the files and discover how many people one trusted had been in the pay of the police," said Mr. Kronin. "Good friends, neighbors, colleagues at work, drinking companions . . ."

He shook his head.

There was a silence. It was like when somebody's died and their name comes up. There was a boy called Mickey in another class at school who'd been hit by a runaway truck last spring. Like that.

"I suppose you had to read them," said Letta.

"Terrible things had been done," said Mr. Dashik. "They could not simply be forgotten."

"As a people we have no talent for forgetting," said Grandad. "Remember 'The Mountain Pasture'?"

"*Anastrondaitu,*" murmured Mr. Kronin, shaking his head again. "I have sometimes felt that there is all our history in that one word."

Another silence, and then Grandad said, "Well, gentlemen, I hope you have time to sample the delights of the British crumpet. You will? Excellent. Letta, my darling, if you would get some more cups and crumpets and perform your office . . ."

When the visitors had gone Grandad said, "What did you mean by calling our friends 'real' Varinians? Am I not a real Varinian? Or Mr. Jaunis or Mr. Orestes? Or your momma and poppa. I will except you, for the moment."

He was amused, but there was a faint sharpness in his tone.

"You are, of course," said Letta. "I don't know about the others. It's sort of shadowy. I mean, Mr. Orestes seems a bit realer than Mr. Jaunis, I don't know why. I suppose Poppa might be, except that he's become a sort of nowhere person . . . What did you call him once? A citizen of somewhere?"

"Exilia," said Grandad. "Never to belong to any country of which there is a map. What about your momma?"

"Oh, I think she's still a real Varinian underneath. Don't you? That's why she keeps trying so hard not to be. Steff's pretty real in his quiet way. I don't know Van well enough to say. What were they here for? Just to see you, like an ancient monument? Oh, sorry, I didn't mean that! Really!"

Grandad was tired but he laughed, which he didn't do often.

"In fact they came to ask me if I would inaugurate a festival of Varinian culture in Potok next year."

"Oh I know all about that."

"You do? It is not yet publicly announced."

"Nigel told me. Momma wanted to talk to Mollie about something last night and she asked me to get the number because her hands were wet, and Nigel said Mollie was out whooping it up with Mr. Orestes at the Varinian Dance Society. You know Mollie's gone really to town about Varina since the vigil? She's learning Field and she's joined Mr. Orestes' Dance Society—he's a hot number at it, Nigel says, and now they're mad keen to take a team out to the festival. Have I said the wrong thing?"

"No, my darling. Tell me about the Dance Society."

"Oh. Nigel's been to see, but he decided it wasn't him. You know what boys are like about dancing."

"English boys. In Varina dance is regarded as a primarily masculine activity. Go on."

"Actually one of the girls told Nigel she thought Mr. Orestes was sexy. Can you imagine? He did a sort of exhibition, playing bagpipes and dancing at the same time with his feet going so fast they were an absolute blur. And he wowed them all along. He's a real fanatic, Nigel said. Anyway he's got

Mollie hooked. She's making herself a national costume, can you believe? Are you going to go, Grandad? Do you think we can all go?"

"I shall have to think about it. The new authorities in Bucharest are unlikely to welcome any manifestation of cultural independence in a minority population. They have a large and restive Hungarian minority in the north of the country, whom they won't want to encourage. On the other hand they will want to prove their liberal credentials, and if the festival brings in a large number of exiles, which I think it may, that will provide useful hard currency. Still, it will take some careful diplomacy. Fortunately Mr. Kronin's brother is a senior official in the new Ministry of Culture. I had better talk to Hector. Mollie too, perhaps, before she looses her organizational fervor on the project . . ."

"But if it happens, can I go? Please? Will you help me persuade Momma?"

"Yes indeed. You must go while you can, on any basis available. So should your momma. I will tell her so."

Letta stared at him. He had spoken quietly, but in the same tone of authority he'd used when he'd stopped the argument between Mr. Orestes and Mr. Jaunis.

"It may be our one chance," he explained. "As far as I can see there is no settlement in the Balkans which all the participants could regard as reasonable. In fact there never has been. So fighting will take place, and it may be severe. But for this year, at any rate, everybody is still too shaken and exhausted and uncertain to start on fresh turmoil, so there may for a while be an illusion of peace. After that, who knows? But certainly while the opportunity is there all who regard themselves as Varinians should return and renew their knowledge of who and what they are. If the festival takes place, they should come to that. If not, they should go as tourists. It may be twenty years before they can do so again."

"All right. You work on Momma. And if she digs her heels in I'll go with Mollie. She's bound to want to. Do you know she's insisting on everyone talking Field at Sunday lunch? And Steff's backing her up. Nigel is not amused."

"She has not started to learn Formal yet?"

"It won't be long now. And I'll tell you what. I bet she'll take it in her stride and when she gets to the conditional optative she'll decide that it's no big deal, and shall *I* be not amused!"

LEGEND

THE MUSTER AT RIQUI

Restaur Vax traveled north and south, east and west through the mountains, and wherever he had not a feud Lash the Golden went with him. At each place Restaur Vax spoke strongly with the chieftain and elders, saying that the time was ripe to drive out the Turks. But each chieftain answered in the same manner, having consulted with his elders: "Gladly would we fight the Turks, but we cannot do it alone. We are too few. When others have come to your standard, we will come also."

"The Kas Kalaz has sworn that he will come," said Restaur Vax.

But the chieftains still said that others must come first. And so they waited each on the other.

Then Restaur Vax said to them, "If all of you swear at one time, then will you fight?"

To that they agreed.

So he sent messages to all of them, saying, "Come to the

chapel at Riqui, so that each may see the other swear upon the shoulder blade of St. Joseph, which is there.[1] Come on the full moon after Ascension, that you may arrive after dusk and leave before dawn, so the Turks will not know of our meeting. Bring your best men to witness the oath."

But to the Kas Kalaz he sent word, saying, "Come with all of your men, and mules, and much straw and sackcloth, and cords. Be at the chapel at Riqui on the night before the full moon."

Moreover, word was brought to the Pasha of Potok, saying, "The chiefs of Varina will muster at the chapel at Riqui on the night of the full moon after Ascension, and there they will swear a confederacy to rise and drive out the Turks. Restaur Vax will be there, who killed your son, and also Lash the Golden."

Hearing this the Pasha gathered his *bazouks*, seven thousand of them.[2] And he set spies on the roads who brought word to him, saying, "Indeed, such-and-such a chieftain has left his place and is traveling with his best men toward Riqui." Thus he knew that the message had been true.

Then he divided his *bazouks* into companies and sent them at rapid march north, west, and east, to come upon Riqui from all sides, telling the commanders, "Find good hiding and wait a few *kolons* away from Riqui until sunset, and then close in on the place when the moon is a handsbreadth up the sky. There will be a full moon to show you your way. Then at the sound of my side drum rush down all together and slay them, sparing only Restaur Vax, that I may slay him with my own hands."

So it was done, and done well. In secrecy and silence the *bazouks* closed in upon Riqui and lay along the hilltops looking down into the hollow. There by the chapel they saw fires, and the shapes of men around, to whom one spoke in a boastful voice.

When all was ready the Pasha ordered his side drum to be sounded, and the *bazouks* drew their scimitars and rushed down into the hollow. But when they came near the chapel they saw that those who had stood by the fires had not moved, for they were not men but dummies of straw and sackcloth, bound with cords, while the man who had spoken to them was not to be seen. (He was Lash the Golden, and at the sound of the side drum he had run into the dark and hidden in a pit that had been prepared.)

Now from behind the *bazouks,* seeing them against the light and not themselves to be seen, the chieftains and their best men shot them down, firing swiftly and hotly, so that they fell like barley before the sickle. Then the *bazouks* lost courage, knowing themselves betrayed, and ran into the dark where the men of Varina met them and slew them with dagger and with sword. Seven thousand *bazouks* they slew around the chapel at Riqui, and not one came back alive to Potok. And the Pasha of Potok was slain in a fair fight by Restaur Vax, before the door of the chapel.

Then in the dawn the chieftains gathered to take their oath, and each said to the other, "How came the Pasha of Potok here with so many *bazouks*? This was no chance coming. A traitor must be among us." For Restaur Vax had told them only that he had learned from a scout that a captain of *bazouks* had seen one of the chieftains on the road, and had recognized him, and was coming with his company to find what was afoot. For that they had prepared the ambush.

Now, however, Restaur Vax stood before them and said, "There is no traitor among us. It was I who sent word of our muster to the Pasha of Potok. His blood is upon all our heads, yours as well as mine, and the Turks will surely take vengeance on all who are here. So whether you choose to swear the oath or not you will do well to forget all feuds and stand by each other in the struggle, or you will all die."

The chieftains acknowledged the truth of his saying, and all of them in turn swore their oath at the chapel at Riqui.[3]

———

1. *At the time of the Phanariote oppression (see page 147) the bones of St. Joseph were removed from the cathedral of Potok, and distributed to a number of holy sites throughout Varina, for safety.*

2. *The numbers are greatly exaggerated. Apart from this the oral tradition of the Riqui Incident, which occurred on 22 May 1819, and is usually regarded as the start of the War of Independence, has remained remarkably faithful to the facts.*

3. *Restaur Vax never admitted that it was he who had lured the Pasha into the ambush at Riqui, but even in his own time it was universally believed that he was responsible.*

SPRING/SUMMER 1990

M r. Jaunis and Mr. Orestes were Joint Honorary Secretaries of VIBI, which stood for Varinians in the British Isles and was pronounced Veeby. Letta had once been telling Biddie and Angel about it when Angel said, "Veeby? Honestly! Only total wimps would belong to something called Veeby! What's with the Isles, anyway? Or are there covens of you in places like Muck and Harris? Why couldn't they call it Varinians in Britain? VIB? I think VIB's got much more punch."

"It means nostril," Letta said.

Biddie had been drinking tooth rot, and choked on it. By the time they'd cleaned her up Angel was away on something else.

Anyway Letta had once asked Mr. Jaunis how many Varinians there actually were in the British Isles.

"According to our records, seven hundred and eighty-three," he'd said. "And six hundred and ninety of them are

members of VIBI, a figure which we believe speaks highly of
our commitment to our homeland."

When Letta went up to St. Albans just after Easter, as
usual, to stay for a few days with Steff and Mollie and Nigel,
she found that almost all seven hundred and eighty-three
seemed to be wanting to make it out to Potok for the festival
of culture at the beginning of August, though it still wasn't
anything like certain that it was going to happen, or if it did,
that the Romanians would let them in. Even so, everybody
was behaving as if it were all fixed.

Letta spent most of her time answering the telephone and
putting brochures in envelopes and helping keep the lists up
to date on Mollie's PC. Using the telephone was thrilling,
because she got to talk to real Varinians in Varina. Mollie's
Field was nothing like up to that yet, nor was Nigel's, and
Steff was out at work all day, so they really needed Letta.

It wasn't easy. The line kept breaking, and the voices when
they came through were crackly and distorted, and besides
that things seemed to be in pretty good chaos at the far end.
There were only two hotels in Potok, so the festival organizers
were borrowing the students' rooms at the university, but
they were overflowing already, as more and more people kept
wanting to come from all over the world. Some of the Varinians could speak a bit of English, but with the lines so bad it
was much easier to be sure about things if the speakers at both
ends were using a language they were comfortable with, so
now Letta found herself talking Varinian—which except with
Grandad had always been a sort of extra in her life, something
she could perfectly well do without but which she kept going
because it was a habit and felt right, though she didn't know
if she'd speak it with her own children—found herself talking
Varinian because she had to, talking to an unseen voice in

Varina, all that way over those terrible lines—and it was *real*.
The first time she put the receiver down she found she was
crying.

Mollie thought Letta must be upset because of the anxiety,
at her age. She didn't really understand when Letta explained.
But Letta called Grandad that evening and told him, and he
knew. Anyway Mollie found her so useful that she asked her
to stay on till the day before the new term started, and by
then Letta was so accustomed to saying *"Oyu?"* when she
picked up the phone that when she got home she had to
remind herself to say "Hello?"

She went up again for half-term, and by then everyone was
almost sure that the festival really was going to take place. In
fact the return of the exiles now seemed like water flowing
toward the sea, something that's got to happen. It will get
there somehow in the end. There'd been an election in
Romania but Mr. Kronin's brother was still high up in the
Ministry of Culture and could pull the right strings. It was he
who'd managed to wangle Grandad his visa. There was still a
chance that the new government would turn tough. They
seemed to be mostly ex-Communists who'd managed to stop
supporting Ceauşescu in time, and they'd won the election by
some fairly dirty tricks, including getting the miners to come
out and beat up the opposition—at least that's what the opposition said. But they were going to land themselves in a fair-
sized international incident if they tried turning the exiles
back at the last moment. There were too many of them for
that, and from too many places, from every country in Europe,
for a start, from the U.S.A. and Canada, from New Zealand
and Australia—a lot of Varinians had settled out there—and a
dozen other countries around the world.

The second half of the term lasted a century. It would have

seemed slow and pointless anyway, because the end of the school year is always a drag, and next term Angel would be living up in Yorkshire and Biddie would be at a boarding school for gifted children to which her parents had decided to send her. All that added to the dreary sense of things ending. At least there was the festival to look forward to.

By now Mollie had found a good Field speaker to help her, so Letta stayed at home for the first week of the holidays, getting herself sorted out, and then went up to St. Albans. It was a typical Mollie exercise, only on a larger scale than usual. There were eleven buses coming from all over Britain and joining up at the ferry. There were also two trucks of supplies and camping equipment. The organizers in Potok were still bouncing with excitement and confidence, and full of assurances that there were going to be food and beds for everyone, but Mr. Jaunis—largely to put a spoke in Mr. Orestes' wheel —had kept shaking his head and wanting to send a VIBI delegation out to Potok to check up. Mollie, despite being so thick with Mr. Orestes, had backed him up. The delegation came back pretty gloomy. Most of the temporary accommodation wasn't yet built and didn't look as if it was going to be; there was very little to buy in the shops; inflation was several hundred percent; you could buy things on the black market, for dollars or marks, but that was illegal; and so on.

So Mollie's PC had clicked into action, dashing off letters to everyone explaining the problem and asking for a bit more money and the loan of good tents, and the last of the answers were still coming in when Letta arrived. Everybody paid up. Not one person grumbled. People volunteered to drive hundreds of miles getting the tents together. An exile who was manager of a Safeways outside Coventry called and said, "Don't worry about the supplies. Just send me the truck and the check and I'll do the rest." There was, unbelievably, a whole two days with nothing left to arrange before the buses departed.

It was five o'clock in the morning and drizzling gently when the taxi took them over to Luton. Each bus had two bus captains, to check the lists and solve problems. Donna, who'd slept all the way from St. Albans, had woken up at last and Mollie was giving her her breakfast when one of the bus captains, a skinny, fussed-looking woman called Anne, pushed past some people who were still stowing their hand luggage and said, "They keep asking if Restaur Vax is really going to be there."

Letta sensed others in earshot craning to listen.

"He's flying out in two days time with his daughter and son-in-law," said Mollie. "He'll be there."

Somebody behind Letta sighed with relief, or content. The bus captain worked her way back up the aisle, repeating the news. Letta caught Nigel's eye. He gave his head a little shake and she nodded agreement. They'd already settled that they weren't going to tell anyone that Restaur Vax was their grandad, unless they were asked. It was lovely that everyone wanted him there so much, but that wasn't anything to do with them. They were just a couple of young Varinians, no different from any of the others.

They sang most of the way to Dover, and waved their Varinian flags (purple and black and white, courtesy of VIBI) at anyone who was looking whenever they came to a halt. The M25 was jammed at the Thames tunnel, which meant an anxious fifty-minute wait, but Mollie's schedules allowed for that sort of thing and they made it to Dover with time to spare. So did the two trucks and the other ten buses, though the one from Liverpool only just. Van was supposed to be on

the Edinburgh bus, but he didn't come and say hello so Letta
and Nigel went to look for him. They found him in one of the
bars with a group of friends. He raised a hand and came over.

"Hi, Sis," he said. "Hi, Nigel."

"Isn't this terrific," said Letta. "I'm sorry Susan's not coming. Mollie says she changed her mind."

"We've split up," said Van.

"Oh! I'm sorry."

"Forget it. These things happen. Tell the others not to
mention it, will you? Okay, see you later."

He turned and went back to his friends.

"That's a pity," said Letta. "I really like her."

"Typical Van," said Nigel.

They spent their first night at three big motels near Co-
logne, and then, because they were going the long way around
through Hungary, they did a tremendous dash down the auto-
bahn almost as far as Vienna. (It would have been quicker to
go through Yugoslavia, but there was some kind of trouble
brewing there, between the Serbs and the Croats, and somebody might have decided not to let eleven busloads of Varinians through.) Next morning they started at dawn and headed
east toward Budapest, and still on east, though Varina now lay
almost behind them to the south.

That afternoon they reached the Romanian frontier at Bors,
and there there was a three-hour holdup while the committee
argued with customs officials, who seemed to think they were
bringing their truckload of supplies in order to sell them on
the black market. They were really hoping to be bribed, Steff
said. At last they let the convoy move on again.

Hungary had been a bit different from the West, but not
too obviously. The roads had been worse, and the towns and
villages had looked strangely old-fashioned, with fewer cars

and a lot more people on bicycles. There'd been horses and mules, and even oxen, working in the fields, or pulling carts, or just plodding along the roads with enormous strange loads on their backs. Romania was the same, only much more so. After Bors they turned south through an enormous level plain, with mountains blue and vague on the horizon to their left. The soil in the fields seemed good, and often the crops were neat and strong, but the people looked poor, sad and exhausted, though they stared and then smiled and waved as the glossy air-conditioned buses rushed by, full of foreigners singing and waving unknown flags. Letta almost felt that it was tactless of the travelers to be there at all, so happy and excited, and so unbelievably richer and more comfortable, even the poorest of them, than the workers in the fields.

The other enormous change, of course, was the heat. She didn't feel it in the bus, but she could see it even through the tinted windows, the fierce sunlight radiating off the baked and dusty earth, or steaming up from marshes, or making hard-edged shadows under groups of trees where tired cattle lay and twitched. The buses stopped every two hours so that the passengers could stretch their legs, and when Letta reached the doorway the heat blasted up at her off the roadway, and going out into the sunlight was like walking through a barrier. Then the bus when she climbed back inside felt not just cool but freezing.

"Those must be the Carpathians," said Steff, pointing at the distant mountains. "If all goes well we should be in Potok by sunset."

But all did not go well. Late in the afternoon, a few miles after Timisoara, there was a holdup. Letta's bus was the last of the line, so that Mollie could keep an eye on the rest of the convoy, and there was an intercom link to the leading bus.

When they'd been waiting a few minutes the driver turned and waved to the bus captains. They went and listened to the intercom and then Anne, the thin and worried one, came bustling back. Mollie met her halfway down the aisle, discussed something briefly, and went forward to the intercom. After another discussion she turned and held up a hand for silence.

"There's a roadblock," she said. "They don't seem to be police or army. They're calling themselves a miners' committee. You probably know that the miners supported Ceauşescu, but Hector says these people are more like bandits. The trouble is they're armed, and they look as if they want to hijack our trucks. But we think if we all get up there and surround them and let them see how many of us there are they won't have the nerve to try anything. It's up to you, of course. Who's coming?"

The whole busload were already on their feet. They crowded toward the doors, Steff carrying Donna on his hip. Ahead of them the other buses were already emptying and everybody was streaming toward the front of the convoy. By the time Letta reached the trucks, which were between the first and second buses, the whole Varinian expedition had gathered around, shouting, booing, and catcalling. Both trucks were solid-sided vans, and she could see their tops above the crowd, but not much else.

A ripping clatter broke through the clamor, followed by complete silence. It was a noise Letta had heard time and again on TV, but it didn't belong in her real world, and it took her a moment to realize that it was a burst of fire from an automatic rifle. A man started to shout angry orders in what she thought must be Romanian. He was answered almost at once by a woman in the crowd starting to sing. Within half a bar they had all taken the anthem up, drowning the man's voice out. Letta sang automatically but with all her energies, not thinking about words or tune, which they all knew well by now, having sung them again and again on the long road south. Grandad had called the tune funereal, but with several hundred voices singing it by the roadside, and meaning it, they made it into a steady, unstoppable march, the march of a nation.

As they drew breath at the end of the verse the man began shouting again. At once they drowned him out with the anthem. More shots clattered out, but their song didn't falter or thin. When they reached the end and stopped, the man didn't try shouting but Letta could hear the mutter of ordinary, angry voices.

"Standoff," said Steff, craning. "They've got a gun to somebody's head. Can't see who."

"They're not going to . . ." Letta began, but her voice trailed off in horror at the thought.

"If they do they won't get away alive," he said. "They've let us get too close."

Her heart clenched. He couldn't mean it. But he did, and it was true. Then he seemed to realize that he shouldn't have said what he had.

"You'd better get clear, kid," he said in English. "You too, Nidgy. Take Donna and go back and wait at the bus."

"But . . ." said Letta and Nigel together.

"Do what you're told, kids. Right?"

Letta would have liked to argue, but there's a limit to how far a thirteen-year-old can stand up to an adult, even when he's only a brother. Nigel would have to do what his father said, anyway, so she'd better, but it didn't stop her being angry about it.

Nigel took Donna and they wriggled clear and then walked down the line of buses, craning back over their shoulders as they went. They weren't the only ones. Other children were coming away too, looking, Letta thought, just the way she felt, shocked and frightened, but hurt too at not being allowed to be part of something very important, something almost that would mark them like a brand or a tattoo, and prove that they were truly Varinians.

When the anthem started again behind them they joined in and marched to its beat, but in the middle of a verse Nigel broke off and pointed ahead.

"Someone's getting impatient," he said.

There'd been almost no traffic on the road, but by now there was a bit of a backup behind the buses, a few battered trucks and the odd car. Beside them, on the wrong side of the road, a larger truck was churning forward. As it neared it slowed, and Letta saw that it was full of men, some armed with guns. More miners, she thought with a sinking heart, but then saw that the khaki they were wearing was actually uniform. Soldiers.

The truck halted beside them. A man leaned out of the cab window.

"English?" he said cheerfully. He must have seen the bus company's address on the backs of the buses.

"Yes," said Nigel and Letta together.

"Why stopping? Accident, eh?"

"It's a roadblock, miners," said Letta.

"They're trying to steal our supplies," said Nigel. "Can you straighten them out?"

"Okay, okay," said the man, grinning and raising a thumb.

The truck roared on. The soldiers in the back waved as if they were going to a party.

"U.S. Cavalry," said Nigel. "They're early. They aren't supposed to show up till the last reel. What are the odds they'll want the supplies themselves?"

They moved into the shadow of a bus and waited, drained by heat and tension. Male voices, furious, broke the afternoon calm. The argument ended and the Varinians started to come back down the road, talking and laughing excitedly among themselves and punching triumphant fists into the air. The first to reach Letta were a pair of newlyweds called Milj and Tara. Milj was Varinian but Tara was dark-skinned, from Madagascar.

"The army showed up and ran them off," crowed Milj. "Took their guns away and all. Were they pissed off about that!"

"Can we go on now?"

"No reason why not."

But there was. The officer in charge of the soldiers decided that they must stay where they were until he got permission from Timisoara for them to move on. The buses pulled off onto the shoulder to let the other traffic through, and then the soldiers searched the entire convoy. They unloaded the trucks and checked everything, and went through the baggage compartments in all the buses, and then crawled about under the chassis banging on bits of metal with the handles of their bayonets. When they opened anything they insisted on the owners being by to see they weren't stealing. They were delighted with things like video cameras and Walkmans and handed them around among themselves, and wanted to be shown how they worked, but they acted more like excited kids with toys, and they always gave them back with smiles and thanks.

"It can't be drugs they're looking for," Letta heard a
woman say.

"Something bigger than that," said a man. "They didn't
bother to open Vicki's vanity case."

"No, it's guns," said another man.

"Guns at a culture festival?" said the woman.

"We're going to Potok, honey," said the second man, as if
that explained everything.

Later, Letta asked Steff about it and he shook his head.

"Doubt it," he said. "More likely they were just going
through the motions, as a way of keeping us here till they got
some sense out of Timisoara. My guess is the Romanians never
did their math and really worked out how many of us were
coming, not just from the U.K., and now they're getting
anxious."

"But could it actually be guns?" said Nigel.

"I suppose it's possible. All these countries are pretty
jumpy about their minorities, and there are a lot of hotheads
around. No doubt some idiots are trying to smuggle weapons
in. But I think they're just being bureaucrats. When a bureau-
crat's bothered, he invariably presses the hold-everything but-
ton. Anyway, it looks as if we're going to have to camp here
for the night, so let's start sorting ourselves out."

Mollie had a contingency plan for just this kind of crisis, so
it all went smoothly enough. A lot of the travelers had emergency rations with them, and there was plenty to spare in the
supply trucks. An old man came by in the evening, and some
of the travelers who could speak Romanian chatted with him,
and he shook hands and left, but came back a little later
leading two mules laden with immense bundles of firewood,
which he sold for several cans of beef stew. They lit fires,
whose smoke drifted up into the dusky air, and ate together,

and sang as they'd sung all the way south. The sun had set in scarlet bands and night rose visibly up the eastern sky, the way it never does in England. Steff pointed at the distance.

Their road must have swung a long way back because the hills, nearer now, were over on their right, a hard-edged ragged line, black against the afterglow of day.

"See that?" he said. "That's Varina."

Well, at least I've seen it, thought Letta as she fidgeted in her sleeping bag, trying to find a place where the iron ground was kinder to her hip. Even if we never get there, at least I've seen it.

LEGEND

FATHER STEPHAN

News was brought to Falje that the Pasha of Potok, with all his *bazouks,* was slain by Restaur Vax and the Varinians at Riqui. Then the Pasha of Falje, though he had little love for the Pasha of Potok, was both angry and afraid, and sent letters to the other Pashas, at Slot, and Aloxha, and Jirin, saying, "Our brother must now be avenged with many lives, or the Varinians will feel strong in their hearts and know they are indeed a people. Then they will rise against us and slay us all. Moreover it is we who must take vengeance, for if we do less the Sultan will send armies from Byzantium, with viziers and generals to oversee the vengeance, and we shall ourselves be called to account. Therefore write each of you to the Sultan, as I have done, saying that we have the matter of vengeance well in hand. That done, come with all your *bazouks* to Potok and we will begin the work."

So the Pashas gathered at Potok. Then the Pasha of Slot said, "Let these Christian swine understand the full measure of our vengeance. Let us take their Bishop, Bishop Pango, and crucify him on the walls of Potok, where all Varina may see him."

The Pasha of Falje said, "I have word that he has fled to the Monastery of St. Valia, where there are many secret ways and many places of hiding."

The Pasha of Aloxha said, "My captain of *bazouks* is a man who does not know pity or fear. Let him take command, and he will find this infidel."

So the captain gave orders and the *bazouks* surrounded the great monastery, and seized all who fled. They broke down the doors and found the fathers at prayer, but with blows and insults they herded them into the courtyard. The captain of *bazouks* looked silently at them.

Then he said, "Where is your Bishop? My masters, the Pashas, would speak with him, but not one hair of his beard will they harm."

But the fathers saw that he lied and did not answer.

Then the captain lined the fathers up before him and said, "Very well, since you are foolish old men, I must show you that I will have my way. Let every fifth old fool stand forward."

He walked along the line of fathers, beckoning each fifth one forward. And a certain Father Stephan, counting swiftly to his right, changed places with the father on his left, pushing him roughly aside, and when the captain of *bazouks* stood before him this Father Stephan shook and trembled as if with fear, and seemed to wish to change his place again. And the captain of *bazouks*, having seen what he did, smiled in his beard and said, "You have missed your count, old man, for it is now you who are the fifth one. Stand forward."

When he had passed in this manner all down the line the

captain made the fathers he had chosen kneel down, with necks outstretched, and he posted a *bazouk* beside each one with his scimitar drawn and ready to smite, and said, "Now which of you will tell me where Bishop Pango is hidden? If none will, then all that I have chosen will die on my signal. Moreover they will die in vain, for I will then burn this monastery with fire, and leave no stone standing on its fellow, and your Bishop will die among the ruins."

Still not one father spoke, so he gave the signal, and they died. Of the rest, some he whipped and some he tortured, but still all held their silence. Then with blows and insults he drove them from the monastery, and his *bazouks* brought fire, and burned it. Levers too they brought and heaved the stones apart. And many secret ways and places of hiding they uncovered, but Bishop Pango they did not find.

But the fathers took the road from Potok toward the Danube, those who were less hurt helping those who were more hurt. At the river they sent word to a certain man who had a boat, which he brought secretly to them by night. And Bishop Pango stood before them at the water's edge and said, "I leave you, and I leave this beloved land so that I may journey through Christendom where I will tell the Princes of the Church and the Princes of the Peoples of the sufferings of our nation under the oppression of the Turks. Be brave, and trust in God, and in a little while I will return."

Now the fathers urged him to go quickly, before the Turks took thought where he might be and pursued and found him, but he said, "I must stay another hour, so that in this place, on the sacred soil of Varina, we may sing a full Mass together for the souls of our dead brothers, and especially for Father Stephan, who knowingly moved into my fifth place in the line, and died so that I might live."

So on the shore of the Danube, above Slot, where the Chapel of the Blessed Stephan[1] now stands, they sang the full Mass for the Dead. None heard, and none came by. Then Bishop Pango boarded the boat and left them.

———

1. *The chapel has recently been demolished by the Communist regime, on the pretext that the site was needed for a navigation light.*

AUGUST 1990

They woke in the dewy dawn, tried to stretch away their aches and stiffness, and took their turns at the improvised latrines, leaving the bathrooms in the buses for the elderly. When they started to cook their breakfasts from the supply truck the soldiers who had been left to keep an eye on them gathered hungrily around. Some of them wanted to try out their English, but mostly they were interested in Western food. They thought the instant coffee was terrific compared to what they could get in Romania. They liked peanut butter, but not Marmite.

"It's funny," said someone as she delicately spread her bread with a thin layer of the dark, yeasty, salty goo. "You have to be English to like Marmite. I know I couldn't live without it."

"So you English now?" said the soldier who was standing by, wolfing his third peanut butter sandwich. "You say before you Varinish."

"We're both," they all said.

"What you want here?" said the soldier, pointing toward the horizon. "Nothing is for you in these mountains, no motor car for all people, no oil well, no swim pool. What you do here?"

Several voices answered. "We're going home." "That's where we belong." "We want to see what Varina is like."

"Varina no place," he said patronizingly, and drew a map with his finger in the air. "Romania here. Yugoslavia here. Hungaria here. Where now Varina?"

"There!" they shouted, flinging out their arms toward the mountains.

He shrugged and held out his mug for more coffee.

They had cleaned up the campsite as best they could and it was already getting too hot for comfort when permission came through for them to move on. The officer who brought it didn't bother to hide the fact that he thought they shouldn't be there at all, and insisted on escorting them the whole way to Potok. Two hours later after they had set off there was another delay at a real checkpoint manned by soldiers, where for a few horrible minutes it looked as if their escort and the checkpoint commander were going to agree to turn them back. Even Mollie gave a sigh of relief as she settled into her seat and the bus moved on.

"They were trying to tell us Potok was full up," she said, "and there wasn't any more room."

"Was that the border, do you think?" said Nigel. "Will there be an actual sign saying 'Varina'?"

"If there's a sign it will say 'Cerna-Potok,' " said Steff. "There is no such place as Varina on Romanian maps."

"Look, there's a flag!" said Mollie.

It hung at an upstairs window, and they all cheered it, and

the next, and the next, but soon they gave up because there were too many to cheer. By then they'd begun to see another sign that they must truly be in Varina now. Letta had more uncertain feelings about this one. Almost every blank surface —the walls of barns, the buttresses of bridges, crags by the wayside as the road snaked up into the mountains—carried the same three letters, as huge as the space would allow, sometimes carefully lettered, sometimes daubed fiercely on in seven slashes of paint:

V A X

"I hope they know which one they mean," said Nigel.

"They mean both," said Minna, twisting around from the seat in front of them. "They are the same. For us he has never died."

About a third of the women in the bus were called Minna. This one was forty at least. Her hair had a lot of gray in it and her clothes were as shapeless as her body, and Letta had decided she was rather sad, but now her eyes were wet and glittered behind the tears, so that she looked almost a little crazy. Her expression crystallized Letta's feelings of unease. Letta knew and loved Grandad and admired him no end. She was sure there wasn't anyone else in the whole world quite like him. She was glad that other people could feel that too. But she also knew that he was an old man, who even when he was feeling fully well got tired quite soon. That he was coming to open the festival was lovely, happy-making for everyone. They would see and hear him, and he would be in his own country again after all these years, and they'd all be glad for each other's sake as well as their own, and so on.

But really there wasn't anything much he could *do*.

One old man can't change everything, but here was Minna looking as if she expected Grandad to take hold of Varina, to pick up the three pieces of it between his hands and mold them gently into a single piece and put them down again in their place, one country now, never to be taken apart again. And Minna herself would happily die if that would help him do it. No, Letta thought. I'm thirteen and you're forty, but I know it's a fairy story and you don't.

At first the road climbed steadily along a mountain flank. The surface was good and the curves gentle, so the convoy sped along. Then they turned off up a narrower, steeper road, with huge potholes unmended since last winter. An endless ladder of hairpins took them grindingly up and up and over a ridge which was a huge spur of the great Carpathian chain. The pass was bleak and barren, between snow-capped peaks. Beyond it the road swooped down toward a wide valley with a fair-sized river wriggling along the bottom.

Letta's ears popped and popped again as they took the downward hairpins. The road leveled and swung around a shoulder, and there, far below them, lay a town, a jumble of red ridged tiles, the domes of small white-washed churches, larger domes on one big church, a ruined something on the hillside beyond with a mess of tents alongside it. She counted the five bridges and knew it must be Potok. The big church must be the Cathedral of St. Joseph, and the ruin was the old monastery of St. Valia.

Everyone was pointing and chattering. Potok vanished and came again several times as the road wound its way down. And then they were there. The town seemed to have no outlying sections. At one moment the buses were passing scrubby precipitous hillsides with here and there a tiny stone-walled field or a terraced vineyard, and the next they were in a street of battered old houses, all plastered the same blotchy orange-yellow, with shuttered windows and heavy crooked doors which hadn't been painted for years, and wide overhanging eaves like hat brims. The street was so narrow that in places, if the bus windows had opened, you could have reached out and touched the walls on both sides.

The street was crowded with pedestrians, who all stopped what they were doing to cheer the buses as they churned slowly through. Two women in black, with lined weather-beaten old faces, climbed through the open door and came down the aisle handing out nosegays of rosemary and bay and marjoram tied with ribbon in the national colors. They didn't want any money. When they got down some of the travelers did so too.

"Let's walk for a bit," said Nigel. "Is that okay, Mum? We won't get lost."

Mollie looked at Steff. She usually left family decisions to him.

"Don't see why not," he said. "Difficult to get lost in a place this size. If in doubt ask for the university, and when you're there look for the British contingent."

So Nigel and Letta jumped down and waited while the bus took the stench of its exhaust slowly away, and then followed up the street. It was slow going as every few yards somebody would stop them and ask where they were from. Letta realized they must be obviously not native Varinians, with their Marks and Spencer clothes and their pale northern skins. It had been a terrific summer back home, but their tans still looked washed-out beside those of the people who lived all the time under these southern skies.

"Where are you from?" they were asked, time and again,

and when they answered "England," the next question, almost always, was "Has Restaur Vax come with you?"

"Not with us," Letta told them. "We came out on a bus, but he's a bit old for that so he's flying to Bucharest. He's supposed to be here tomorrow."

Next, people wanted to know about England, and to try out the English they'd learned in school, and just be friendly. They didn't seem to find it odd either that Letta could rattle away in Field or that Nigel couldn't, but there was something about their smiles which gave Letta a feeling that they thought the way she spoke was a bit peculiar. Or perhaps they were simply amused by her eagerness and excitement, which she certainly felt. Being in a country where everybody spoke Field, as the normal thing, was wonderful. She felt like a bird released into the air.

Nigel was tugging at her sleeve. She looked ahead. The buses were out of sight.

"Come on," he said. "I don't want Mum worrying."

(Typical Nigel. He was the worrier, not Mollie.)

So they hurried as best they could until they found the road blocked almost from side to side by a mob of people milling around a center where a man was being hoisted into the air, amid cheers which mingled with hoots and laughter as he was dropped and then hoisted again to sit on his bearers' shoulders, waving both arms overhead in triumphant greeting.

"Hey! It's Uncle Van!" said Nigel.

It was too. He'd had his back to them, but the churn of the crowd turned him until Letta could see her brother's long, normally moody face, now smiling and excited.

"What's he think he's doing?" said Nigel. "This isn't *The Prisoner of Zenda*. Bet you he's told them who his grandad is."

Letta found Van interesting, and thought she might have

liked him if she'd known him better, but Nigel naturally
enough had picked up Steff's attitude. And certainly Van
didn't just look like the star of some old swordplay romance.
He seemed to feel like that too, the True Heir come back to
his oppressed people. They'd be storming the castle next,
while he held twenty men-at-arms at bay on the stairway to
the young Queen's bedroom.

"Who do they cheer?" said a woman crushed against the
wall beside her.

"His name's Van Ozolins," said Letta. "He's just come on
the bus from Scotland."

"Scotland?" said the woman, impressed. "Still he is one of
us. He has the face of our men."

Letta knew what she was talking about. She'd already seen
dozens of versions of it on the streets of Potok. Grandad had it
too. He used to joke about it and quote a poem by the other
Restaur Vax about Varinian men which started off "Combat-
ive, wiry, hound-faced, crazed with honor . . ." Yes, that was
Van all right.

They broke through at last and jostled on up the street.
When Letta asked for the university the woman she'd chosen
insisted on guiding them all the way.

The university had one lovely old building, stone as yellow
as honey, with a pillared front and three red-tiled domes.
Bishop Pango had built it, their guide said, but everything
else had been pulled down by the Communists and rebuilt
with modern blocks. These were like grimy vast shoe boxes
set on end. Despite their size they were depressingly mean and
dingy.

The buses had unloaded and Mollie was sorting things out.
The British contingent had been promised a hundred and
ninety beds, and there were fewer than half that for them, but

from what the earlier visitors had told her she'd guessed something like this might happen, so now it was a matter of putting the contingency plans into action, seeing that the elderly got first pick, and the families with small children had what they needed and so on. In theory her principal helpers knew what to do, though of course there were some of them who were ditherers or botherers and kept running back with problems for her to sort out, which she did, coolly, never looking irritated or blaming anyone. (A rumor went around the party that evening that one of the local Varinians had watched Mollie in action for a bit and then turned and asked—seriously, according to the story—"This is your Mrs. Thatcher, then?" For the rest of the trip everyone, including the local Varinians, called Mollie Maggie, which as a passionate Liberal Democrat she found trying. That was later, of course.)

It was obviously going to take hours to get it all sorted out, so Letta decided the best thing she could do to help was to take charge of Donna, who was tired enough by now to be sleepy but too cranky to sleep. She read her *Asterix and the Goths* for the umpteenth time until she dropped off, and then she put her in the stroller and found her way to the official campsite, which was on the other side of the river, spread out along the hillside below the ruined monastery. Letta had arranged to share a tent with a girl from her bus, a couple of years younger than herself, called Janine, who had a Varinian mother and a Welsh father, and a tiny baby brother, who was why Janine was delighted to have Letta to share with. Steff was going to come and put their tent up for them, but he was still helping Mollie, so Letta found herself a narrow patch of shade beneath an old wall and settled down to wait.

She felt dreamy, dazed, but not sleepy, though she should have been exhausted after the long journey, and the holdups,

and the night on the hard ground. Her whole body brimmed
with happiness. The wall was part of the ruins, and the sun
must just have left it, so that the old stones still breathed out
warmth in a caressing, welcoming waft. People moved between the mass of tents calling and laughing. There were
transistors going, and what sounded like live music, twangy
ethno-rock, down by the river, which she could sometimes
hear muttering over its boulders though it was shallow and
skimpy now. She guessed it must be a real torrent during the
snowmelt.

Over to her right lay the town, all tiles and domes, with a
few harsh concrete towers as a reminder of what the Communists had done. From there too came a steady muttering, almost too faint to be heard except when some of the thousands
of voices that made it burst into cheering or laughter. The
smells of the south floated on the hot and golden air, sun-
baked dust, dung that dried before it could rot, wild aromatic
bushes on the slopes. The whole steep valley purred with her
contentment.

Two boys, fifteenish, came by on the new-worn path below
where she sat, walking with that self-conscious swagger boys
use when they want the world to think of them as men. The
difference from English boys was that they made a good job of
the swagger, despite the fact that they were holding hands.
They glanced at Letta, checking her out, then away, either
because of Donna or because they thought she was too young
for them, and then back with a different look, having registered through some slower mind channel that she didn't belong. They stopped.

"You American, huh?" said the taller one, in English. He
had the hound face, like Van, and obviously thought he was

hot stuff. Mentally Letta named him God's Gift. The other one was shorter, and anxious about most things, a classic henchman. Hench.

"No, from England," she said, also in English, waiting for a proper long sentence she could use to spring her Field on them.

"You come in airplane, huh?" said God's Gift, giving her her chance at once.

"No, we came in a bus. We were supposed to get here yesterday, but the miners held us up with a roadblock at Timisoara and then the army kept us there all night."

The effect wasn't quite what she'd wanted.

"Hi! Who taught you to speak like that? You sound like some real old auntie, used to be a teacher or something."

"That's how we talk at home. My parents left Varina before I was born."

"Bet you talk Formal too," said Hench. "You know, my momma says her poppa tried to make them talk Formal Sundays."

"Can't see the use," said God's Gift. "Bloody *leave*."

"My grandad says they used to call it the pig verb," said Letta.

"Use is, teachers got to have something to teach," said Hench. He was brighter than he looked, thought Letta.

"Pig verb is right," said God's Gift, not apparently noticing that Hench had come up with a genuine thought. "Hey! You got any tapes? Genesis? Sting? Bon Jovi?"

Angel was a Genesis fan, as it happened, and had coaxed Letta into going along when her father had given up an evening of lawn bowling to take her to a concert in Southampton the summer before. Letta wasn't a fan of anyone—didn't in her heart of hearts much care for music—but she felt she'd better take a bit of interest so as not to feel left out, and she'd enjoyed the Genesis concert much more than she'd expected, not the music itself, but the sense of being carried along on a tide of excitement—nothing like as fake as she'd expected—and looking at the weird clothes the fans wore—all that.

It really paid off now. They squatted on the grass beside her. Even God's Gift was impressed as she told them about it. Soon he was wanting to know where she was staying, and whether she had to look after Donna the whole time, and then how many cars her family had and how big their swimming pool was. No swimming pool! They were astounded. Two cars, and eight separate rooms in the house, and Genesis concerts just down the road, but no swimming pool. It didn't make sense. Everybody in the West had a swimming pool. They knew that because they'd seen it on *Dallas* and *Dynasty*—old, old episodes, from what they told her about the plots.

She put them off about meeting again, saying she was in a group and she didn't know what they'd be doing, and yes she expected she'd have to look after Donna most of the time (liar —Steff loved doing that). God's Gift actually seemed disappointed. An English girl who'd been to a live Genesis concert would be something to boast about, even if she wasn't startlingly beautiful and a bit young and hadn't got a swimming pool. Then somebody whistled from down the slope, friends of the pair, and they got up. God's Gift had one last try.

"Know what you're doing this evening?"

"We're all going to a folk concert, I think."

"That old stuff! Twangle ping, twingle pung, my goat is dead. Can't stand it. Have fun, though. See you."

They machoed away, holding hands again, to join their friends. Letta thanked her stars that Nigel hadn't been there.

He'd have felt challenged to outmacho God's Gift, and that would have been really embarrassing. And at least it had been a change to talk to someone who didn't want to know if Restaur Vax was coming.

LEGEND

The Hermit of Lapiri

ow the Pashas of Falje, of Slot, of Aloxha, and of
Jirin said in their hearts, "There is no Pasha in
Potok to oversee the taxes, and to leave to the people
enough for next year's seed to be sown, so that next year's
harvest may be taxed in its turn. Soon the Sultan will send a
new Pasha to Potok, so let us at once strip from the town all
that we can, and carry it to our own Pashaliks. But let us do it
under pretext of law."

They summoned the aldermen of Potok and said, "By your
treachery was your Pasha slain, for you warned Restaur Vax of
his going to Riqui. Therefore you must pay the blood price of
a Pasha, and that is seventeen thousand *kronin.*"

Then the aldermen implored them and said, "How shall we
find such a sum, when the yearly tax of Potok is but seven
hundred *kronin?*"

The Pashas said, "It is for you to answer your own question.
You have treasure, all of you, hidden below your stairs. Your

wives wear gold pins in their shawls. And take heed to gather the blood price by St. Axun's Day, for should you fail we will take the blood price in blood. Every fifth man we will slay with the sword, and your sons we shall take for slaves, and your sisters and daughters for our own uses, and your roof-beams we will burn with fire. See to it."

At that the aldermen of Potok despaired, and took counsel. And one said, "Let us send to Restaur Vax to come to our rescue, saying that it is he who has brought this vengeance on us by slaying our Pasha."

So they agreed, though some thought in their hearts that they would betray Restaur Vax to the Pashas, and so save their town.

When the message was brought to Restaur Vax he said, "We must go to the aid of Potok."

His chieftains answered, "What are these townsmen to us? They are Greeks and Magyars and Croats.[1] They buy for three *stija* and sell for ten. They have treasure of their own below their stairs. Let them pay their own price."

Then Restaur Vax spoke strongly with them, saying, "Potok is the heart of Varina, as the mountains are its soul. How can the soul live without the body, and how can the body live without its heart?"

But they would not hear him.

Then Restaur Vax said, "Your choice is your choice, but I will go. Alone I will go if need be."

Lash the Golden said, "Body, heart, and soul are all one to me, and mine are sworn to you. I will come also."

And Kas Kalaz, not to be shamed by Lash, said he would go with them, and so said some few others, but with doubting hearts, for they were not enough to fight the Pashas on a level plain.

But Restaur Vax cheered them and said, "What we cannot win with our swords we must win with our wits. Moreover we must bind these merchants to us with ties of blood and of gold, or when the chance comes they will think to betray us. Gather therefore with your best men into the wood above St. Valia, and I will come to you there on the Eve of St. Axun."

Then he took horse and rode to Lapiri, where lived a hermit who had been once sub-Prior of St. Valia's, and knew all its secret ways, but now was of great age and blind, and to him he told what was in his heart.

Then the hermit said, "For what they have done to St. Valia's, and what they will do to our sacred land, I will help you as I can. But even to the Turk I will tell no lie, lest I peril my soul."[2]

To that Restaur Vax agreed. He put the hermit on his horse and led him by goat paths and the paths of the hunter until on the Eve of St. Axun's they came to the wood above St. Valia. Thence a boy led the hermit down into the town and took him to the alderman. To them he spoke thus.

"I am the Hermit of Lapiri, who in former days was sub-Prior of St. Valia's. I have heard of your need, and I will go to the Pashas tomorrow and tell them of a secret place where they will find a treasure of seventeen thousand *kronin,* and that they may take as the blood price for the Pasha of Potok. But hear me, these Pashas are men of insatiate greed, and they will ask me if there is any other treasure in Potok."

"To that you must answer that there is none," said the aldermen.

"That cannot be while you have treasure, each of you, below your stairs. For I will tell no lie, even to the Turk, lest I peril my soul."

"Then what can we do?" asked the aldermen.

"You must send it out of Potok to a safe keeper," said the hermit, "and by the will of God Restaur Vax is even now in the wood above St. Valia. Send it to him this very night, and I swear to you that he will return to you, when the Pashas have taken their blood price, all that is yours."

Then they said, "This Restaur Vax is a brigand and the friend of brigands. He will steal our gold."

The hermit answered, "I am the Hermit of Lapiri and I do not lie. All that is rightly yours will be returned. Do as I tell you, or I will go back this night to Lapiri."

Seeing no help, the aldermen then took up their treasure from under their stairs, and the gold pins from the shawls of their wives, and sent them to Restaur Vax in the wood above St. Valia's.

On the morning of St. Axun's the aldermen came to the Pashas and said, "There is no treasure below our stairs to pay the blood price. But look, this old man who is now blind was once sub-Prior of St. Valia's, and he will show you a place where is hidden a treasure of seventeen thousand *kronin,* and that will be your blood price."

Then the Pashas questioned the hermit, and he told them that it was as the aldermen said, so they carried him to St. Valia's and there, feeling the ground with his staff, he led them to a place in the vineyard and said, "Dig here. At a shin bone's depth is a great stone in which is an iron ring. Lift it up and you will see a staircase. Let torches be brought and lit, for it is very dark below."

So it was done, and they found the stone and heaved it aside and saw the stairs leading down into the dark. Then they sent down a *bazouk* carrying a torch, and called to him, "What do you see?" And he cried out, "I see boxes of gold, and many gold pins, spread about the floor."

Hearing that, the Pashas rushed down the staircase, each fearing that the others might cheat him of his share. As they knelt to gather up the gold Restaur Vax and Lash the Golden fell upon them from behind and slew them. For the hermit had told them of a secret passage which led from St. Valia's Chapel in the wood into that place, and there they had lain hidden in the shadows until the Pashas came. And then Kas Kalaz and the rest came out of the wood and slew those who were aboveground, all but three *bazouks* who escaped back into the town.

When these three told their fellows what had happened at St. Valia, and that all four Pashas were slain, the *bazouks* were afraid, and fled from Potok, and from all Varina north of the Danube.

Then Restaur Vax told the aldermen to come to St. Valia's, and gather up the treasure, which was the same treasure as that that had lain below their stairs. And they counted it and said, "One tenth is not here."

Then Restaur Vax said to them, "All that is rightly yours is here, as the hermit promised. But I have taken a tenth by way of taxes, for I am now master of Potok and of Varina. Moreover, think in your hearts. The Turks will know that it was you who told the Pashas to come to St. Valia where I slew them. That blood is on you, as on me. Therefore you have need that I should be strong, with cannon, and food to feed my army, so that I may defend you when the Turk comes to take vengeance. We are now bound each to the other with ties of blood and of gold."

The aldermen wept and said, "The tax upon Potok is seven hundred *kronin* only, and you have taken seventeen hundred."

Restaur Vax laughed and said, "If I had not come to your

help you would have paid the Pashas seventeen thousand, and still you would not have been ruined."

<hr>

1. *Potok has always had a number of non-Varinian citizens, many of whom were successful merchants. There have been frequent episodes of friction and some bloodshed as a result.*
2. *The trickster who has to deceive without actually telling a lie is a popular motif in Varinian folklore.*

AUGUST 1990

The folk concert took place in the ruined cloisters of St. Valia, a large square open space, its rough grass hummocky with buried masonry and its yellow walls patterned with the remains of archways and illegible tablets. The English contingent had not yet adjusted to Varinian notions about time. They arrived about half an hour before the concert was supposed to start and found almost no one else there and the sound system still being set up.

"I'm dead beat," said Mollie. "I'll have a nap. And let's find somewhere near an entrance so that we can slip away."

"Not in front of that speaker, Nidge," said Steff. "I value my eardrums."

"I've got some earplugs," said Mollie.

"It's *meant* to be loud, Mum," said Nigel.

They found a bank of turf against the outer wall. Donna slept, sprawling and inert, and Mollie did her trick of having a nap sitting bolt upright with her head balancing on her neck. She said anyone could learn to do it and it was just as refreshing as sleeping lying down.

Steff read. Letta and Nigel chatted and watched the crowd beginning to stream in. The sun went down and the ruined bell tower glowed with floodlighting against the darkening sky. By the time the stars were fully out the cloisters seemed crammed, but more and more people kept pushing their way in, squeezing the mass tighter and tighter, or scrambling up the crumbling walls and perching along them.

Mollie woke and muttered to Steff, who glanced around and then said, "Okay, listen. This might get out of hand. If it does, don't try and get to the door. We'll go over the wall here. I'll lift Nidge up and then pass Donna to him. Then Letta, then Mollie. Somebody will give me a leg up. Shouldn't happen, but just in case. Got it?"

They nodded. It was another of those differences. In England there'd have been crush barriers and marshals, and ambulances ready, because they'd been doing this sort of thing for years and knew what might happen. In Varina everything was new. This was the beginning of a new world, before rules, before problems, before disasters. It was alarming but exciting too, and somehow, Letta felt, pure.

"Hey! There's Uncle Van!" said Nigel.

"Where? I want to talk to him," said Mollie.

She cupped her hands around her mouth and called. It was another of her tricks. Nigel said he'd seen her hail a taxi across Piccadilly Circus in the rush hour. She did it without yelling. She just flung her call and it carried. Like now. Van looked around, wildly at first, then spotted Mollie and came struggling over, causing a commotion in the crush as half a dozen other people tried to follow him. He arrived panting and tousled, but obviously on a terrific high.

"How's everyone?" he shouted. "Isn't this great! Got some friends here want to meet you."

He introduced them as they arrived. They were native Varinians, all at the same fever pitch of excitement as Van. Everybody had to shake hands with everyone. A pretty young woman gave Steff a smacking kiss and cried out, "Now I have kissed both grandsons of Restaur Vax!"

Her friends all cheered.

"And where is Letta?" she asked, and flung her arms around her and kissed her and then stood back, holding her by the shoulders.

"And you, you live with him in the same house!" she said. "Van says you have tea with him every day! And is he well? Is he still . . . ?"

She couldn't bring herself to say the words but instead held her hands cupped but rigid, a few inches apart in front of her, and made them quiver, as if there were some precious object between them which she was testing to see if it was sound still.

"He's fine," said Letta. "Bright as a bird. Of course he gets tired sometimes. But mostly you wouldn't guess he was anything like eighty. I'm very fond of him."

"Fond?" said the woman with a startled laugh. "You aren't supposed to be fond of a hero. That's quite wrong. What you do with a hero is worship him."

"Oh, look," said Mollie. "Something's going to happen at last. Listen, Van. Message from Poppa. Grandad will be at the Palace Hotel at twelve tomorrow. Opposite the cathedral. He'd like to say hello, and he's not going to have much time for us after that."

"I'll be there."

"Allow a bit extra. The square's going to be packed solid."

(One of Steff's family's complaints about Van was that he was hopeless about keeping appointments.)

"Don't worry, Mollie. Historic moment. Wouldn't miss it for the world. Okay, Steff, Nigel, Sis. Be seeing you."

"Typical Uncle Van," said Nigel automatically as the group plunged back to join their other friends, but it wasn't typical at all, Letta thought. She'd never seen her brother in that kind of state before.

Now the spotlights came on and a band appeared, a standard small group with guitars, bass, drums, and a primitive synthesizer. The singer was a pale, hungry-looking blond woman in jeans and crazy high heels. They waved to the crowd, fiddled with their mikes, and were just set when one of the spotlights popped. Everyone laughed. Then they were off. Letta reached across to Mollie for earplugs. The speakers were large, but they'd been turned up well beyond the point where they could take the bass, so every chord was threaded with an appalling, tooth-rattling metallic buzz—just like a Western concert, only far, far worse. All around her the Varinians were bellowing their national anthem, rejoicing.

The songs from then on were rock versions of old Varinian folk songs, most of which Letta had heard, but not of course like this, with electronics and a band which kept trying to liven things up with a heavy rock beat. But she thought the singer was pretty good, with throaty bubbling low notes and soft trailing-away high ones which made her spine tingle. The lead guitarist, on the other hand, was doubly dire, a pretty awful musician, and an older version of God's Gift, but ten times worse.

After the band there were bagpipes. Varinian bagpipes are the sort you work with a little pair of bellows under your elbow, instead of blowing into the bag like Scottish pipes.

This is just as well, as half the point is the dancing. Varinians would regard standing-still pipers, or even marching-around ones, as shirkers. The pipers were all men, but they wore short frilly skirts so that everyone could see the steps, a sort of twiddling jig, starting pretty fast and getting faster and faster until the fingers on the pipe were a blur and the legs were almost a blur too. And all the time the top half of the body, which was dressed in a stiff jacket with buttons all up the front and complicated patterns of gold thread, had to stay as still as a statue, with a calm statue-face above it, and only the tassel on the little round hat flopping wildly to and fro. Several pipers started together, playing the same tune, and the crowd picked up the beat by clapping, and then gradually clapping faster until one of the dancers missed a step and dropped out, and so on until just one dancer was left, piping and twirling, and he was the winner.

"Is Mr. Orestes this good?" whispered Letta.

"Nothing like," said Nigel. "It's amazing. It ought to be in the Olympics. Then we'd be sure of getting at least one gold."

After the pipers came a real folk band with weird but beautiful instruments. The male singer had a strange, bleating tenor, but apparently that was how the songs were supposed to be sung. Letta enjoyed them but she sensed that the crowd wasn't so keen. To them this was pretty ordinary, something they could do for themselves at home.

Then there was another round of piping, and then an old woman was helped onto the stage. She looked pretty frail and needed a stick to walk, but she held herself straight and wore a wonderful long back dress, covered with sequins, which looked at least as old as she was, and a feather boa. Her hair was shining white, her face thin and beaky, with heavy eye shadow and thick pale makeup. Everyone had started cheering

the moment she appeared, and she stood there looking surprised but gracious while the master of ceremonies—a fat,
anxious, smiling man—tried to introduce her through the
clamor.

"Who is this?" Letta asked Steff.

"Minna Alaya," he said. "She was a film star in Germany.
Silent films, you know, so the accent didn't matter. Grandad
told me she's the most beautiful woman he's ever met."

The woman held up her hands and the cloisters fell silent
for her, while the MC adjusted the microphone.

"They asked me to do something," she said. "I didn't know
what. These are such happy times at last, aren't they? All I
could think of was to read a poem they taught me at school.
So long ago. Some of you older ones will know it too, I think.
But then the Communists took these poems away from us.
Why? They are not about politics. No, but they took them
away because they wanted to stop us being the people we are,
and these poems are one of the many things that make us the
people we are. Us Varinians. Don't be afraid because it's in
Formal. It isn't difficult."

With quivering hands she took out a pair of spectacles and
put them on her nose and then unfolded a piece of paper and
held it so that she could read it by the spotlights.

" 'The Stream at Urya.' "

A slow, long sigh breathed from the crowd, followed by
utter silence. Letta had felt her own lungs join the sigh, because this was so right. Grandad had chosen "The Stream at
Urya" to read with her because he said it was the easiest of all
Restaur Vax's poems, his last, written as he was dying in
Rome, remembering the stream below his father's farm. There
seemed to be nothing to it, only short simple sentences about
the hot sky and the hard bare hills, and the naked rocks, and

the thin stream tumbling through. Because it was easy, Grandad said, it was the first piece of proper Formal, not counting silly little stories like the goat boy book, which children used to be taught in school.

The woman read the first two lines in a clear voice, but halfway through the third she faltered, and went on, but choked again, and stopped. Her glasses seemed to be misting up, and she was finding it difficult to see the words. She stumbled through a half line from memory, and this time when she stopped again somebody in the crowd prompted her. With a gesture of thanks she went on, and next time she faltered it was as if the whole audience picked her up and murmured the words with her. Letta saw Steff's lips moving, and beyond him the reflected spotlight lit a row of faces, and almost every one of them was saying the lines too.

But they were young! They couldn't possibly have learned "The Stream at Urya" in school before the Communists came. And yet they knew the words. Almost everyone in the audience, though many of them must have been born in a time when it was dangerous to have the book in your house, knew the whole poem by heart. In carefully faint murmurs, so as not to drown the thin old voice, they carried the woman through to the end.

Then they cheered her for about ten minutes. Slowly the cheers changed to cries for an encore until she held up her hands for silence. Her makeup was streaked with tears. The MC produced an enormous yellow handkerchief and she wiped the tears away and held herself erect.

"No," she said in a clear voice. "Please don't ask me to read it again. I think my heart would burst."

So they cheered and cheered while she limped to the edge

of the stage, where hundreds of arms reached out to help her down.

Letta was wiping her own face with Kleenex when Nigel said, "What was all that about?"

"You'll have to learn Formal," said Letta smugly.

LEGEND

The Captain of Artillery

Restaur Vax sent letters to Bishop Pango, saying, "Now I hold Potok, and all Varina north of the Danube. Soon the Turk will come against me with armies, and to fight them I must have cannon, and also a Captain of Artillery to teach us the use of them. I have money from the merchants of Potok, and can pay well."

Winter fell, with great snows, and there came in secret to Restaur Vax one who said he had fought in the French Wars as a Captain of Artillery. He was small of stature, and slim, like a boy before manhood. He studied the land and said, "For mountains such as these you must have mule guns, which may be carried by goat paths and the paths of the hunter, and with those you will fall on the Turk unawares. Such guns I can supply, and then teach your people the use of them. Now let us make terms."

Restaur Vax said, "It must be done quickly, for when the snows melt the Turk will come, and our need will be great."

The Captain of Artillery said, "Then I will bring your guns under wool packs, on a barge, down the Danube. Tell me of a place where there is a quay with good landing."

Restaur Vax said, "We hold Slot, where there is a deep-water quay and many barges load and unload, for there are merchants there to whom our people sell stuff that they have made in the winter."

"So be it," said the Captain of Artillery. "My price is seven hundred *kronin,* half now that I may buy the guns, with shot and powder, and half when I bring them."

Then the Kas Kalaz, who was there, said, "These terms are too hard. How shall we trust this little foreigner? He will take the money and we shall not see him again."

And so said others. But Restaur Vax said, "Trust him we must, for we have no other help. What else will you do with the money? Will you melt it into gold bullets and fire them at the Turk? Moreover, small though he is, he has the look of honor."

The Captain of Artillery departed. Winter gripped the land, so that the Danube froze and no traffic could pass. While the ice was yet solid the Turk crossed the river with armies and cannon and captured Slot. At that Restaur Vax sent letters to the Captain of Artillery in Vienna appointing another place, but the messenger was eaten by wolves, so that the Captain of Artillery did not learn of the need to change plans.

Then a message came from the Captain of Artillery to Restaur Vax, saying, "The river melts, and the river traffic is moving. Your guns are laden and ready. We wait only for the powder. Be at Slot on the day appointed. You will know my barge by a yellow standard."

Then some said, "He does not know that the Turk has taken Slot. We must look for fresh cannon elsewhere."

But Restaur Vax said, "There is no time. Take my horse, Lash, and ride by the river till you see a barge with a yellow standard and hail it, and tell the Captain of Artillery what has befallen."

This Lash did, and found the barge, but it could not come near the shore because there were shoals, so he set the horse into the water and though he did not himself know how to swim he held on to the harness and so came to the barge, and bade the horse swim back to the shore and return to Restaur Vax. By this Restaur Vax knew that the barge was found.

Meanwhile Restaur Vax had sent through the hills and gathered from many houses the hangings[1] that the people had made in the winter. On the day appointed he came with eighty men, all weaponless and in the likeness of farmers, to Slot. By twos and threes they came, driving mules laden with hangings, and gathered at the quay where the merchants bought. And at the same time the Kas Kalaz and all the others lay in hiding around Slot, having set a man to watch for the barge with the yellow standard.

When it was seen, the man fired his musket as a signal, and then the Kas Kalaz and the others rose up from their places of hiding and fired on the walls, as if they would attack the town. At that the *bazouks* who guarded the quay ran to the walls to defend the place. Then Restaur Vax and his men took their weapons from among the hangings and seized the quay, and on the barge the Captain of Artillery held a pistol to the steersman's head and told him what he must do, while Lash the Golden carried up from the hold two guns, the barrels being of such weight that two ordinary men could not have lifted them. These he assembled and loaded, as the Captain of Artillery had shown him.

Then the barge came to the quayside and the guns were

carried ashore and made ready, the Captain of Artillery standing by one and Lash by the other, while the rest of the guns
were brought up from under the bales and set upon the mules.
And now the Turks, seeing what was afoot, returned to the
quayside, many hundred *bazouks,* but the way was narrow and
the Captain of Artillery fired with his cannon into the mass of
them, as did Lash in his turn (this having been shown him too
by the Captain of Artillery as they came down the river), and
there was great slaughter and the Turks fled.

So the guns were brought out through the town, but the
bazouks upon the walls fired hotly at them as they passed
under the gate, and the Captain of Artillery was struck in the
side and fell down with a great cry. Thus his hat fell from his
head and the long hair which had been hidden beneath the hat
streamed down, and all saw that it was not a man, but a
woman of great beauty, like the mother of St. Valia, but that
her hair was as red as a cloud at sunset.[2]

They set her on a mule and fled and took her to a farm
above Drogo where lived a woman skilled in herbs, who
washed and bandaged the wound and declared that she would
yet live.

But the chieftains came to Restaur Vax and said, "When
she is recovered she must be sent away. We cannot fight with
a woman among us."

Restaur Vax said, "She is our Captain of Artillery, and
where shall we find us another before the Turk is on us?"

Then Lash the Golden said, "To fight beside a woman is not
honorable. Our courage will be less."

But Restaur Vax said, "I did not see that your courage or
your honor was less when you fought beside her on the quay at
Slot. And who taught you the management of cannon?"

1. *Weaving hangings in elaborate geometrical patterns is a traditional winter occupation among Varinian peasants. They are then sold at riverside markets in the spring, when the Danube melts.*

2. *Marie McMahon (1779?–1841) is a historical figure. Half-French and half-Irish, she disguised herself as a man and followed her lover into the French army. After he was killed at Jena she continued to serve, though not apparently quite undetected, as she seems to have borne at least three children on various campaigns. Her highly unreliable memoirs (Paris, 1835) represent her as having been a great beauty in her youth. By the time of her exploits in Varina she must have been around forty-five. Several observers remark on the striking color of her hair.*

AUGUST 1990

St. Joseph's Square was the heart of Potok. On one side stood the cathedral, not very grand, crumbly and homely, built of gray-gold stone with three red-tiled domes. Opposite it stood the Palace Hotel, which at first glance looked far more imposing, but at second glance had something fake about it. Steff had insisted on a quick tour of Potok their first evening, before the concert, so that they could find their way around without getting lost, and being Steff he'd already looked everything up in an ancient guidebook. The Palace Hotel, he said, looked like a fake because it was one.

When the War of Independence was over and the Turks agreed to let Varina become semi-independent, provided Restaur Vax went into exile, Bishop Pango had become the first Prince-Bishop. The old Bishop's palace had been part of St. Valia, which the Turks had destroyed, and there wasn't enough money to build a new one, so he'd taken over five of

the merchants' houses opposite the cathedral and got an archi-
tect to design a grand facade, with a great porch and curling
double stairways. The facade was symmetrical, but the houses
behind weren't so some of the windows were blank, and several of them were half-blank, with bits of the old windows
showing behind the new ones. Letta didn't like anything to do
with Bishop Pango, so she thought his palace was just right
for the old fraud.

After the First World War, when Varina had been split in
three, it had become the governor's palace for the Romanian
Province of Cerna-Potok, and when the Germans invaded
they'd taken it over as their headquarters, and then the Communist Party had moved in, and now they'd gone and nobody
knew what to do with it so some enterprising person had
borrowed enough money to buy a job lot of beds and furniture
and turned it into the Palace Hotel.

Mollie and Steff had one of the rooms in the university,
partly because of Donna and partly so that Mollie could be at
the center of things.

"Come and pick us up by half past ten at the latest," she'd
said. "Grandad's due to arrive at eleven, and he's making the
opening speech at twelve."

They set off in plenty of time, Steff carrying Donna in a
backpack, but for once Mollie had got it wrong. Normally it
was only ten minutes' walk to the square, but not when every
single person in Varina seemed to be heading that way. It was
difficult to get into the center of Potok at all, and the nearer
they struggled the tighter the crowds were jammed and the
slower they all shuffled along.

"This is no good," said Steff, and struck off down a side
alley which led to another street just as solid with people as
the first, and so on, with increasing difficulty, until they were

right around at the back of the hotel. The policemen who were posted to stop unauthorized people trying to sneak in that way were quite unimpressed by Steff's pass and told him to go around and try at the front. But when Steff explained he was Restaur Vax's grandson they became smiling and jolly and insisted on everybody shaking hands with everybody.

One of the policemen led them through the kitchens, where a banquet was being prepared, and then through a warren of corridors formed by the five houses needing to be joined up. It didn't feel much like a hotel, more like depressing old offices or a really grungy school. And then their guide opened a small door and stood aside, and they were in a grand entrance hall with red carpets and gilt mirrors and potted palms and a sweep of stairs with gleaming brass banisters. Fifty or sixty people in their best clothes were standing around. Letta spotted Mr. Orestes talking to a large, blond, red-faced man in a bright blue suit. The main doors were open and the midmorning sunlight dazzled in. From where she stood Letta could see one of the domes of the cathedral, but not the square itself. Despite that she was at once aware of the immense crowd standing shoulder to shoulder, waiting there. They made a steady murmur, quiet but huge, so that the entrance hall was like the chamber of some giant seashell, filled with the shushing mutter of the ocean.

Steff led them to a side alcove.

"Hang on here a moment," he said. "I'll check where we're supposed to be."

Nigel nudged Letta and gestured slightly with his head. She glanced around and saw that they weren't alone in the alcove. Sitting in a corner on a stiff chair, half-hidden by one of the palms, was Minna Alaya, who had read "The Stream at Urya" the night before. Letta hesitated and went over. Miss

Alaya turned her head without moving her body and nodded, like royalty.

"I just wanted to say how lovely that was last night," said Letta. "Thank you very much."

"Oh, I felt such a fool," said Miss Alaya. "Imagine! Crying like a baby in front of all those people!"

"We were all crying too. It didn't matter."

"For you it is permitted, but I am a professional. I cry only to order. You are one of our exiles?"

"Yes. We live in England."

"And you too know 'The Stream at Urya'? That is good."

"I don't know it by heart. I read it with my grandfather. He's teaching me Formal."

"Good, too. These things must not be lost. And why are you here in the palace on this grand occasion? Do you perhaps, in England, know my friend Restaur Vax?"

"Well, as a matter of fact—I mean, we're trying not to make a fuss about it so we can just be ordinary visitors—but he's my grandfather. He lives with us in our house."

Miss Alaya smiled and nodded, royal as ever, but obviously pleased. She glanced toward Nigel, who was rather pointedly looking the other way. Perhaps his English half couldn't cope with going straight up to famous strangers and starting to chat.

"And that is another grandson?" she said.

"A great-grandson, actually. He's older than me, but he's my nephew."

"I would like to talk to him, please."

"You'll have to speak slowly. He's half English, and his Field isn't very good."

Miss Alaya nodded her understanding. Letta turned to beckon to Nigel but he was watching something on the other side of the room, so she went over. He looked around as she came and pointed.

"See that big guy over there?" he said. "Talking to Hector Orestes? Any idea who he is?"

"No. Why?"

"Hector's fawning like a puppy, far as I can see. Some of the others too. And the big guy's lapping it up. He doesn't even look Varinian."

"I don't know. I see Lash the Golden a bit like that."

"Another blond thug."

Nigel knew the Legends only from what Steff had told him. Being dark and slight and cautious, Steff had never had much time for Lash. Letta grinned, and gestured with her head.

"Minna Alaya would like to say hello," she said.

His eyes widened, but he came obediently over and waited while Miss Alaya gravely inspected him.

"Very like my friend Restaur at that age," she said. "A distinct family likeness, despite the English blood."

Nigel hadn't quite followed so Letta translated.

"Tell her she should see Uncle Van," he said. "He's supposed to be the spitting image."

Letta did so, and Miss Alaya nodded, still amused.

"Do you know who that is over on the far side?" said Letta. "The big blond man in the blue suit? I think he looks a bit like Lash the Golden."

Miss Alaya didn't bother to turn her head. Her face became severe and her tone chilly.

"So he would have us believe," she said. "His name is Otto Vasa. He has made a great deal of money since the war, in Austria, where he lives. It is he who is paying for this festival, out of his own pocket. Tell your grandfather when you see him that he is a dangerous man. He would like to be President when your grandfather is dead. He is not . . ."

She broke off because Steff had arrived to collect Letta and Nigel. Recognizing who they were talking to he gave a foreign-looking little bow and held out his hand, which Miss Alaya touched graciously with the tips of her fingers.

"Forgive me," he said. "We were much moved and honored by your reading last night."

"It is nothing," she said. "Please convey my respects to your grandfather."

"I'm sure he will wish to see you," said Steff.

"He says you're the most beautiful woman he ever met," said Letta.

"It is true," she said. "They all said so. Now you must go and prepare to welcome our hero, and I must wait here. This is what it means to be in one's second childhood—one must learn again to do what one is told. Good-bye."

"How did she know Grandad?" asked Letta as they climbed the stairs. "I thought he was just a schoolmaster then, and she must have been famous."

"It's a small country," said Steff. "Everybody knew everybody, among the intellectuals, at least. And then in the war—she'd been a German film star, remember, so a lot of the German officers had had a crush on her, and she played along and let them think they could trust her, but all the while she was sending information out to the Resistance. The trouble was, when it was over, some of the Varinians wanted to shoot her as a collaborator, but Grandad got her out of that . . . all highly romantic and probably untrue, but that's what Poppa told me."

"Of course it's true," said Letta. "It's got to be. It fits."

"Only in stories, Sis. In here, apparently."

They had come to a wide landing with a new red carpet
running a few paces to the left and right. Beyond that
stretched a tattered old brown one. Opposite the top of the
stairs were some big double doors, through which came an
odor of fresh paint. Letta followed Steff through and found
Mollie and Donna in a grand, uncomfortable great room with
more of the little gilt chairs, and some shiny tables, and huge
gilt-framed mirrors with black blotches on them, and enough
flowers for a funeral. Three tall windows looked out onto the
square, with a balcony outside. In front of the middle one was
a podium with microphones. The man who'd led them up,
some kind of hotel manager, started fussing around opening
doors and showing them the rest of the suite. There was a
bedroom with a vast pink bed and a lacy pink canopy covered
with artificial roses; a little den with a desk and two easy
chairs, where a workman was installing a telephone; a terrific
bathroom with a tub about eight feet long and four feet deep
and several vast brass taps controlling a shower device which
looked like something from a Jules Verne film; several immense cupboards; and yet another bedroom, this time with
twin beds but also frothing with lace and roses, pale violet.

Letta had an urge to pretend she was six again and rush
around trying out all the beds and turning on the taps and
gadgets, but at that point Van came in, tousled and panting,
and said, "I think he's almost here. I heard them cheering."

Nigel began to open one of the windows but Steff said,
"Hold it, Nidge. That comes later. We don't want to spoil the
great moment."

Letta craned, but the balcony was in the way so she took off
her shoes and pulled one of the idiotic chairs over and climbed
onto it so that she could see over the rail. The whole square
was crammed with people. Despite the closed windows she

could hear that the cheers were louder and more intense, and over in the far right hand corner the crowd was churning around. She could see the helmets of outriders trying to force a path through the mass. After them came the roof of a black official car. It stood still, then moved on, and behind it appeared the cab of a truck, painted black and purple and white, with flags flopping listlessly on either side. Slowly it edged forward. It carried what seemed to be a festival float, swathed in the Varinian colors. The cheering crashed out like falling waters and the crowd became a forest of waving flags. On the float was a platform with a rail round it, and standing there, holding the rail with one hand and waving cheerfully with the other, stood Grandad.

He had to be dead tired, tired with the journey, tired with the sheer emotion of homecoming, but he held himself straight and turned to the left and right and waved, and whenever the truck was forced to a halt he bent down to shake a few of the thousands of hands that reached up to greet him. He was wearing a black beret over his bald head, an open-necked shirt, and gray slacks. The extraordinary thing, Letta thought, was that he looked exactly like himself, no different from the Grandad who had crumpets with her at teatime, as if this too was something he did every day of his life.

At last the truck moved out of her line of vision. As it did so she noticed that the color of the crowd had changed from darker to paler beneath the layer of flags, as all those heads turned to watch it and she was now seeing faces, not hair. The cheering never stopped, but after several minutes its level dipped for a while and then rose again. In the quiet spot she could just hear a band playing. It had to have been the National Anthem, as Grandad climbed down from the float and up the steps and turned beneath the porch and stood there

waving while the cheers rose even louder than before, and at
last died away as he turned and disappeared into the hotel.

There was a bustle below, but while it was still going on,
the door opened and Momma rushed in, laughing and crying
at the same time, not acting like herself at all, but throwing
her arms around everyone and hugging them with easy joy.

"Isn't this wonderful!" she cried. "Oh, Letta, my darling,
how are you? I'm so happy you're here! We've all come home,
and you've never even seen it!"

"Is Grandad all right? He's not too tired?"

"He's fine, fine!"

And she rushed away to hug Van and Nigel and the others.
After a while they fell silent and just stood there, too keyed
up for chat or laughter, but listening to the murmurs below
and the unending ocean-mutter of the crowd outside.

Time passed. Without warning the doors opened again and
Grandad came through, with Poppa behind him.

"Well, here I am at last," he said, smiling and erect. But
after the doors had closed they all saw his shoulders droop as
he let the wave of exhaustion wash through him. Steff had a
chair ready and helped him into it. Letta knelt and unlaced his
shoes. He leaned back with closed eyes.

"I would give all Varina for a cup of tea," he murmured.

"Bet you Mollie's got a thermos," said Poppa.

She had too. The tension broke and they laughed and
talked about their journeys while Grandad sipped at his cup
and nodded and smiled, though he still looked almost as old
as he really was. But then he began to peer around the room
and a curious amusement came into his face.

"You know," he said to no one in particular, "I have spent
sleepless nights trying to devise some method of getting a

bomb under this floor. This was the German commandant's office."

He handed his cup to Letta, sat up, and looked at his wrist-watch.

"I have a few minutes still," he said. "Time for a wash, at least. Letta, my darling, in my bag there are clean socks . . ."

"I'll find them. What happens next?"

"At noon I have to go out onto the balcony and make a little speech. I won't offer to take you with me . . ."

"I'd much rather be down there."

"Me too," said Van. "Is that okay, Momma? Mollie? If I take Sis and Nigel down and keep an eye on them? You can find Grandad's socks, uh?"

"You may have trouble getting back in . . ." Steff began.

"No problem. I'll find a way. Come on, kids."

He rushed ahead of them down the stairs, paused, surveyed the group in the entrance hall, and plunged through. By the time Letta and Nigel caught up with him he was explaining his needs to the manager, who kept glancing aside, as if he were hoping for an escape route to open up. Van was relent-less. They were Restaur Vax's grandchildren, so he must find a way of getting them out into the square and then back in. Rescue! Some kind of minion passed with a cardboard box full of dead flowers. The manager grabbed it from him and gave instructions. The minion, happy to be relieved of his box, led them off into the maze of corridors, down into cellars, and along a stone passage which seemed to take them almost to the end of that side of the square. Here he unlocked a creaking door and took them deeper down still, switching on lights as he went. This corridor led into a wider space. Along one side were several iron doors with small barred grilles. Their guide walked to one of them, bowed his head, crossed himself, and muttered. He crossed himself again as he turned away.

He pointed upward.

"That was the Communist police headquarters," he said. "Here my mother's cousin died. First they tortured her. I am sorry. You are children. I should not tell you this. But those years are gone. Now it is time to honor the living."

He led the way up another stair, unlocked a door, and led them into a bleak entrance hall with a reception desk and an ancient telephone exchange. A fence of heavy iron bars ran across the hall from floor to ceiling, just inside the door, with a kind of cage like a giant humane mousetrap to keep visitors waiting till they had shown their passes or whatever and then let them through one at a time. As their guide showed them through a sort of turnstile in this barrier Letta, still shocked and chilly after what he'd said in the cellar, asked him, "Where did the Communists come from?"

He stared at her, puzzled.

"I mean were they Romanians? Russians? Serbs?"

"They came from here," he said. "I know which cell was Illa's because another cousin told us. He was one of them. He would have liked to help her but he was afraid. We were all afraid. All of us."

He was a small, plump, worried man, about forty, she guessed. He hadn't liked telling her what he did, but she could see he felt he had to. She was going to apologize when he smiled and shook his head.

"Those years are gone," he said again. "This is a happier day."

He let the others through the trap and unbolted the door, holding his foot against the bottom so that the people crowding on the top step of the flight that led up to the doorway didn't tumble through but had time to stand clear. They looked over their shoulders, surprised, but didn't stir or make room, so all Letta could see was the solid wall of their backs.

"Wait," said their guide. "You come, mister."

He and Van went back through the trap and returned with four chairs, for Letta, Nigel, and themselves. They climbed up with the chill, grim room behind them and the sunlit square in front, and waited.

They were now at the side of the square, with the cathedral on their right and the hotel facade stretching away on their left. The cathedral clock stood at two minutes to noon. Many of the crowd had their backs to the hotel in order to watch the minute hand edge around. As it crept toward the mark they began to make shushing noises. The murmur of voices dwindled and died. Silence filled the square, not mere absence of sound, but positive silence, a great pool of stillness which the Varinians had willed into being and which now lay brimming between the buildings in the sunlight. A baby cried. A far dove called and was answered. The first quarter donged out, followed by a shuffling of feet on stone as the crowd turned to watch the balcony. The central windows were now open. The second quarter donged, but no one heard the third, or the fourth, or the solid boom of the noon bell, because Grandad was standing on the balcony and the cheering drowned them all. Sheets of flags waved above the close-packed heads, the noise went on and on, unstoppable. Letta half fell but their guide caught her and set her back on her chair. She realized that she had been jumping up and down, and her throat was hoarse with yelling. The cathedral clock said almost ten past twelve, but it seemed to her that Grandad had come out barely a minute ago. She was dazed, drunk, drugged with the

shared, immense emotion. A crowd like this could do anything, anything . . .

It *was* shared too. It wasn't just a lot of different people's
excitement all totaled up. It was one thing, like the silence
had been, something they made between them all. And with
it they shared a purpose and a will. Grandad had been making
quiet-down gestures with his hands for some time, and they'd
paid no attention, but now they had had enough and all together, in a very few seconds, they fell silent. Here and there a
hoarse cry of greeting rose, but he waited a moment or two
more raised his head and began.

"My friends, my countrymen . . ."

Another burst of cheering crashed out, and another after the
next few words. They never let him get through a whole
sentence, but that didn't matter. In fact it barely mattered
what he said. He was there, officially, to open a festival of
Varinian culture, and Letta thought he must have talked
mainly about that, but to be honest she wouldn't afterward
have been able to tell you what it was about, if anything. All
she could have said was that it was wonderful, and that it was
in simple Field except for the last three words, and those
nobody heard at all because of the crash of cheering that
greeted the first Formal syllable. But everyone in the square
knew what he was saying.

"*Unaloxatu. Unaloxotu. Unaloxistu.*"

This was the motto embroidered on the battle standard of
the first Restaur Vax. You could see it in the cathedral again,
after fifty years, because somebody had managed to hide it
away when the Germans came, and kept it hidden all the time
the Communists were in power. It was the real thing, Steff
said. He'd told Nigel the words meant "One nation we were.
One nation we are. One nation we will be," and they did, but

the English wasn't the same, because *una* meant "whole" as well as "one," and "lox" meant "country" as well as "nation," and in Formal it took only one whole word to say each part (which you couldn't do even in Field) so that you felt you were making it true by the very way you said it.

At length their guide decided it was time to go back, so he managed to get the door closed and bolted and let them in through the trap, then led them back the way they had come. Letta's family didn't go to church, but she remembered a bedtime prayer which Biddie's mother had said with them when she was staying there last year, and whispered it now as they passed the place with the cells in it. When they got back into Grandad's room he was still out on the balcony, and the cheering was roaring on, as loud as ever.

LEGEND

The Riddle

Now that the five Pashas were slain, the Turks were afraid to face the Varinians in battle. But Selim was Pasha of Virnu, across the river, and he was subtlest of all the Turks.[1] He said in his heart, "I will send spies against this Restaur Vax, Greeks and Bulgarians and Croats, who yet speak the language of these dogs and may pass themselves off as true Varinians, and so join his bands, and be trusted until they are permitted to stand by his side, and then they will strike him down. Moreover, to give them courage, I will put a price on his head of seventeen thousand *kronin*. Very like, these spies will be found out, but that too is good, for Restaur Vax will see that he cannot any longer know which volunteers he can trust."

Then one came to Restaur Vax saying that he was a Varinian from beyond the river, and talking good Field. Restaur Vax questioned him closely, and he answered well, but in the middle of questioning him Restaur Vax cast his glance down by the man's feet and cried *"Phidi!"* which is the Greek word for viper. At that the man leaped clear even before he cast his own glance to the ground, and by this he was seen to be a Greek. So they took him away and slew him.

Restaur Vax said, "This is Selim's doing."

His chieftains answered, "We must therefore trust no new recruits."

Restaur Vax took thought and said, "Not so. We will test all who come to us with a riddle. We will say to each man, 'What were you? What are you? What will you be? Answer us now with the words that you learned in your mother's arms.' "

So it was agreed. Seventy-seven spies came, speaking good Field, pretending to be true Varinians, and saying they wished to fight the Turk. But not one of them could answer the riddle, nor did they return alive to their own pastures. But of all the many Varinians who came, none failed the test. Had they not learned the answer in their mothers' arms?[2]

═══════

1. *Selim Pasha (1712–1777) was not a contemporary of Restaur Vax. Pasha of the western province from the early age of twenty-six until his death, he earned a justifiable reputation for both efficiency and ferocity, and continues until the present day to be a general bogeyman of Varinian folklore.*

2. *"The Lame Girl's Lullaby" has the refrain "Tutunatu tutu-notu tutunistu," which is popularly explained to be in Old Varinian and to mean "Asleep you were. Asleep you are. Asleep you will be." That is to say, before birth, in the cradle, and in the grave. The point of the story is that an impostor would be unlikely to know the nonsense refrain of a cradle song.*

Old Varinian was the literary language developed by the trouba-dours in the Middle Ages from the even older language of which modern Field is a simplification. Almost all traces of Old Varinian were effectively destroyed by the Phanariotes, Greek Orthodox officials of the Turkish Empire during the seventeenth and eighteenth centuries. Modern Formal was developed in the period leading up to the War of Independence in an attempt to create a literary language to replace the lost Old Varinian. It is unlikely, however, that the refrain of the song was ever more than nonsense.

AUGUST 1990

Letta was escaping up a mountainside. Her companion was a bandit. Somebody had told her she mustn't trust him. The Turks were spread out below, tiny with distance. They hadn't seen her yet. Her heart was hammering. People were shouting, running around on the now dark hillside, calling for her . . .

"Letta! Letta!"

She jerked awake and sat up, her heart still hammering.

"Letta! It's Parvla!"

It was still dark, but people really were running about, and shouting.

"Oh do shut up. What's going on?"

That was Janine, in English, groaningly, on the other side of the tent. It had been a hot night, so Letta had slept on her bag rather than in it. She crawled out through the flaps and stood up. Parvla was there in her folky cotton nightgown. (Letta was going to try and find one like it before she went

home, only they didn't sell them in shops—they were something you made for yourself.) She'd met Parvla at a camp sing-
along a couple of nights before. She lived near a village about
twenty miles out of Potok. She was two years older than Letta
and felt older still in some ways but younger in others. In
spite of that they'd hit it off at once, looked for each other
next morning, spent time together, and agreed to meet again
today. But not this early, with stars still out and only a faint
gray line to the east, behind Mount Athur.

"They've taken him away!" gasped Parvla. "They came in
the middle of the night, two long black cars, and rushed into
the hotel and took him from his bed, wrapped in a blanket,
and drove away."

"Grandad! Restaur Vax?"

"Yes."

Letta was dopey, unable to think or feel. This seemed to be
still part of her dream, with the dark hillside and the people
moving around with angry cries, and her heart still uselessly
hammering.

"What's everybody doing?" she said.

"We're all going up to the square, I think."

Letta pulled herself together.

"Oh. Right. Thanks. I'd better find Nigel. You go and get
dressed."

While she was groping for her clothes she told Janine what
had happened, but Janine simply groaned and turned over.
She pulled her jeans and shirt on over her pajamas and started
down the hill, but before she'd gone more than a few yards she
heard Nigel's voice, calling for her as he climbed.

"Here," she shouted, and found him.

"What's happened?" he said. "Something to do with
Grandad, I gather. Is he all right?"

"I don't know. Somebody came and took him away. They're all going up to the square."

"Us too? We'd better check in with Mum and Dad. They'll be worried sick."

Blundering among tents they made their way down to the main path. People were already streaming along it toward the town. Their voices were mostly low, but Letta could feel their anger like a thickening of the air. The crowd grew denser and slower, but then she and Nigel were able to branch off toward the university, where a lot of lights were on and yet more people were pouring away toward the town. Mollie was in her room with a knapsack packed and Donna ready and dressed but fast asleep, waiting for them.

"Well done," she said. "Steff's gone up to the hotel. He called the desk here five minutes ago and said he's arranged for us to be let in at that back entrance. Apparently you can't get to the front at all. Ready?"

Even by the back way they barely made it. All the streets in the center of Potok were jammed with furious Varinians. At one place they passed there were crashings of glass and yells of rage from a courtyard. In the thin dawn light Letta saw a man run forward and hurl something. Another crash, and more yells. She heard a bystander ask what was up and somebody tell him that Romanians lived there. The bystander immediately rushed into the courtyard yelling, and looking for a missile of his own.

Letta and Nigel had paused for a moment to watch, and Mollie had gone ahead. In panic, Letta thought they'd lost her, but then she spotted her craning back to see where they'd got to. When they caught up she said, "For God's sake don't get separated. Keep with me." There was a snap in her voice, which Letta had never heard before. As they struggled on Letta realized that Mollie, too, was afraid.

Steff was waiting for them at the kitchen doors. He was obviously extremely relieved to see them. He took Donna onto his shoulder, still totally sogged out with sleep, and as he led them toward the front of the hotel, talked over his shoulder to Mollie.

"Not as bad as we thought. Kronin's brother—you remember, the guy in the Ministry of Culture—says it's all a mistake and he's furious about it."

"Are they going to send him back?" said Mollie.

"If they've got any sense, but nothing's open yet. We got Kronin's brother out of bed."

"It's really nasty out there, Steff. We saw a gang of people breaking windows. Does anyone know where they've taken him?"

"Timisoara, I should think. Bucharest in the end. They may just shove him on a plane and send him home."

He led the way into the entrance hall which had groups of people standing, talking in low voices. From beyond the doors rose a dull, deep roar, not much louder than the noise the crowd had made the opening day, but quite different. They didn't wait but went straight upstairs to what had been Grandad's room. Momma was coming out of the bathroom with a sponge bag. She'd been crying.

"Oh, darlings!" she said in English. "Isn't this too awful. I'm so relieved to see you. Has anyone seen Van?"

At that moment the telephone in the little den rang, and stopped. Poppa appeared in the doorway with the receiver to his ear, beckoning them over.

"Right," he was saying. "We'll do that. . . . Not a chance —it'll never get near the hotel. No, it'll have to be somewhere

right outside the town. . . . All right, Min and Letta . . .
They'll have to have an escort—I'll see if anyone here can fix
anything. But listen. Do they realize what they've stirred up
here? If they don't let you come back . . . I'm sure you are
. . . If they don't see that, then they're crazy . . . Kronin's
called his brother. He says it's a mistake. So . . . Right, here
she is."

He passed the telephone to Momma, who listened and murmured her answers, crying again now. Poppa moved the others aside so as not to interrupt.

"He seems all right," he said in a low voice. "They've
stopped at Paçel, just over the border. They're giving him
breakfast. They haven't told him anything except that he is to
ask for some clothes and two members of his family to escort
him, so it looks pretty certain they're going to put him on a
plane . . ."

He broke off and went over as Momma beckoned, but she
seemed to change her mind and started talking in a language
Letta didn't know—Romanian, probably. She asked questions, but mostly listened. At last she gave a heavy sigh and
just stood there, shaking her head. Poppa took the telephone
out of her hand and put it back in the den.

"I don't understand," she said. "That was a captain, army, I
think, not police. As far as I can make out—it's a terrible line
and my Romanian's rusty—he wasn't in charge of the people
who took Grandad away, but he's somehow taken over. He
says he's got to wait for orders. They're taking him to Timisoara. They want me and one other to go with him.
Letta . . ."

"I want to stay here," said Letta.

It was all she knew. The nightmare from which she'd
woken kept lurching back around her, swallowing her, drown-

ing her, and then ebbing away. Had she really struggled along
through the furious crowd, watched the men hurling stones in
the courtyard, almost lost Mollie? Yes, of course, but still it
all seemed full of the shapeless terror of dream. Even here, in
the big, lit room, watching Momma stand shaking her head
and saying she didn't understand . . . All she was certain of
was that she must stay and face whatever danger Varina faced.
Parvla was out there, somewhere among the roaring
crowd. . . .

"You'll do what you're told," snapped Momma, and then,
"I'm sorry, darling. I don't want him worrying about you.
Don't you see?"

Letta pulled herself together.

"I'm sorry," she managed to say. "Whatever you want.
. . . It's just . . ."

Then Van came rushing through the doors, hair tousled, a
smear of dirt down one cheek, but with glittering eyes and a
fizz and fever in his movements.

"Oh, there you are!" cried Momma. "That's wonderful!
How did you get in?"

"Climbed," he said. "Some of the gang gave me a leg up to
a bedroom window around the side. Isn't this terrific! Isn't
this just what we wanted! They couldn't have done it better
for us if we'd asked them!"

Quite unaware of the appalled hush that filled the room he
rushed to the window and stared out. It was almost light now,
with the stars gone and the topmost points of the ridges on
either side of the valley tipped with the first rays of the sun.
Below them stretched the shadowy slopes and lower still came
the tiles and stone of the cathedral, not warm red and gold as
they would be at noon but dull brownish and gray. And then,
below everything, the immense, dark, roaring crowd.

"You're not going to ask if we know anything about what's happened to Grandad?" said Poppa quietly.

Van turned, making at least a pretense of shame.

"Oh yes, of course. I'm sorry. Anyone know where they've taken the old boy?"

Poppa told him the news.

"That sounds all right," he said. "Provided they haven't beaten him up or anything. If they just ship him out."

"If they've got any sense at all they'll send him straight back," said Poppa.

"Well let's hope they haven't got any sense at all," said Van. "This is just what we wanted. Otto Vasa's going to make a speech to them in a bit. They asked me downstairs to check if that was okay with you. He'll need the balcony."

There was another silence. Momma and Poppa and Steff looked at each other. Letta could see they didn't like it at all, but it was difficult for them to say anything. They'd always kept out of Varinian politics, partly not to make things difficult for Grandad and partly because it wasn't their sort of thing.

"What's going on?" whispered Mollie, who hadn't been able to follow Van's rapid Field. Letta told her.

"Is this a committee decision?" she said. She was talking about the main Festival Committee, who'd run everything so far.

"No time for that," said Van. "Anyway, it's not just culture anymore. And we've got to strike while the iron's hot."

There was a knock on the door and two men came in with the podium Grandad had used, and microphones. The loudspeaker system was still in place because there was going to be a closing ceremony in the square before they all went home. Again Momma, Poppa, and Steff looked at each other. Poppa shrugged unhappily and stood aside to let the men through. They opened the central windows, and when the crowd outside saw the podium going into place their steady angry roar swelled up and rose in pitch. Van strode across to one of the side windows to watch, but the rest of the family moved to an inside corner of the room.

"I want no part of this," said Poppa.

"I think we're stuck," said Momma.

"What do you think Grandad would like us to do?" said Steff. "You met this Vasa chap, didn't you, Poppa?"

(They'd all seen him, of course. He'd seemed to be everywhere throughout the festival, always with the same big, benevolent smile and booming voice. Sometimes his wife had been there too, looking like a film star, with a fixed, winsome smile on her lips.)

"He was perfectly polite," said Poppa. "Momma didn't care for him."

"I thought he was gruesome," said Momma. "I wouldn't trust him an inch."

"That's what Minna Alaya told me," said Letta.

They looked at her in surprise, and she was just about to explain when the doors burst open and again and Otto Vasa himself stood there, looking huge and stern, with four or five other men behind him. After a moment's pause he strode across to them and shook hands, first with Poppa and then with the others.

"This is a terrible business," he said. "I grieve for you, Mrs. Ozolins. My wife sends her condolences. Once again these swine have shown that they are no better than the Germans, no better than the Communists."

"My father's just telephoned from Paçek," said Momma. "It looks as if they're putting him on a plane back to England."

"They will say anything," said Mr. Vasa, dismissively. "So great a man, so noble. After all that he has done and suffered for Varina. Now you must come with me. You must be at my side. You must show your faces to the people at this hour of their need."

Poppa was about to say something but Mr. Vasa simply gripped him by the elbow, put his other arm round Momma's shoulders, and without exactly dragging them marched them toward the window. Mollie looked at Steff. He hesitated, as if he might have refused to follow, but just as Momma stepped onto the balcony she turned and gave a pleading backward glance, so they all trailed out behind.

The roar of the crowd rose still further, reached a steady, raucous pitch and stayed there. The sunlight had moved halfway down the hillsides, but as the sky brightened the mass of people below seemed darker than ever, with the white bars of the Varinian flags which they waved looking like flecks of foam on a stormy lake. Mr. Vasa took up his position at the microphone and motioned the others to the places where he wanted them, Momma on his left, and then Poppa, and then Letta and Nigel; on his right Van, then Mollie, then Steff. He ran both hands through his thick blond hair, which looked like a natural, unthinking movement but still bushed it out into a romantic, golden mane, and then held up his arms for silence. Letta remembered Grandad doing the same five days ago. Gradually the roaring died away.

"My friends, my countrymen . . ."

He paused for the roar of voices to crash out, and waited impressively for silence.

"Five days ago those selfsame words were spoken from this balcony by our great leader, Restaur Vax . . ."

Another bellow of voices, one huge voice.

"Five days ago it was a time of hope. After a lifetime of suffering, his suffering, our suffering, we were together again, one people."

Again the roar, but this time changing, getting a rhythm, becoming a chant yelled defiantly from ten thousand throats. *"Unaloxatu! Unaloxotu! Unaloxistu!"*

Again, and again, and again. Ten thousand fists punching the air in rhythm to the chant. Mr. Vasa with both arms raised, conducting the chant until with a wide-sweeping gesture he cut it short.

"Our rulers pretend to be democrats. They hold elections. We send Varinians to their parliament. They say they will listen to us and do what we, the people, want. But these are words. What have they given us? When have they listened to us? How are they better than that swine Ceauşescu, these rulers who come like thieves in the night and snatch an old man from his bed? This is not words. This is what they do! Why? Because they are afraid!"

By now the yelling was almost continuous, but he carried on, bellowing above the din. At times Letta, though she was only a few feet away, could barely hear what he said, but it didn't matter. He could have said almost anything, provided he'd said it in that harsh, aggressive bark, in those snapped-out sentences, with his clenched fist smashing down on the podium to hammer the points home.

Letta loathed him. She hadn't realized it was possible to hate anyone as much as this. She glanced up at Steff and saw that his face was stern and angry, and Mollie's too, but Van beyond them was tense and thrilled.

". . . in what dark prison, in what torture cell, does Restaur Vax, that good old man, now lie? What are they doing to him, my countrymen?"

She felt sick. She was going to faint. Wasn't there anyone in the roaring crowd below who could see what a liar he was? Momma had told him, only ten minutes ago, that Grandad was all right and they were probably going to put him on a plane to England . . .

She couldn't bear it anymore, but turned and slipped away behind the others and back into the room. A man said something to her but she simply shook her head and pointed and let him take her arm and help her to the bathroom door.

She went through and locked it and then stood gripping the basin with both hands, with her head bowed over the bowl, wondering if she really was going to be sick. After a while she decided she wasn't, so she sat on a chair with her fingers in her ears trying to blot out the roar. Then it struck her that Momma might miss her and be worried, and then that she was ashamed of herself for running away when the others were all sticking it out, and she didn't want to be caught skulking in the bathroom, at least, so she unlocked the door, still not having made up her mind whether she could face going back out onto the balcony.

The question didn't arise. As she was just going through into the main room Otto Vasa came striding in from the balcony, wearing a grand, heroic look. A small, dark man with a moustache was waiting for him. Neither of them noticed Letta. The small man made a rapid thumbs-up gesture. Mr. Vasa dropped the hero mask for an instant and winked like a smug schoolboy, then turned, stern and serious, to help Momma gallantly through the door.

LEGEND

THE DANUBE PILOT

Now Selim Pasha sent for his captains and said, "Restaur Vax holds Potok and all Varina north of the Danube. Soon the Sultan will hear of his doings, and he will send armies with generals, and he will say to us who live here, 'Why have you allowed our rest to be disturbed by a mere bandit?' And he will take from us our estates, and our sons he will send to his galleys and our daughters to harems, and our names will be no more."

The captains said, "We cannot fight Restaur Vax, though we are many more than he. He is too strong in his mountains, where he knows the goat paths and the paths of the hunter, and can fall on us unawares."

Selim said, "Then we must bring him across the river to our own lands, where the mountains are less, and strange to him. Go now through the land with your *bazouks,* and demand of the people more taxes than they can pay, and when they

refuse punish them with great cruelty, so that they cry out to
Restaur Vax to come to their aid."

As he commanded, so it was done, until the West Varinians
sent word to Restaur Vax saying, "Come to our aid, or we are
no more a people." And Restaur Vax said, "We will go." But
his chieftains said, "Selim will set watch on the river and send
his *bazouks* against us while some of us are yet on the water
and those who have landed are as yet unready."

Restaur Vax said, "We will cross in the dark of the moon."

His chieftains said, "This is madness. Who crosses the Danube in the dark of the moon? Only the hardiest pilots, and
how can we trust them? All the pilots are Serbs and Bulgars."

Restaur Vax said, "Let boats be gathered at Vosh. Selim
will no doubt send us a pilot."

And so it was, for a man came to Restaur Vax saying, "I am
the hardiest pilot on all the river, from the White Mountains
to the Inmost Sea. I will lead you over in the dark of the
moon."

Restaur Vax looked into his eyes and said, "You are a fine
man. I guess you have many fine sons."

The pilot said, "I have three fine sons."

Restaur Vax, still holding his gaze, said, "I trust they are
well."

The man said, "They are indeed well."

But Restaur Vax saw his eyes narrow as he spoke, and by
that he knew that the man's sons stood at that very hour in
Selim Pasha's courtyard, with ropes around their necks. Nevertheless he told him that he should be their pilot, and settled
a price, and gave him food and wine. But as the man ate,
Restaur Vax said to Lash the Golden, "Have this man watched
in secret, and bring me word of all that he does."

Then Restaur Vax took his horse and rode on the banks of

the Danube, some *kolons* below Vosh, studying the farther shore for a landing place. On the second dusk as he rode he saw an old woman rowing toward the shore, but the current was swift with rains and she was weary with rowing, for she was indeed old, and in her struggle she let go of an oar and it was swept away. She too would have been swept away had not Restaur Vax ridden his horse out along a sandspit and plunged into the river and thrown her a rope and so towed her ashore.

Then the old woman thanked him, but still she wept and said, "Now I have lost an oar, and I shall never see my sister again, for the winter is near and the current is already too great for me, and before the ice forms hard my sister will be dead, with none to care for her."[1]

Restaur Vax said, "Mother, you are old to be crossing this great river alone. Are you not afraid?"

She answered, "All my life I have lived by the river. I was born on the farther shore, and on this shore I was married and widowed, and on the farther shore I would wish to die, only I have no means to carry my goods across and now I have lost an oar. But I know this river as a farmer knows his fields. If I had my strength I could cross it in the dark of the moon."

"So you shall cross it," said Restaur Vax. "You and your goods. Soon I will send some friends, with a fine boat. They will load your goods aboard and then they will bring you to Vosh to wait for me."

"Nothing is given for nothing," said the woman. "I am old, but no fool. Why should you do this for me, who have nothing to give you?"

"You are richer than you know," he answered. "You have half my country to give me. I am Restaur Vax."

At that she blessed him, and said she would do all that he wished.

When Restaur Vax rode back to the mountains he asked Lash what their pilot had done.

Lash said, "He has built a signal fire on the point above Vosh, which cannot be seen from the quayside. Furthermore he has sent word to his brother to come to him."

"All goes well," said Restaur Vax. "Now this we must prepare, and this, and this. Let it be seen to."

As the dark of the moon came near Restaur Vax and the chieftains and their men, all save a few, traveled to Vosh, for they knew that Selim had spies still north of the river. Those few took a boat to the widow's house and loaded her goods and gear aboard while it was still day, and then she went willingly with them to Vosh. As night came on they all gathered at the quay and boarded the boats which lay ready and set sail, calling from boat to boat so that they should not be lost to each other. The pilot went with them, but when they were well clear of the quay his brother ran to the place where the fire was laid ready, and lit it, as a signal to Selim on the farther shore that the crossing had begun.

Then Restaur Vax put his pistol at the pilot's head, as did the chieftains to those who were steering the other boats, and the old woman stood beside the tiller and said this way, or that, and so brought them down to the place where the boat lay with the old woman's goods aboard. That they took also, and then crossed the river, still calling softly from boat to boat, and with the old woman still standing by the tiller and saying this way, or that, until she had brought them to the landing place below her sister's house.

It was still then night, so they made ready for battle, and the sister's son guided them by goat paths and the paths of the hunter to the landing place opposite Vosh, where Selim lay in wait.

Then in the dawn the Captain of Artillery fired her cannon upon the *bazouks,* who had lain waiting all night and now slept, and Restaur Vax and the chieftains and their men fell upon them with pistol and with sword and slew them. Only Selim escaped, in a swift boat down the river, and fled to the Sultan in Byzantium, who flew into a rage at the news he brought and threw him into his deepest dungeon.

But Restaur Vax and the chieftains went hither and yon through the mountains and fell upon the *bazouks* wherever they were, before they could gather themselves into one army, and slew them.[2] And until all was done Restaur Vax ordered that a guard be set on the house where the old woman now lived with her sister, to see that none should trouble them.

———

1. *The encounter with the old woman may be borrowed from* The Adventure of Prince Ixil, *an ancient magical romance, now lost, apart from a few fragments.*
2. *The crossing of the Danube for the winter campaign of 1823–24 was accomplished by means of a ruse. Apart from exaggerations of her own role, the account in Marie McMahon's* Memoirs *tallies with several of the details in the Legend.*

AUGUST 1990

The car drove right out to the farthest corner of the airport, where a plane was waiting, guarded by a dozen soldiers. When they climbed aboard they found Grandad sitting with his eyes closed at the back of the first-class compartment. He looked old and ill, but smiled and let himself be kissed and patted their hands, but then lay back and closed his eyes again while the plane taxied around to the terminal to pick up the rest of the passengers.

The passengers were in a very bad mood, as they'd been kept waiting six hours for Momma and Letta to arrive. Two soldiers with guns stood beside the cabin crew and watched them keenly as they shuffled past. The soldiers left only when the doors were about to shut for the plane to leave.

It was evening, and as the plane climbed, Letta could see farther and farther into the west, across a vast, already darkening landscape to the final barrier of mountains, hard-edged against fiery-banded sky. Some of that was Varina, she knew.

One of those distant hummocks could be Mount Athur. She wondered whether she would ever see it again.

There was no one else in the first-class compartment, so they had a stewardess to themselves. She stood and went through the motions with the usual plastic smile while the safety instructions were read out on the intercom, in French and English and Romanian. When the seat belt sign went off she came and asked if they would like anything to drink. It took Letta a long moment to realize that she had spoken in Field.

Grandad opened his eyes and smiled. The stewardess glanced swiftly to see whether any of the other cabin staff were in earshot and whispered, *"Unaloxistu."* There were tears in her eyes.

"May you live to see it," said Grandad, and then, in English, "Will you try to make us some tea. Real tea. My daughter will show you how."

"Mollie gave me some Jackson's tea bags for you," said Momma.

"She should rule the world," said Grandad.

Being in the first class their seats were in sets of two, not three. Letta had automatically put herself next to Grandad, with Momma on the other side of the aisle, but now that she'd talked to him and touched him and decided that he wasn't hurt, only very tired and sad, she realized this wasn't fair to Momma. She must be just as worried. So when Momma came back from showing the stewardess about warming the pot and putting enough tea bags in and seeing that the water was really boiling—oh, such English things to be doing, and it would still be horrible fake milk!—Letta stood up and gestured silently that they should change seats. Momma shook her head.

"I'm dead," she whispered. "All I want to do is sleep. Thank God that's over. I wish we'd never come."

She said it in English. For a moment Letta's heart seemed to stop. Her mouth half opened and she felt her face go white, but Momma didn't seem to notice. She was already turning in to her seat. Letta stayed where she was, in the aisle, too stunned to move. A picture of Lapiri formed in her mind. That had been only two days back.

It had started with an argument, almost a fight, the evening before. Momma had said "Tomorrow I'm going to Lapiri. I'd like you to come too, Letta. There's something I want to show you."

Letta had said, "Oh, but . . ."

There'd been plans she'd made, friends she'd arranged to meet. She'd started to explain, but stopped, because she could see Momma was upset. And then it had been Poppa, who almost never let you see what he was feeling, who had said "I'm afraid you'll have to miss that. We'd like you to go."

There'd been something in his voice. Letta hadn't understood what, but she'd known it mattered so she'd stopped arguing and gone out to try and find one of her friends to tell them she wasn't going to make it.

Then, next morning, they'd left Potok and the festival, just Momma and Letta, in a weird old taxi which someone had painted bright yellow with Marlboro ads on the side to try and give it a sophisticated New York look. They had driven, juddering on every pothole, twenty miles along the flanks of Mount Athur and then, almost at a walking pace, along a winding unmetaled road, over a shoulder of the mountain and down into a still and secret wooded valley. They had come through the wood and found a small dark lake with a few houses and a tiny white church reflected from its surface, and a single immense sweep of mountain rising beyond. Momma had asked the driver to stop.

"This is Lapiri," she had said. "This is where I grew up."

They had climbed out and stood and looked. When Letta had got her camera out Momma had put her hand down without a word and stopped her. Then, though the track went on, no worse than before, they had walked around the lake and into the hamlet.

Nobody came to Lapiri. Certainly no foreigners. People had stared, and fallen silent. Momma had walked up to two elderly women and said, "Is Minna Vari still alive?"

The women had gazed at her, still silent, not even accepting that they had understood her.

"I am Minna Kanors," she had told them.

Their looks had changed to amazement, and then to smiles and handshakes.

"This is my daughter, Letta," Momma had said, and Letta had found herself being kissed by crones and hugged by smelly old men with bristly chins while the news was cried from house to house and more old people came hurrying out for more kisses and hugs and greetings, with Letta still trying to guess why Momma, whose unmarried name had of course been Vax, had told them she was Minna Kanors. And now small gifts began to be brought—a couple of figs, an almond biscuit, strips of dried fish from the lake (practically pure salt), doll-size mugs of fiery clear peach brandy. At last the whole gang of them, about fifteen, all old (anyone under fifty was probably in Potok for the festival), had led them off to a one-roomed house, barely bigger than a kennel, leaning against the church, and there in a wooden bed they'd found an old woman, quite blind and almost deaf, and they'd bellowed in her ear to tell her that Minna Kanors had come to see her, bringing her daughter.

"This was my foster mother," Momma had whispered.

The blind woman had smiled and nodded and whispered Momma's name, and Momma had sat on a stool by the bed. Letta had bent and kissed the chill, shriveled cheeks, and then they'd all gone back into the sunlight leaving Momma and the old woman together. They'd asked Letta questions, not about England or America, not about swimming pools (she didn't see any TV antennas and later Steff had told her that they probably couldn't get any signals at Lapiri because of the mountains) but about family. How many sons? Two only? And just the one daughter? Well, one daughter was enough to look after the parents in their old age. And only two grandchildren? Tsk tsk. She'd mentioned Grandad. Restaur Vax? Ah, yes, a very great man, but she hadn't been sure they'd been talking about the right Restaur Vax because two of the old men insisted on leading her off to see the cell where the Hermit of Lapiri had lived, four or five mossy stones beside a dribbling stream in the middle of the wood . . .

Momma had allowed her to take photographs when they went back to the taxi, but she obviously hadn't wanted to talk. They were off the cart track and onto the metaled road before she said anything, and even then, though there was no way the driver could have heard her above the growls and rattles of his cab, she spoke in English and kept her voice down, almost to a whisper, low and strained.

"There is something I have to tell you," she said. "I don't want to, but it's important to both of us. It may help you to understand why things aren't . . . aren't easy, quite, between us . . . not like they ought to be with a mother and daughter. There's a sort of block, isn't there? Something in the way?"

"Not really. Well, yes, sometimes, I suppose . . . Honestly, you don't have to worry, Momma. I'm used to it. It doesn't matter."

"It does matter, but I can't help it . . ."

She paused, sighed, drew a breath and began.

"Well, I was born about three years before the Germans came. No, four, it must have been. Your grandfather was teaching at Virnu, in Yugoslavia. I don't remember any of that time. When the Germans came he joined the Resistance—he had no other choice, I accept that. He sent me and my mother to Lapiri because Romania was pro-German and he thought we would be safer there, but soon there were Germans in Romania too. My mother had been born in Lapiri, so she used her family name, Kanors. If anyone asked, I was her illegitimate daughter. As far as I knew I had no father, though I remember being woken at night once, and a man being there who took me onto his lap and talked to me. The villagers knew who I was, of course, but they don't tell things to strangers. Lapiri was my childhood, the only world I knew. I had a friend of my own age, Junni. She had no father, too. We were like twin sisters, never apart. I think I was as happy as a child can be.

"Then the Germans were driven out, and I remember a confused and frightening time, car journeys, and cheering crowds, and huge rooms, and town smells, and strangers looking after me, and my mother when I saw her seeming unhappy and worried, and pretending not to be. And this man who said he was my father . . . I didn't want a father, I wanted Junni. But there was a day when the man took me onto his lap and told me stories, and when important people came to talk to him he sent them away. My mother was there. I could see she'd been crying. Then the man said good-bye.

"And then my mother came to my room and woke me and helped me to dress in the dark and we crept through passages and down stairs and through cellars and came out in a dark street where men were waiting, with guns. They led us, stopping often, through twisting streets. We got into a car, my mother and I and two of the men, and drove without any lights through the dark. It was very bumpy, not a proper road, but I fell asleep. To my joy I woke in my own room at Lapiri.

"I ran out to look for Junni, but I found her house in mourning. She had missed me as much as I'd missed her, and she'd gone off one morning alone. They thought she must have gone to look for me, but she'd fallen into the lake and drowned. Her mother was all in black. She didn't tell me about the lake. She held me close and said that Junni had gone to the Virgin and St. Joseph. I thought these must be places like the town where I had been, and soon she'd come back, like I had. I didn't understand anything. Nobody told me anything true. They thought they were being kind to me, I suppose, not telling me. All I knew was that Lapiri wasn't a happy place anymore, and everyone was afraid.

"Then, next day I think, my mother said I must hide for a while, and she might be going away too, but I mustn't worry. She smiled and patted and stroked me, but I could feel she was frightened like everyone else. Her cousins took me to a cave in the mountain. They said I mustn't come out. They brought me food at night. I don't know how long I stayed there. I don't even remember being there. Only sometimes in a shadowy way I can see somebody, a child, sitting in a dark place and staring at a big white patch—that would be the mouth of the cave, I suppose—with her knees drawn up to her chin and her arms around them and just rocking, rocking, rocking . . .

"The next thing I remember is being back at Lapiri, but not in our house, in Junni's. It was several months later, but I didn't know that. I only learned much later what had happened. Almost as soon as I had hidden, the Communists had come. The villagers had seen their cars across the lake and were ready. Junni's mother took off her mourning and my mother put it on. They told the Communists that it was I who had drowned. They showed them Junni's grave. The Communists made my mother watch while they dug the body up. She identified it as mine. They took her and it away, my mother blindfolded and the body in a sack which they tossed in the back of one of their cars as if it had been potatoes. The people of Lapiri watched in silence.

"You met Junni's mother just now. Minna Vari. When they went to fetch me from the cave they found me crazed, so I became Minna's crazed daughter. She cared for me, watched over me, was utterly patient with me, as if I had been her own child. I don't remember any of that time. It's like the cave. I can—I don't know—*feel* in a shadowy sort of way somebody looking after me, my guardian, who would never let anything else that was bad happen to me. I suppose I thought it was my mother, but it can only have been Minna. I think without her I might have stayed crazed all my life.

"But when I came to myself she sort of withdrew a little. She told me that I must now be called Junni Vari, and that I must never tell anyone that my real name was Minna Kanors . . ."

"Why not Minna Vax?" said Letta.

"I'll come to that."

"I'm sorry. It must have been . . . oh, there aren't words!"

"Yes, it was very bad. Even I understood it was very bad, though they still didn't tell me anything. Minna was always afraid I might go crazed again. I did, once or twice, for a few days. All I knew was that my mother had left me and something very bad had happened. I didn't want to know what that something was. I tried to bury even the knowledge I had, to hide it away. I wanted Minna to *be* my mother. I wanted to *be* Junni, but she wouldn't let me. I was Kanors, not Vari. Worse trouble would come if I tried to be Vari—bloodlines are very important in these remote villages. Furthermore, she told me that my mother and father had been scholars, so I must be one too. My mother had taught me to read and write —Minna couldn't—and the Communists had set up schools so that they could teach everyone to be Communists too, but our little school was very primitive and our teacher wanted to send me to a grander school. Minna agreed at once, and the villagers clubbed together to pay for my needs.

"I was delighted to go. It was a way of hiding, of burying, the bad secret which I must never know. It was a way of starting to be somebody new. I felt I had no name. I wasn't Junni or Minna, Vari or Kanors. I think that is why I worked so hard at school. I was a prize pupil. I hadn't been that before. I was a kind of new person. Do you see?

"Anyway they sent me to the university, here in Potok, when I was barely sixteen. I met your father. We had known each other only a fortnight when he asked me to marry him. He had reasons of his own, but for me it was a door into a new world, and I could go through it and close it behind me and forget everything I had been before. I would have my own

name at last. Minna Ozolins. We bribed officials to let me
marry so young.

"So I went through the door and closed it behind me. Only,
at night, when I was asleep, it would open again and dreams
would slip through and come to me. I would be standing by
the lake, looking across at the houses and the church below
the mountain, beginning to walk around toward them, knowing all the while that something was going to happen . . .
and then I would wake moaning and shuddering and your
father would hold me in his arms and try to comfort me.

"In the end he persuaded me that I must go back and make
my peace with Lapiri. We borrowed bicycles. The journey
took almost all day. Minna welcomed me, but when I told her
we were married she was obviously upset. I thought it was
because we had not been married in a church—she was very
religious. She asked us to wait and went out. We heard the
church door open and shut—you saw how close it was—and
we thought she was praying for our sinfulness. When she
came back she asked your father to leave us alone as she had
something to tell me. That is when I learned what had happened to my mother, and to Junni, and what my true name
was, and what it meant to be the daughter of Restaur Vax.

"You see, in the eyes of the Communists your grandfather
was a no-person. There was only one Restaur Vax, an old hero
who had fought the Turks. We were told some of the stories,
but not others, not in schools. He had written no poems—
none of that. But your grandfather, no, nothing at all. And
no-persons can't have living children. If the Communists were
to learn who I really was, I would become a no-person too.
Remember, I was a Communist. We all were, the prize students who were going to run the country one day. Minna
hadn't sent your father away because she wanted me to hear

the story alone. She didn't know if she could trust him not to
inform the authorities."

"That's awful! Your own husband!"

"It was the world we lived in, darling. . . . Well, when
she'd finished we held each other close and wept for what we'd
both lost. I don't believe anyone had ever seen Minna weep,
but she did then. She said, 'When you were crazed, you were
my own daughter.' I knew what she meant. I said, 'And you
were my own mother.' And it was true."

She paused. Her face worked at the memory. Letta took her
hand and Momma squeezed back and shook her head and
went on.

"It was dark. I found your father and walked with him by
the lake and told him. We ate with Minna and slept on her
floor. Next day we rode back to Potok. But as soon as we were
able we went out to Lapiri again and were remarried, by the
old rite, in the church. Minna made the lace for my veil and
baked the bride-bread. I made my peace with Lapiri.

"After that I was happy—happy for the first time since my
childhood. We were elite, we had good jobs, good lives compared to most people. We took the trouble to seem loyal little
Communists, though like everyone else we made plans about
how we might escape to the West if ever the chance arose.
And when the boys were born we sneaked off and had them
baptized in the church at Lapiri. I still had my nightmare
from time to time, but now that I knew what it meant I could
bear it. Then we made a friend, an official in the security
ministry. I asked her, not telling her why, if she could find
out anything about what had happened to my mother. I don't
think it was she who betrayed us, I think she was just indis-
creet, but another friend warned us that the secret police now
knew of my interest. We decided to leave. We spent all the

money we had on bribes, and we were lucky too—I think you
know that part of the story."

"Poppa told me. He made it sound funny, as if it had all
happened to somebody else. I suppose it was terrifying,
really."

"If it had gone wrong I should never have seen my sons
again. But your father was brave and clever, and it was all
right in the end. Only when it was over I started having my
nightmare again, as bad as it had ever been. It took me a long
time to get rid of it."

She looked down at her hand, still twined into Letta's, and
gently withdrew it.

"Well, that's all," she said. "If there's anything you want to
know, ask now. I don't want to talk about it again if I can
help it. But I thought—we thought, your father and I—that
you've a right to know why . . . well, why it's been difficult
for me to have a daughter of my own. Do you understand?"

"Not really . . . well, sort of. When you were my age,
you mean . . . ?"

"That's part of it. I've got no maps, no clues, about what
it's like to be an ordinary child, growing up in safety and
comfort. It's almost as if I couldn't afford to know. Suppose
I'd never had a mother I could remember, I think that might
have been easier. But I do remember her. I adored her. We
were very close. We slept in the same bed—there wasn't room
for another one. And then we were punished. Dreadfully,
dreadfully punished. When you're a child, everything happens
for a reason. It's always somebody's fault . . . Oh, Letta, I've
longed to love you, love you easily, I mean. I *do* love you,
really I do! But I daren't let it be easy. Do you understand?"

"I think so," said Letta. She knew she didn't really. She
could see what Momma had been telling her, but it was out-

side her. She couldn't take hold of it, draw it into her, make it her own. Not yet, anyway. The whole terrible story, and how it went on and on, ripple after ripple, through life after life, all because Grandad had been who he had been. That must have been difficult for Momma too, more difficult than Letta had ever realized, welcoming home this old man she barely knew, but who had shaped her whole life by being who he was, bearing the name he bore.

"And thank you for bringing me," she said. "And for telling me. I think it's going to be a help . . . when I'm used to it, I mean. I . . . I always thought it was just because I came so late I was a bit of a nuisance."

"Oh, no, darling."

"But it's true."

"It isn't true in any way that matters."

The road was twisting beside the river now, the cab growling around the sharp bends. Any moment they'd be in Potok.

"Have you tried to find her again?" said Letta. "Your mother, I mean. I asked Grandad about her once, but he just shook his head and I knew I mustn't ask again."

"He has not forgiven himself. He's trying to find out something, now that the barriers are down, but so many people have disappeared . . . I'm not sure I any longer want to know . . ."

They were silent again until they rounded the last bend and saw the old East Gate of Potok—the only one left—ahead of them. On either side of it the battlemented walls showed here and there among the red-tiled roofs. In front of it several hundred people were dancing a *sundilla*, the weaving chain dance it took only a dozen dancers to start, and then anyone who felt like it could join in while the bystanders clapped with the music. All the traffic had slowed and was nudging through as the dancers wove in and out among the cars.

Letta watched them pass. She didn't know what to think or how to feel. Lapiri had seemed so pure, so simple, but it was there that Momma's own momma had stood by a grave in somebody else's mourning and watched somebody else's daughter being dug out of the ground, and known that she would probably never see her own daughter again. That was the picture that kept coming back.

Two chains of dancers went snaking by on either side of the cab. One group wore national dress and carried baskets of flowers which they tossed across the roof of the cab to the other group. They were laughing with excitement and happiness, but some of them, Letta thought, might have had fathers or grandfathers who had driven out to Lapiri and carried Momma's momma away, blindfolded, with Junni's body in a sack in the back of the car.

"If Junni hadn't been drowned," she whispered, "I wouldn't be here today."

"Try not to brood about it, darling," said Momma. "It was a long time ago and we might as well enjoy our last few days in Varina."

Deliberately, as if to show what she meant, she had begun to clap her hands in rhythm to the dance. But two nights later black cars had come and men had taken Grandad out of his bed and whisked him away. Just like the old days.

Still standing in the aisle of the airplane Letta bent and kissed Momma's forehead and whispered, "I'm sorry."

"At least you can now see why I prefer to live in England," said Momma, grimly, and closed her eyes.

Letta felt her way to her seat and sat thinking about Lapiri until the stewardess came back with tea. Grandad, who seemed to have been half asleep, straightened and looked decidedly perkier.

"There is champagne also," she whispered, "since you are traveling first class. We keep a little French champagne for the VIPs. I will say I made a mistake . . ."

"At the moment tea means more to me than all the vintages of France," said Grandad. "Sugar, please, but not that plasticized milk. Ah!"

He smiled at her and cradled the cup beneath his nose to sniff the steam. He looked relaxed and calm, like an old man Letta had noticed on the road to Lapiri, sitting at his door in the sun with his dog's head on his lap, both fast asleep.

"What happened after they took me away?" he asked.

Letta pulled herself together and started to tell him all she'd seen, being woken, finding Nigel and then Mollie, struggling through to the hotel, his telephone call, Van, Otto Vasa's speech, and then waiting and waiting for the car . . .

". . . in the end they didn't dare bring it into Potok," she said. "The crowd would have wrecked it. We had to walk out to the Jirin Gate. They gave us an escort, real heavies. We saw other cars burning, and shops being looted. Then there was a roadblock, a barricade, you know. Some of the men there had guns. And they wouldn't let us through till they'd checked again with Otto Vasa. After that it was easy. Somebody went and fetched the car and we drove the rest of the way."

"Did you see any signs of military activity?"

"They'd pasted newspaper over the windows so that we couldn't see out, but we had to stop twice and the officer got out for a bit and came back and I heard orders being given."

"And you thought Otto Vasa was horrible."

"Yes. I hope Lash wasn't really like that."

"In what way horrible?"

"I don't know. Oh yes, I do. At first I just decided he thought much too much of himself, as if he *was* the festival—I know he'd paid for most of it so he was a bit entitled—but I couldn't stand the way people like Mr. Orestes fawned on him —Van too, I'm afraid—and you could see how he loved it at the same time he despised them for it—all that. And of course Minna Alaya had warned me about him . . . But really, it was the way he talked about *you* when he was whipping the crowd up, as if you weren't a real person, just something like Restaur's banner which he could say big, noble things about . . . and then lying, too. I heard Momma telling him you were all right and they were treating you okay, but he talked about you being in prison, and tortured . . . and he talked about you as if you were *dead.* And then, when he came back into the room after he'd been pouring out all this sob stuff and he didn't think anyone was looking, he was so pleased with himself that he winked! I hate him!"

Grandad sipped and nodded and sipped again.

"How do you interpret the wink?" he said. "He winked to someone in particular, I take it."

"Some kind of a henchman who'd given him a thumbs-up. I think they were saying, 'We've done it. We've brought it off. This is what we wanted.' I mean that was what Van was saying too."

"Interpret further, my darling. Did the wink celebrate a chance opportunity successfully seized, or a deliberate plan carried through?"

"I don't know. The plan, I suppose. I'm just guessing. Why?"

"Naturally I asked many times what I had done to deserve

this treatment. In the end I was informed that I had broken the conditions of my visa, which I took to mean that I had taken part in political activities. I had been extremely careful not to, but I was aware from the first that efforts were being made to provoke me into political statements, in particular by one or two of Otto Vasa's entourage."

"The one he winked to was a skinny little man with a big moustache."

"That could be Nirvan Orestes, a cousin of our Hector's. He is certainly of the party which would like to provoke an immediate confrontation with the Romanian government, if not outright rebellion."

"You mean one of them actually told the Romanians."

"I'm afraid it is all too probable, my darling. As always, I am much more useful to them as a name and a symbol than as a living person with opinions of my own. Ah, well. What about you, my darling? It is sad for you that our lovely adventure should end like this."

Letta didn't say anything.

"No?" he asked.

"I've been thinking," she said. "Something had to happen. It was too lovely. It wasn't real. Did Momma tell you she'd taken me to Lapiri?"

"She did."

"And on the way back she told me what happened there?"

"Yes."

"At first I wished she hadn't. It seemed to spoil everything. And then I thought it's better to know. You can't pretend everything's a pretty dream, when it isn't. Those people out in the square—there must be a lot of them who'd do things like that to each other. I expect some of them have. You've got to know that too."

"Yes, my darling. But when you have learned that lesson you have a still harder one to learn. There are also a lot of people who would not."

They landed at Heathrow in the late evening. The other passengers were made to wait while two men came aboard and led Grandad and Momma and Letta away, not through the usual passenger channels. The men were polite. Grandad knew one of them. They were shown into a small bare room and Momma and Letta were asked to sit down while Grandad was taken through into another room. After a while one of the men came back and beckoned to Letta. The man behind the desk in the second room was the same one who'd brought Grandad back to Winchester last year. He asked Letta to tell him what she'd seen when Otto Vasa came back from the balcony after making his speech. He made a note, stood up, and shook hands with Grandad.

"Well, sir," he said. "I'm sorry for you that it's ended like this, and we'll do the best we can with the Romanians. I'll talk to my colleagues in Paris. They have a bit more influence there. I think that's all. There's a car ready to take you back to Winchester. Good-bye, Miss Ozolins. It was nice to meet you again."

LEGEND

The Pomegranate Trees

Restaur Vax sent letters to Bishop Pango in Rome, saying, "Return, for the Pashas have fled, and our country is ours."

Bishop Pango answered, "In a little while."

Restaur Vax wrote again, saying, "Return, for we need both your counsel and your blessing."

Bishop Pango answered, "My blessing is always with you, and my counsel is that the Pashas are not fled forever."

A third time Restaur Vax wrote, saying, "Return. Your counsel is wise, but we are strong in our mountains. The Pashas cannot drive us out. All that is needed is your presence among us."

Then Bishop Pango sent for the messenger and told him, "Say this to Restaur Vax. 'There was once a king who married a woman from the far south, and he loved her greatly and gave her many gifts, but still she repined. And when he asked her why, she told him that she yearned for the things of her own land, and above all for the sight and scent of a pomegranate tree in the spring. So the king sent south for pomegranate trees, enough to fill an orchard, but it was a far journey and a hard one, and when they came at last all but four of the trees were dead. These he gave to his gardener, saying, "Make me a garden, and let there be a pomegranate tree at its center, for my queen to see and smell when it flowers in the spring."

" 'The gardener had never grown such a tree, and knew nothing of its culture, but he knew his king for an angry man when his wish was not fulfilled. Therefore he built for his king four gardens, each with a pomegranate tree at its center. One tree he both pruned and dunged. One he pruned and did not dung. One he dunged and did not prune. And the fourth he neither dunged nor pruned. So the trees prospered or stayed or failed according to their nature.

" 'Then in the spring the gardener led his king and his queen to a garden filled with roses and with lilies and with amaranth, and at its center a young pomegranate tree heavy with blossom, so that it scented all the garden. The queen clapped her hands with pleasure and the king rewarded the gardener with praise and with gold. So the gardener left them to delight in their tree, and sent for his workmen and said, "Let the other three gardens be plowed, and wheat sown in their place, that my master may not know of them, the two gardens where the tree at the center is a poor thing with only few leaves, and the fourth where it is dead.' "

"My son, that gardener was a wise man. Moreover he had four trees of which to make trial, and we have but two. Let us not grow them in the same garden."

By this Restaur Vax knew that the Bishop would not come.

AUGUST 1990

Letta was trying to write to Angel. It should have been a way of helping her settle down, but it wasn't. Nothing was. Nothing would be, either, at least not until tomorrow, when Grandad got back from the health farm which Momma had insisted on his going to, as soon as they were home from Varina.

Tomorrow. So that meant it was exactly a fortnight since she'd been sitting in the plane staring out at the mountains of Varina, dark beneath the sunset. The buses hadn't come till almost a week later, with everybody on them except a few fanatics who'd insisted on staying behind. Van was one of those. According to Nigel he'd had some kind of shattering argument with Poppa, which was extraordinary, because Poppa never had arguments with anyone, but it mightn't have been just about not coming home.

Apparently as soon as Grandad was arrested, Otto Vasa had completely hijacked the festival, turning it into a series of rallies to demand total independence for Varina. He'd organized a sort of bodyguard for himself, who wore yellow sashes and paraded at the rallies like soldiers, drilling and marching to shouted orders. He'd actually tried to have it hushed up that Grandad was safely out of the country, because it would be more of an outrage if he were in prison in Bucharest. Worst of all, he'd taken Van around everywhere with him, and talked about him as the third Restaur Vax. According to Nigel, Van had lapped it up, but Letta knew he mightn't be being fair, because of the permanent needling between Van and Steff.

Then the Romanian army had shown up and tried to take charge, and there'd been a terrifying confrontation just outside Potok, with a great mass of unarmed Varinians facing up to the soldiers with their tanks and guns, but Otto Vasa's henchmen seemed to have known they were coming and had got some foreign TV crews there, so the army had backed down because of the cameras and Otto Vasa had taken all the credit.

Then Mollie had managed to get the buses organized to bring everyone home early, so that was the last anyone knew.

The maddening and extraordinary thing was that though the radio and TV and the papers were full of what was happening in the old Yugoslavia, even the World Service hardly ever mentioned Varina. Letta found a short bit in the *Independent* about Grandad getting thrown out, and once or twice, in background articles about how dangerous things were getting between the Serbs and the Bosnians and the Croats, there were mentions of Macedonia and Varina being places waiting to explode, but there was nothing ever about how, or why, let alone what it was like to be there. Letta felt that she had been part of something huge and wonderful—the most important thing in her life, maybe—which had then gone wrong, like a good dream turning to a nightmare. But it was real, it had happened, it was still happening, still huge. Only if she walked down into Winchester there were all those people, shoppers, tourists roaming dazedly about, street musicians playing folk instruments, and as far as they were concerned it wasn't there.

And now there was this letter from Angel, making jokes about it. Typically Angel, about the horrors of having to live in darkest Yorkshire, where she'd never be able to make friends with anyone because she couldn't understand the weird way they talked, and how she was going to pine away in exile and die, so she'd decided to run away and turn up on Letta's doorstep talking in a foreign accent and saying she was really a Varingian freedom fighter on the run from the secret police . . . A month ago it might have been funny, even the joke about spelling Varinian wrong might have been funny, but it didn't work for Letta now.

She struggled through two sides of her answer. She had to do at least four, which wasn't fair because Angel's writing was twice the size of hers, and on top of that she'd finished up with one of her poems. Letta didn't write poems, and if she had she certainly wouldn't have made everyone read them, the way Angel did. This one was called "Christina." It was from a film they'd all seen on the box last Christmas, one of those terrific old film stars standing in the prow of the ship which is taking her away into exile, but of course in Angel's poem it was Angel . . .

They'd gone to visit Grandad on his health farm a couple of days ago, and Letta had asked him if there was another poem like "The Stream at Urya" which she could have a go at until he came back. He'd suggested one called "Receding Moun-tains." It was only fifteen lines long, but two of them were a bit tricky, he'd said. The old Restaur Vax had written it, not long before he died, remembering how he'd leaned on the rail of the boat and looked back when he'd left Varina for the last time. Letta thought she might try turning it into English and sending it to Angel. It would fill a page, anyway.

She got the book down and read the poem through again. She still couldn't see how the two tricky lines meant what she thought they had to, but the rest of it she liked almost more than "The Stream at Urya." Despite the strange old words and the twiddly bits which gave them their exact meanings, there were still lines which could make her skin crawl and prickle the hair on her nape. Hopeless, of course, to try and do that in English . . .

She stopped writing and fell into a daydream, a fantasy. She was in a small, dark room in Rome, standing invisible behind a chair where an old man sat at a table. No, he wasn't old, not really, just poor and tired and ill, and everyone had forgotten him, but you'd never know that from what he was doing now. Letta watched the long-nibbed pen scratch its way across the paper. The man had left Varina almost forty years before, but he remembered the moment and made it all new, the young fighter saying good-bye to the mountains, the mountains which had been his allies and friends, unchanging in defeat and victory. Good-bye for a little while. Soon he would return . . .

Only he'd never been allowed to. Letta reached out her invisible hand and laid it weightless on his shoulder. He paused for a moment in his writing, then went on.

Forty years in exile, and all because of that dreadful old fox, Bishop Pango. First thing Letta would do when Grandad got home was tell him what she thought of Bishop Pango.

. . .

"You do him an injustice," said Grandad. "Without him we might not be a people at all today. Sixty years ago, you know, when Romania was at least nominally a democracy, our northern province sent two members to the parliament in Bucharest. They were not on speaking terms with each other, because they belonged to opposing parties. One was a Vaxite and one was a Pangoist."

"That's silly."

"Silly but normal. It is nothing exclusive to Varina. It happens wherever there isn't enough of something important to go around—money, justice, power. There will always be some who will settle for nothing less than what they believe to be rightfully theirs. They are the Vaxites. The Pangoists are the ones who calculate the most they are likely to get, and settle for that."

"But Restaur Vax had done all the work. He'd made it happen. Then they booted him out."

"It was what they could get. There is never enough justice to go around. Besides, there are times for heroes, and times when it is better for heroes to do the decent thing and recede into legend."

Letta looked at him, puzzled. He'd changed. Only slightly —perhaps she wouldn't have noticed if she'd been seeing him every day. He was still brown from the Varinian sun, and sat as straight as ever in his stiff chair, but he seemed somehow smaller. His hands looked older than she'd remembered, with hummocked veins under the loose, blotched skin. And his voice sounded sad—nothing a stranger would have heard, but Letta's ears caught the note.

"Are you all right?" she said.

"The doctors say I am doing very well for my age. Why?"

"You sound unhappy. Underneath, I mean. Or angry."

"I'm sorry. I've missed you. And now, instead of having worthwhile conversations with my granddaughter I shall have to spend my days doing what I can to prevent our modern Vaxites and Pangoists from ruining everything with their stupid quarrels."

"Which are you?"

He smiled and put his hands together in the old way, with the ghosts of his left-hand fingers resting against the living ones of his right hand.

"You will tell no one?" he asked. "Very well. Between us two only, I am an onion. At the outside you have my name, like the brown onion skin you throw away. Next there is a Pangoist layer, not thick, because I want those I talk to to believe I am someone they can do business with. But inside that I am a Vaxite. I demand everything we are entitled to. No, wait, this is still not the center, but it is a good thick layer, and it means that those who wish to do business with me must realize that I too mean business. If I demand less than everything they will fob me off with less than they might have yielded, and I shall find that I have betrayed both myself and my country. Then, inside that I am a Pangoist. In the end I will take what I can get."

"Oh."

"I'm sorry to disappoint you, my darling. But suppose there had been no Bishop Pango, no treaty of Milan. Suppose my namesake had insisted on fighting on, demanding complete independence, what would have happened? The great powers who imposed the treaty would have lost patience, sympathy with little Varina would have ebbed away, we would have become no more than the naughty child in the European nursery, and the Turks would have been left to crush us out of existence. There might well have been no Varina at all today."

"I suppose so."

"The same is even truer now. We would not be fighting against muskets and scimitars and clumsy cannon. The Serbs and Bulgarians and Romanians all have modern armies, with modern weapons. How many rocket attacks, how long an artillery bombardment, do you think it would take to reduce the buildings around St. Joseph's Square—our lovely cathedral, our ridiculous palace—to heaps of golden rubble?"

"Don't! It won't happen, will it? Not nowadays?"

"Nowadays is a very frail notion. It certainly could happen, though I believe the odds are still on the side of reason. But if Otto Vasa is given his head, I will no longer think so. He already has a considerable following."

"Parvla went to a huge rally of his."

"Parvla?"

"Didn't I tell you? The friend I met at the festival. I got a letter from her this morning. Van made a speech at the rally. She says every girl in her valley is in love with him."

"She doesn't live in Potok?"

"No. I write to a place called Kalavani, but that's only where she goes to collect the letters. She lives on a farm up a side valley—it's an hour's walk, she says. It must be perfectly lovely. She says you look right out down the valley, and there's a waterfall that comes over the cliff beside it so it's cool in the summer . . ."

"Saludors."

"That's right! Parvla Saludors. You've been there! She never said!"

"No, I've not been there, but my friend Miklo Saludors

used to talk about that waterfall on hot days in the mountains."

"Parvla's father? No, her grandfather?"

"Her great-uncle, I should think. He was some years younger than me. He had no children. He was engaged to be married, but he was one of my companions on the peace mission, whom the Russians shot and buried in the clay pit."

"I don't understand how people can do things like that."

"May you not. May you simply be aware that such things happen, and that ordinary-seeming people are capable of doing them. What else does Parvla tell you?"

"Oh, everything is wonderful and they're going to try and have a referendum on independence—that was what the rally was about—but bread is getting terribly expensive because the Romanians are making things difficult and her geese have just hatched and her sister is pregnant again. I'm afraid she thinks Otto Vasa's wonderful. I don't know what to say to her about that."

"Tell her it's hard for you to judge, as you're not there."

"Could you tell me a bit more about your friend Miklo? She'd be thrilled to know you knew him."

"I imagine she is already aware of that."

"She'd have told me."

"Not necessarily. For all our excitability, we are a reticent people."

"You mean she might have thought it was pushy to tell me?"

"Perhaps."

"But is it okay if I . . ." Letta began, and stopped when Grandad held up a finger. He thought for a few moments.

"All right," he said. "This is perhaps a little unwise, but I will write a note on Miklo for you to send to your friend."

"That would be terrific! She'd be thrilled! Why is it un-wise?"

"Because if she were to show it to the wrong people it could be taken by them to make it seem as if I were approving the use of Miklo's name as that of a martyr for the cause of free-dom. This is exactly the sort of thing that Otto Vasa is doing when he speaks at these rallies."

"Oh, in that case . . . couldn't you just tell her things that don't matter, you know, the sort of jokes you tell about friends?"

"Perhaps I could, but then, well . . . I owe it to Miklo not to deny what he meant to me. That is more important than being wise. But if I do this, then perhaps—who am I to complain about the use of Miklo's name for political ends?—if I do this, then perhaps it would not be out of place for you to suggest in your letter that you are not absolutely sure how far Otto Vasa is to be trusted."

"Not absolutely sure, hell! I wouldn't trust him as far as I could throw an elephant. He's the most absolutely world-beating utter downright untrustworthy jerk anyone could hope to meet!"

"I respect your judgment, my darling, but if you put it in those terms your friend will close her mind. For the time being all we can do is work by hints and suggestions. We must sow the seeds of doubt and hope they grow. Vasa at some point is going to reveal his true nature. We cannot make it happen, but we can help our countrymen to be ready, when it does, to see him for what he is."

"What is he, anyway? I mean, a Vaxite or a Pangoist?"

"Neither. Both Vax and Pango were patriots. They loved their country, in their different ways, worked for it, fought for it, and if need be would have died for it. Vasa is also a patriot, but of a different kind. His country is simply an extension of himself. Varina must will what Vasa wills. There is no other source of right or wrong. He is a Vasaist."

LEGEND

RESTAUR'S BRIDE

Now for seventeen years[1] the Pashas left the mountains in peace. Nowhere did any Turk dare to come, no rooftree was burned, no children taken for slaves, no flocks seized without payment. So the chieftains dispersed, each to his own valley, and the men put their guns above the rafters, and all was well.

At the beginning of this time Lash the Golden came to Restaur Vax, holding in his hand a lamb fleece which had been dipped in blood, and said, "This I found at my door in the morning dew. It is from the Kas Kalaz. The last Turk has been driven from the mountains and his oath is fulfilled. He seeks my death."

Restaur Vax said, "Let me go to the Kas Kalaz and ask him, for all that we have done and suffered together, you and he and I, to forgo his oath and let the feud sleep."

But Lash said, "Am I to see you kneel at my enemy's feet? Never while my honor lives shall I endure that. Besides, I am no merchant or farmer. I am a bandit till I die, and now there are no Turks to rob, nor will I any longer rob my countrymen. I will go elsewhere."

So Restaur Vax took a silver coin and laid it on a log and smote it in two with his sword, cleaving the log also. One half he kept, and one half he gave to Lash the Golden. So they wept and parted.

Then Restaur Vax mounted his horse and rode west, but he had gone only a small way when he saw a woman coming toward him, wearing the veil of mourning.[2] He took a coin from his purse and cast it in the road before her, at which she blessed him. Then by her voice he knew her for his mother, but he saw that she did not know him.

He leaped from his horse, but fearing to slay her with sudden joy he asked first who she was and why she wore the veil of mourning. She answered, "I do not know who I am, nor why I must wear this veil, nor why my feet are on this road. All memory has been taken from me."

He said, "Your name is Parvla Vax."

She said, "It is as good a name as any."

He said, "You travel this road to find your son."

She said, "It is as good a reason as any."

He said, "I am your son, Restaur."

She said, "No doubt you will be as good a son as any."[3]

Then he took the veil from her face and kissed her and put her on his horse and led her west until they came to the bridge over the Avar. There he saw that the house that had stood beside the bridge was empty, and its roof-beams burned and its walls black with flame, so he asked other travelers where was the woman who had kept the house, and one said, "She fled from the Turks and now lives in a cave in the mountains."

So Restaur Vax turned aside and went by goat paths and the paths of the hunter until he came in sight of the cave. The woman sat on a rock with her two daughters in her lap, and a book before her from which she was teaching them their letters. Restaur Vax said to his mother, "Now it is your business to find me a wife. Go to that woman and ask if she is spoken for, for she is a widow. If she asks you what she must bring as a dowry, say to her three good fields and twenty-seven sheep."

His mother said, "One woman is as good as another, and that is a fair price."

She went to the woman and spoke as she had been told and the woman looked up and saw Restaur Vax standing in the pathway beside his horse, with his musket on his back and his sword and pistols in his belt.

"Am I to marry a bandit?" she said.

Then she looked again and said, "There was a certain priest who came by the bridge and brought my troubles upon me, though he paid a fair price."

She looked a third time and said, "I have need of a husband and my daughters have need of a father."

"But where are your sons?" asked Restaur's mother, in the voice of one speaking in a dream.

"I have no sons," said the woman.

Then Restaur's mother looked at the children and said, "I had two sons," and as she spoke the bolts of her memory were drawn and she knew all that had been done to her, and fell to the ground and mourned. The woman raised her up and Restaur ran to her side and now she knew him and wept again. Then the woman went into the cave and brought out wine and bread and olives, and they sat and ate.

The woman said, "So you would be a farmer? Can you shear a ewe? Can you prune a vine?"

Restaur said, "I was a priest who learned to be a warrior. Now I am a warrior who will learn to be a farmer. And your daughters will be my daughters and my mother will be your mother, and I will build your house by the bridge over the Avar, and all will be well with us, as it is with all our people."

So the woman lit a fire at the cave mouth and baked the betrothal cake, and they ate from the same dish and drank from the same cup and kissed each other and were agreed.[4]

———

1. *The full independence of Varina lasted from the battle of Tresti (1 March 1826) until Bishop Pango's acceptance of Turkish hegemony with himself as Prince-Bishop at the Milan Conference in October 1828.*

2. *Traditional face covering of widows without immediate family to support them, enabling them to beg without loss of honor to their clan.*

3. *This encounter and its sequel are probably entirely fictional, reworking a traditional tale, now lost. Restaur Vax's own poem "Meeting" (op. cit.) uses the tale up to this point, but treats both son and mother as nameless figures of mythic stature.*

4. *Restaur Vax married in 1824 Mariu Kori (1799–1893). She had been betrothed to Vax's elder brother until his disappearance at the start of the War of Independence (see* Legend: Lash the Golden*). By custom Restaur took the family obligation on himself as soon as he was free to do so. It is to Mariu that we are indebted for the preservation and publication of almost all the poems.*

AUGUST 1990

One good thing, nothing to do with Varina, happened. The recession, which had taken Angel away, brought Biddie back. Her parents were feeling the pinch, and decided that in order to pay for their own holiday in Greece they would have to rent out their Devon cottage for the priciest part of the season and spend the rest of the summer holidays in Winchester.

Biddie called at breakfast.

"Hi," she said. "How was Romania? Don't tell me now. We got back last night. What are you doing this afternoon?"

"Nothing special."

"Shall we choose presents? In time, for once?"

"Great."

"Pick you up at two?"

"Make it one-thirty. I want to get back and have tea with Grandad. He's been at a health farm. He's only just back."

"What about Richoux?"

"Do that first?"

"Fine."

They hung up. That was a fairly typical Biddie call. Her parents were extremely tough with her—medieval, Angel used to say. They were tough about homework, tough about being out after dark, tough about clothes, tough about dragging her off to Devon all the holidays and most weekends, and fiendishly tough about the telephone. At one point there was trouble with Angel, who didn't think that anything less than an hour and a half counted as a serious telephone call, but then Biddie's dad, who was a thoroughgoing gadget nerd, attached a timer to the telephone which cut it off after three minutes whether you called her or she called you, unless she used a special key which she had to ask for. What's more it kept it cut off for another five minutes, so you couldn't just make a series of three-minute calls. This meant that Letta's friendship with Biddie had been almost entirely a school thing, so it was especially pleasing and comforting that Biddie had called pretty well the moment she got back.

Choosing birthday presents was a ritual, much more important than the Christmas-present ritual. Because of the way their holiday comings and goings had worked out they'd usually had to wait for the start of the winter term, and then they'd cruise the gift shops on High Street looking for things under five pounds and awarding them points on a scale of one to ten for idiocy. If they couldn't find two objects scoring at least eight they bought each other cards instead. Then they'd finish up having hot chocolate at Richoux.

Letta loved Richoux, even crammed with tourists, as it was in August. It was a bit posh and a bit ye-olde, but nothing like as fake as it might have been. They were lucky and got a table in a niche, where they settled down and looked at each

other. Biddie had hardly changed at all, Letta decided. She
had a very square face with coarse black hair, black eyebrows,
dark brown eyes, whitish freckled skin, and a wide mouth.
Letta guessed that if she never saw her again till she was sixty
she's still recognize her at once. In their old school everyone
had known that Biddie was about the cleverest pupil they'd
had there, ever, and she was going to get all sorts of scholar-
ships, and finish up famous. It was lovely now to be with her.
Theirs wasn't the sort of friendship you had to work to keep
going, like the one with Angel. It was simply there, a fact.

"You've changed," said Biddie.

"I was just thinking you hadn't."

"I have, too. At least I've gone on strike. I've told Momma
and Dad that now we're going to different schools they've got
to let me have other ways of getting to hang out with you. We
get home for weekends from this school, so I've said I won't
always be coming down to Devon with them. I'm going to be
staying with you instead, if it's okay with your mum."

"That's great! I'm sure Momma won't mind. What did
your parents say?"

"They're thinking about it. They'll say okay in the end.
They know what matters and what doesn't. Tell me about
Romania. I found your card when I got home."

"Not Romania, Varina."

"It had a Romanian stamp."

"It won't next year. Don't you remember, I spent most of
last hols helping my sister-in-law in St. Albans fix buses and
hotels and things to get to our culture festival?"

"Oh, yes. How did it go?"

"The first half was brilliant. Best thing that's ever happened in my life. I can't imagine anything as exciting, ever
again. I felt as if I'd come home, as if a huge piece of me had

always been missing and now I was all joined up again. And my grandad was there—he was our last real prime minister—and everyone cheered him everywhere he went. He was total hero. And then, out of the blue, the Romanians arrested him in his pajamas and took him away. They let Momma and me come along after, to see he was all right, but they practically kept their guns pointing at us all the time until we were on the plane and out of the country."

"Wow!"

"Our people—the Varinians, I mean—were pretty well rioting about it when we left. Burning cars and smashing foreigners' houses. And after we'd gone the Romanians sent the army along, and the Varinians went and stood in front of them and wouldn't let them into the city."

"It sounds pretty scary."

"It is. And there's a horrible man called . . ."

"I mean real armies. That's big guns and tanks and airplanes doing rocket attacks if things go wrong . . . What's up?"

Letta had felt the blood drain from her face. She closed her eyes and bowed her head. It was almost the same words Grandad had used, bringing this sudden lurch into horror, here in the snug, smug, coffee-scented tearoom in a town where there hadn't been actual fighting—war, blood, bodies, cannon-shattered homes—since heaven knows when. Vivid as a nightmare she saw three warplanes screaming over the shoulder of Mount Athur. She saw St. Joseph's Square, the crowds racing for shelter. One of them was Parvla. She tripped and fell. The crowds milled over her.

"Are you okay?" said Biddie.

"It mustn't happen," whispered Letta. "Nothing's worth that, nothing."

She shook her head violently, willing the nightmare away, and pulled herself together.

"I'm sorry," she said. "I'm okay."

"Of course it isn't worth it," said Biddie. "I wish I knew why anyone thinks it is. We're all the same underneath, aren't we?"

"I am more different than you think," said Letta, in Field. Biddie looked blank. Letta said it again in English.

"But that's just language," said Biddie.

"No it isn't, it's . . . let me think . . . yes, listen. Sometimes I dream in English, and sometimes I dream in Field, like I was talking just now. I've always done it, but since I came back from Potok—I don't know—well, it isn't quite the same me doing the dreaming. I've got a sort of overlap. You know, like a shaky TV signal, with a sort of shadow line because you're seeing two pictures. . . . It isn't just language. It isn't just having our own cheeses and legends and dogs and our own kind of Christianity and things like that. It's something that's kept us going on being Varinians for hundreds of years, when everyone else was trying to stop us. We aren't like anyone else, and nobody can make us."

"Just now you said it wasn't worth it. Now you're sort of saying it is."

"I don't know. I really don't know!"

Then the waitress came and they ordered their chocolate and to calm herself down Letta asked about Greece, and then they talked about Angel until it was time to go present hunting. As they came out to High Street Letta glanced up at the low, drab cloud base and felt a vague sense of release, then realized that at the shadow edge of her mind she had still been seeing that intense blue southern sky across which the warplanes had swept.

• • •

When she got home she found a motorcycle blocking the driveway, a huge, brand-new beast of a thing, glistening purple and white and black. There were black leathers draped on the banisters and a crash helmet striped with the Varinian colors on the hall table. Hell, she thought, I'd much rather have him to myself, but at least it might mean there's news from Potok. She made the tea, put an extra mug on the tray, and carried it up.

A man was talking as she climbed the last flight. She knew the voice. Steff. Steff on a bike like that? Grandad answered, called to her to come in when she knocked, and went on as she backed her way through the door.

". . . never been natural traders. We have relied on outsiders living among us to create wealth, and then of course have envied them. How many of the crowd in the square last month were aware of standing in a place where there was a major massacre of Jews in 1852? They had come to the Prince-Bishop's palace for protection but he had shut his doors against them."

"Was that horrible old Pango?" said Letta, still with her back to the room as she nudged the tray onto the cluttered table. (It couldn't be Steff—he'd have been on his feet, helping her.)

"His successors," said Grandad. "Pango had encouraged the Jews to settle in Potok."

"Hi, Sis," said the other man.

"Van!"

"Didn't want you to jump like that with the tray in your hands. How's life treating you?"

"That's not your bike!"

"It is, too."

"Bike?" said Grandad.

"A great glistening monster painted our colors," said Letta. "Where did you get it? How fast does it go?"

"A hundred and forty, supposed to," said Van. "I haven't been over a hundred. It's a BMW."

"A gift?" said Grandad in his quietest voice.

"And then some," said Van. "Otto made quite a splash of handing it over. He sprang a farewell party on me in Vienna, and handed the bike over when the champagne was flowing. There's a few things he wants me to do for him over here, and I've got to have transport, but mainly it's to make up for being booted out of Varina."

"Booted out!" said Letta. "Like Grandad?"

"That's right."

"In your pajamas?"

She'd asked that seriously, without thinking, just trying to imagine the scene, but laughed at herself when Van laughed. Even Grandad smiled.

"We had a tip-off," said Van. "We've been getting pretty good intelligence, so we had a couple of hours to set something up. I talked it over with Otto. I wanted to go into hiding, but he said it was too soon for that sort of thing, so we made them come and get me. We let them think I was just drinking with a few pals in this *torno,* the one with the pink umbrellas in Jirin Road, and they came swooping up in three of those black stretch limos to grab me, but our people poured out from every house in the street and blocked them in, so they radioed the army for help and I got up on a table and did my young-hero bit and said I was going quietly to save bloodshed. Then I let them take me and put me on a plane to Vienna. It was supposed to be only a stopover for me there, but Otto had fixed things up for us both to get off so that he could spring the party and the bike on me."

"You mean they threw him out too?" said Letta, with a leap of the heart.

"He'd got some business to see to. They can't sling him out that easily—he's a Romanian citizen."

"I thought he was an exile, like Grandad," said Letta.

"The difference is that he chose to live in Austria," said Grandad, still in that quiet voice which Van appeared not to notice. "I, for my part, was forced to live in England."

Letta decided to change the subject.

"Are you going back to Glasgow?" she said.

"No point," said Van. "I haven't got a house, I haven't got a girlfriend, and I haven't got a job."

"What!"

"When I decided to stay on in Potok I called them up and resigned. They'd have fired me anyway for overstaying my leave. Don't worry, Sis. I shan't be out begging on High Street. Sue's selling the house, so there'll be a bit of money after the mortgage is paid off, and I've got a few things to do for Otto, so he's paying me a retainer."

"Where are you going to live?"

"Here, if Momma will let me. You're in my old room, but Steff's looks empty. Don't look so baffled, Sis—it's only a couple of months."

"I'm sorry. I was just surprised."

"Let us establish an island of calm in the hurricane of events," said Grandad. "Let's have our tea and crumpets."

"God, you're not going to light the fire," said Van. "It's roasting in here already."

"Yes, of course," said Letta. "You can't have crumpets without it. If you don't like it you can go and move your bike.

You'll have to anyway before Momma gets home. She comes swooping in there. You don't want it scrunched, I imagine."

"Oh, all right," said Van. "Do a couple for me. Plenty of butter, please. Drooling with it, okay?"

He lounged out and clumped down the stairs.

Letta heard Grandad sigh.

"Is this all right?" she whispered. "I don't like it."

"It's not entirely Van's fault," said Grandad. "Popular enthusiasm is hard to resist. I had a visit from my policeman this morning."

"The tall thin one who met us at the airport?"

"Yes. He is a good friend, insofar as he can afford to be. He has been putting together a file on Vasa. Some of this I knew already, but some I did not. After the war there was a penniless, parentless urchin who ran away from a camp for war orphans and showed up in Vienna . . ."

"Was he really a Varinian?"

"He seems to have spoken Field as his first language."

"Bother. I suppose that pretty well proves it."

"I'm afraid so. Anyway, he ran errands for black marketeers, and then worked for himself in the black market. There was a shortage of building materials. He found ways to supply them. He got to know the government officials who awarded the state building contracts, and became wealthy. All this I knew. But now my friend tells me that there is evidence that at some stage Vasa contacted the Ceauşescu regime and undertook various financial dealings for them when they were salting away their fortunes outside their country. Some of that money will have found its way into his pockets. So now he is genuinely enormously rich. He has several houses, a vast castle in Carpathia, a wife who is an archduchess in her own right or some such nonsense. But he has no country. He is trying to buy himself one."

"He can't do that!"

"If we succeed in making Varina free, we will be citizens of the poorest country in Europe. And to the truly poor the rich are rich by magic. They have a secret. If you make a very rich man your president, he will use his magic to make your country as rich as he is."

"That's nonsense."

"It is powerful nonsense. However, we think Vasa is not relying solely on his wealth. There are well-placed people in Bucharest who were once members of the Ceauşescu regime, with which Vasa had many contacts. Van himself has told us that Vasa is getting good intelligence. And does it not strike you that this motorcycle was bought and painted in our colors in a remarkably short time? Perhaps Vasa knew sometime earlier that Van was about to be expelled."

"You mean he arranged it himself?"

"Perhaps. Your friend Parvla has already told us that Van is a very popular figure, more popular with some than Vasa himself. He would not tolerate that for long, I think."

"But it still doesn't make sense. Why should the Romanians be helping Otto Vasa stir things up? Don't they want it all to simmer down?"

"Of course. That is what the Romanian government wants, officially. But the army itself contains many nationalist extremists, and there are local politicians who would be glad to gain popularity by whipping up anti-Varinian sentiment. I now think it may have been a combination of these which originally abducted me, and the central government then took over and decided to spirit me out of the country."

"So it wasn't Otto Vasa's idea after all?"

"I don't know. As I told you, he has many contacts with powerful officials who are still in place. He knows things which they would much rather keep secret, so he is in a strong position both to bribe and blackmail them."

"But what's in it for him? He doesn't want the Romanians to crack down on us either, does he? He wants Varina independent, just like we do, only he wants to be boss."

"He has the mentality of a bandit. He will believe that when the time comes he can ride the tiger."

"It sounds terrifying."

"It is."

"Why don't you tell Van?"

"He will have heard stories of this kind and dismissed them as lies to discredit Vasa. He will not believe them, even from me. I must—"

"He's coming back."

". . . forty-three Jews died in the square. Others were hunted down in their homes."

"*We* did this?" said Letta as Van came panting in. "Us Varinians?"

"The great-great-grandparents of many of those whom you saw."

"Ancient history," said Van. "What can you expect if the price of bread goes up ten times in a month. Crumpets ready?"

LEGEND

SELIM'S RETURN

There was a girl of matchless beauty born in the valley of the Spol.[1] When she was five years old the Turks took her and offered her for sale in Jirin market. There the slave captain of the Pasha of Jirin saw her, and bought her for his master. Years passed and each year she became yet more beautiful.

When she was almost a woman Restaur Vax drove the Pashas from Varina, and they fled, taking their households with them to Byzantium. There they found the Sultan greatly vexed for the loss of Varina, and he cast them into his dungeons and ordered their goods to be taken from them and sold, but reserved for himself the best.

Thus it was that the warden of the Imperial Harem came to the Sultan and said, "A young woman of matchless beauty has been entered in the inventory." And the Sultan said, "Let us see her."

She was brought and stood before him and looked proudly

at him, and without fear, so that he was amazed and said, "We are the Sultan of all the world. Are you not afraid?"

She answered, "I am a Varinian. How should I be afraid?"

He asked her, "Are you Varinians then afraid of nothing?"

"None of us knows how to be afraid," she answered.

"Not even the little children in the dark of the night?" he demanded.

At that she laughed and said, "When I was a little child, sometimes in the dark of the night I was afraid that Selim Pasha would come for me, but now he is in your dungeons, so I have nothing to fear."

Then the Sultan sent for his chief vizier and said, "We have a man called Selim Pasha in our dungeons. Let him be taken from the rack, and set free, and restored to his household and his honor. Let gold and armies be given him, as much as he may ask, and say to him that he has a year and a day in which to restore to us by what means he may our lost province of Varina. And if he should fail, then his state shall be ten times worse than it is now."

So it was as the Sultan commanded, and before the ice had melted from the great river Selim Pasha raised his standards outside the walls of Potok, and behind him stood an army of seventeen thousand *bazouks*.

———

1. *The women of Spol Valley are still proverbial for their beauty, as the men are for their stupidity.*

AUGUST/SEPTEMBER 1990

Van rode his new bike north to settle things with Sue and arrange for having his own gear moved to Winchester. A few days later he was back, in time to come and have tea with Grandad and Letta. It was a Saturday, so Momma came too, not because she particularly wanted to see Grandad but because Van was there. Since he'd been home from Potok, Letta had realized for the first time how much Momma cared about Van, in a way she didn't seem to about Steff or Letta herself. It was the sort of thing that happened in families, Letta knew—not that Momma made a parade of it, in fact she'd probably have denied it completely if you'd asked her, but all the same she was different when Van was around, brighter and less concerned with the business of keeping the household going.

It was a lovely late summer afternoon and they had the window open, with the roofs and treetops of Winchester spreading away below them. They weren't talking about anything much, just sitting peacefully there, when Van said, "Will Poppa be home in time for St. Joseph's?"

Poppa was in Bolivia, advising about bridges.

"When's St. Joseph's?" said Momma.

"Oh, Momma!" said Van.

"Twenty-seventh," said Letta, "and he better had be, because it's my birthday the day after."

"Of course it is," said Momma. "I don't know why I said that. Yes, he'll be home."

"Can we have *kalani?*" said Van.

"To welcome home our various prodigals it really ought to be *trozhl,*" said Grandad.

"You get me the goats' udders and I'll do you *trozhl* tomorrow," snapped Momma. "I could do *kalani,* I suppose, though the lamb's nothing like the same here . . ."

"Not tough and stringy enough," said Grandad.

"As a matter of fact Poppa did bring a bottle of bitter sauce home from Potok," said Momma. "I was keeping it for the goose at Christmas. And I saw some figs at Sainsbury's, so we could have *dumbris* for afters . . ."

Letta was delighted it wasn't going to be *trozhl,* which was a slithery sort of stew which she'd found disgusting. *Kalani* was just *kebabs* with green peppers, but you dipped them in this sauce which almost shriveled your mouth first go but made you want to try again. *Dumbris* were whole figs inside a jacket of spiced dough, deep fried and coated with honey, intensely sweet and delectable. "Eat three and die in paradise" was the saying about them. The point was that it was almost impossible to swallow more than one. However much your mouth wanted to, your throat refused.

"No fields like Father's. No food like Mother's," said Van.

They all laughed. It was another saying, much the same as

"Home Sweet Home." In fact Letta had seen it again and again on plates and plaques and even T-shirts on the souvenir stalls in Potok. She could almost hear Momma purring.

"We'll be all right for wine," said Van. "Hector brought some home from his uncle's vineyard. He gave me a couple of bottles."

Grandad had been sitting back in his chair, looking benign and relaxed, but now he flashed a sharp glance at Van.

"Old Paul Orestes has got the vineyard back?" he said.

"A couple of months ago," said Van.

"They used to make really good wine," said Grandad. "It will be interesting to see whether the Communists managed to ruin that also. When did you see our Hector?"

(*That* was what he really wanted to know.)

"Last night. I stayed with him on the way down."

"Why didn't you stay with Steff and Mollie?" said Momma, refusing, as always, to notice the fact that her sons didn't get on with each other. "It's only a few miles difference."

"I took a cup of tea off Mollie," said Van. "Don't you want the wine, Momma?"

She shrugged and spread her hands with a twisting motion, as if she were wringing out an invisible cloth, a gesture she never used to make but which Letta had seen again and again on the streets of Potok. It meant almost anything you wanted it to mean.

Grandad was still watching Van.

"Wasn't I given some almond brandy?" he said. "Did that find its way home? We will need it after the *dumbris*."

"In any case," said Van, "Mollie's spare room is pretty well chock-full of paperwork for next year's festival."

"Next year's festival?" said Momma.

There was a silence.

"They aren't seriously going to try and have another festival next year?" she said.

"It has been suggested," said Grandad, "but I for one was not aware that the project was sufficiently far advanced to fill a whole bedroom with paperwork."

He spoke dryly, but Letta could hear he was both surprised and angry.

"It isn't like that," she said. "At least according to Nigel. He says they were hardly back before people were calling up wanting to book places. Mollie kept telling them how iffy it was, but they still insisted on putting their names down and some of them are sending money. She's just keeping track."

"It's not at all iffy," said Van. "It's going to be in Listru."

"Oh, for God's sake! Listru's in Bulgaria!" said Momma.

"Listru is in the Southern Province of Varina and we have a perfect right to hold a festival there," said Van.

"What do you mean 'we'?" snapped Momma. "This is childish. You can't do anything. It isn't your business anymore. I'm not talking about you, Poppa, but . . . oh, Van! Letta! You've got British passports. This is where your life is going to be! This is where you belong! Varina's over!"

"You wouldn't have said that a month ago," said Van, teasing, not seeming to notice how upset Momma was becoming. "Half Potok saw you dancing the *sundilla* in the square."

"Yes, I know. Yes, I had a good time . . ."

"Tears streaming down your face," said Van.

"Listen. I was saying good-bye. I was happy once in Potok, long ago, when Steff and you were born. And now I was saying good-bye, because I knew I could never go back. It wasn't real anymore."

She banged her fist onto the table so that the teapot rattled on the tray.

"I think it was the realest thing I've ever known," said Letta.

She couldn't help it. She had to say it. It was true, and it mattered to her not to pretend, in spite of understanding why Momma felt the way she did. Momma drew a breath to yell at her, held it, and let it out.

"Of course it was lovely, darling," she said carefully. "Especially lovely for you, with everything so happy, and no memories from before."

"Until they came for Grandad," said Letta.

"Exactly," said Momma. "And that was when it stopped being a lovely dream and started being real."

"I don't buy that," said Van. "That happened because our country is occupied by foreign powers. It's got nothing to do with being real. In a real Varina it wouldn't have happened."

"In a real world it did," said Momma. "And trying to hold a festival in Listru will only make it happen again, worse. The Bulgarians can be just as nasty as the Romanians—nastier, if anything. And anyone who tries to get there from outside will be just wasting their money. All they'll do is sit in a bus for four days and then get turned back at the border."

"There are ways past borders, if you know how," said Van.

"Van, please!" said Momma. "Can't you see what dangerous nonsense you're talking? Poppa, do say something."

"It need not be dangerous, or nonsense," said Grandad. "For myself, I think we should attempt to hold a second festival—"

"We're going to hold one," interrupted Van. "We're not talking about a few buses being stopped at the borders, we're

talking about a hundred thousand native Varinians from the
Northern Province all crossing the Danube together."

"This isn't the Thames," said Momma. "Have you *seen* the
Danube?"

"Course I have," said Van. "There's quite a few boats. We
can build rafts and tow them. How are they going to stop us?
Are they going to turn their guns on raft-loads of women and
children?"

"If they thought no one was looking they might well," said
Grandad. "If we were to reach such a confrontation, I would
not take the risk. I would prefer to negotiate with the Bulgarian regime. We could for instance offer to postpone the pro-
posed referendum, which they certainly see as provocative—"

"Not on your life!" said Van, cutting in again. "That's
going to happen. It's not negotiable."

"Oh, Van!" said Momma. "You're talking as if you could
make the Bulgarians do what you want. And the Serbs and
Romanians. You can't. Do you imagine you can fight them?
They've got armies, with tanks and guns and warplanes. It
won't be like old Restaur Vax fighting the Turks anymore. It
will be hell."

"It's not going to be like that," said Van. "In any case
Restaur Vax didn't win that war—not by himself. What he
did was make enough of a nuisance of himself for long enough
for the British and the French and the Austrians to get tired of
having this mess on their doorsteps and tell the Turks they'd
got to lay off. That's what we've got to do now. The trick is to
stir things up and keep them stirred until everyone, even the
Americans, realize we're not going to go away and they make
the occupying powers give us what we want. If we can't stir
things up one way we'll stir them another."

"What do you mean?" snapped Momma.

Van just looked at her, saying nothing. He wasn't simply teasing. There was something else, some meaning in the tense silence, which Letta didn't understand.

"As Van says, that is the trick," said Grandad quietly. "I think there is very little difference among any of us over that. The argument is about how the trick is to be performed. Ideally we should persuade the outside powers that our cause is just, which it is, that we are prepared to be obstinate about it, which we are, but also reasonable, which we are not. To attempt to hold a cultural festival in the old capital of one of our three provinces fills the bill as neatly as can be expected. I think we shall be prevented, but I will certainly act as if I intended to go, and if I am allowed to I shall do so."

"So will I," said Letta.

"Good for you," said Van.

Momma rose, grabbed everyone's mugs, and banged them onto the tray.

"I think you're all mad," she said in English. "I see I shall have to talk to Steff. Open the door for me, please, Letta."

She marched out, catching a pleat of her skirt on a loose screw on the door plate. She ripped it free and tramped on down the stairs. As Letta was closing the door she turned and caught Grandad's eye. He made a minute gesture with his hand for her to go away, so she took the pack of crumpets and left. As she went down the first flight she heard Grandad's voice asking a question, and Van's answering, cautious but obstinate. Then they were out of earshot.

Momma was already on the phone, saying, "Hello, darling. Is your father there? Can I have a word with him?"

Letta patted her shoulder comfortingly, but got no response, so she went into the sitting room and started flipping through the TV channels. There seemed to be nothing but dreary cricket and ancient Westerns. Van used to be good at cricket, she remembered. When she was small Momma had once taken her to watch him having a trial for the Hampshire 2nd XI. Cricket was like the *sundilla,* she thought. Probably all countries have something like that, meaningless and boring to anyone outside, but really important to people inside. Look at baseball, for heaven's sake! Momma thought cricket was meaningless and boring—she'd only gone to watch because Van had been playing. But she'd cried while she'd danced the *sundilla.* Despite what had happened at Lapiri, she wasn't really free, and she never would be.

She wanted to keep Varina as a kind of frill, a flavor, an old book you don't read anymore. It was cooking *kalani* and dancing at midnight in St. Joseph's Square. If Potok fell to ruins, if nobody remembered the dances, or knew how to cook *kalani* and *trozhl* and *dumbris,* if nobody dreamed in Field, if no one could ever be pierced to the heart again by the single word *anastrondaitu,* Momma would say it was a pity, but that was all. She would say that she and her family had their own lives to live, here, now, in England. That was what really mattered. She would mean it, too, but still she would be lying.

Letta shook her head. I'm not going to tell myself that lie, she thought. Even if something like what happened at Lapiri happens to me, I will never tell myself that lie.

I hope.

LEGEND

The Daughter of Olla

Men came to Restaur Vax while he was shearing his sheep by the bridge of Avar, and told him that Selim Pasha was besieging Potok with seventeen thousand *bazouks*. He said nothing until he had lifted the fleece cleanly from the ewe between his knees. Then he laid his shears aside and stood.

To each of the men in turn he said, "Go now to such-and-such a chieftain and tell him what you have told me. Bid him come to the Old Stones of Falje on the eve of the next new moon."

But to the last man of all he said, "Go west and south, beyond the farthest border. Ask those whom you meet for the place where the mountains are wildest and the law is least. There you will find Lash the Golden. Give him this half piece of silver, and say no other word."

So the men departed. Then Restaur Vax said to his wife, "You are my treasure and my joy, but Selim Pasha is besieging Potok with seventeen thousand *bazouks,* and I alone can hold the chieftains together, to drive him out once more. So give me your blessing and your leave, and when it is done I will return."

She said, "If you must go, you must go. I give you my leave and my blessing."

He said, "Men will seek you here to use you, because I am who I am. Take your daughters and our son to the cave where we were betrothed, and you will be safe."

So they loaded three mules with all that they could carry, food and gear and guns, and Restaur Vax with his son in his arms led his family to the cave below the ridge of Avar, and saw them well housed, and journeyed on to the Old Stones of Falje.

Now in Potok there were certain Greek merchants who feared for their lives and their goods should the city fall. They said among themselves, "Restaur Vax is no help. He is no more than a mountain brigand. Let us open the gates to Selim Pasha and he will protect us."

So two of them went secretly to Selim in his camp and stood before him and said, "We will open the gates to you, if you will protect us and ours when you sack the city."

But Selim smiled in his beard and shook his head. He took a peach and crushed it in his hand so that the juices ran between his fingers and said to them, "I hold Potok in the palm of my hand. My *bazouks* could take it in a morning were I to give the order."

He tossed the spoiled peach aside and said, "What use is Potok to me, while Restaur Vax is alive in the mountains? Bring him into my hands, and then I will protect you when the city falls."

At that the Greeks were dismayed and returned to the city

and took counsel. And one said, "A summer ago I traveled in the mountains, and at the Bridge of Avar I traded with a woman who nursed a newborn child, her man being away. She spoke to me pleasantly but told me nothing of herself. There was, however, another woman, old and wandering in her wits, who told me that the first woman was the wife of Restaur Vax, and the child was his son,[1] and that during the wars the woman had hidden in a cave far up the mountain until Restaur Vax had come to claim her as his bride. Now, no doubt, the woman has returned to that cave to hide. Let us therefore ask Selim for a safe conduct through his lines and take our Greek servants, whom we trust, and go and find this cave and seize this child, and then we can make Restaur Vax do our bidding for the child's safety."

So they agreed. But there was in this house a servant woman, a Varinian named Olla, who mistrusting the Greeks and knowing that they had stolen secretly from the town and returned, lay on the boards above, listening through a crack. And she had a small daughter, not eight years old. Olla took thought about how she should warn Restaur Vax, but the Turks ringed the city close about and she could see no way through, for herself. So she took a butter barrel, just large enough for her daughter to curl within it, and she made a fastening for the lid so that it could be opened from inside, and since she could not herself write she taught her daughter what to say, and carried the barrel down to the river by night and set it floating on the current, which carried it away.

But the river was swollen with the snowmelt and the barrel jarred heavily against a boulder, so that the child was stunned and the barrel itself broke and the child was washed away down the stream and cast up on a sandbank far from the city. There she was found by Lash the Golden, who was journeying to join Restaur Vax and fight the Turks once more. He had slept among bushes and woken at sunrise and gone to the river to bathe his face. Finding the child he turned her over and at first thought her drowned, but hoping that perhaps she yet lived he made a fire and dried her and wrapped her in his coat and rubbed her limbs until she choked and opened her eyes.

Then, not knowing where she was or to whom she spoke, she whispered the lesson which her mother had taught her, saying, "I am the daughter of Olla, who is a servant maid among the Greeks of Potok. My mother has heard her masters planning to seek the cave where the wife of Restaur Vax is in hiding, so that they may take his son and give him to Selim Pasha in exchange for their own safety."

She closed her eyes and opened them again and said her lesson through, and again a third time, and then she died. At that Lash wept, and carried her to a priest, giving him silver for her burial, and then, going by goat paths and the paths of the hunter, he hastened all day and all night and came at noon on the second day to the ridge above the Avar below which lay the cave. There he heard shots, and ran with all speed, and saw men attacking the cave while one held them at bay from within.

Seeing by their dress that these men were Greeks he lay down and took good aim and shot one man, and a second, and a third, so that the rest turned to flee. Then Lash the Golden drew his sword and fell upon them, cutting them down as they ran. When they were all slain or fled away he returned to the cave.

There he found Restaur's wife and saluted her as the mother of heroes, for it was she who had held the cave until he came, using two guns, with her daughters loading one while she fired the other. He took them to a place of safety and journeyed on to the Old Stones, where he found Restaur Vax speaking strongly with the chieftains who had gathered there. Now, many were reluctant to take weapons once more and fight the Turk. They said, "What is Potok to us? It is spring, and we have our fields to sow and our flocks to drive to the high pastures." But Lash stood up before them and told them of the child who had carried the message, and they were shamed. For they said in their hearts, "If this child, this daughter of Olla, can die thus for Varina, how should not we, who are grown men and chieftains, do as much?"

———

1. *Theodore Vax (1825–1890). Restaur Vax's poem "Prayer for My Son" (op. cit.), refers to the baby as having been born on the mountain, and baptized in blood, with the smoke of gunpowder for incense.*

SEPTEMBER 1990

"I think that's absolutely horrible," said Letta, putting the book down. "I mean, she was only eight! She didn't know what she was doing! She didn't choose! He mother stuffed her into this barrel and threw her in the river and it went wrong and she got drowned, only she lived just long enough to give the message. And I bet she didn't even know she was doing that, or what it meant, or anything. It was just something she had to get rid of before she could die. So they blubber over her and think how noble they are and decide to go and fight the Turks after all. They just *used* her! It's disgusting!"

"One of the functions of legend is to make the disgusting tolerable," said Grandad. "There is in fact a poem by my great-grandfather about the daughter of Olla which makes much the same point. It's called 'Patriotism.' In fact it's a difficult and obscure poem, very gloomy in tone, but I think what he's saying is that patriotism is like the child's message, something we don't understand but we've still got to pass on, at whatever cost."

"He was using her too."

"I suppose so, but in his case—"

"Hold it. That's the telephone."

Letta jumped up and ran downstairs. She and Grandad were alone in the house. It was the last day of school vacation. Momma was at work. Poppa was back in Bolivia, and Van was off on his bike somewhere up north. In fact he was supposed to have been back for lunch, and Letta was a bit angry with him for not letting her know, as she'd got it all ready, and she and Grandad had waited for him, too, when she'd been really hungry. She guessed the telephone would be him now, saying where he'd got to, all charm. She picked the receiver up, ready to snap, and gave the number.

"May I speak to Letta Ozlins?" said a woman's voice.

"Ozolins," said Letta automatically. "That's me."

"I'm afraid I have some bad news for you," said the voice. "Will you please sit down?"

Letta's heart gave a desperate thud and her throat went dry. She groped for the chair and sat.

"All right," she managed to say.

"This is the Royal Hospital," said the voice. "It's about your brother Van. Is that his full name?"

"Yes. Is he all right? What's happened?"

"He's had a serious accident. I don't know the details, but I understand he was wearing motorcycle gear when he was brought in. His condition is stable. He's now conscious, and he's asking to see you."

"Me? Has anyone told Momma? My mother?"

"Your mother?" said the voice, surprised. "We understood

. . . Hold on a moment . . . No, it's Letta, his sister, he is asking us to get hold of."

"He probably didn't know her work number. I'll call her, then I'll come. It's only five minutes. Which ward?"

"Nightingale."

"All right. Thanks."

Letta hung up, gave herself a few seconds to calm down, and phoned IBM. Momma was in a meeting, said the man who answered. He'd ask her to call back. He made it sound like a favor. Letta said no, it was urgent, and told him about Van and the accident. Grumpily the man said he'd see what he could do. Letta sat waiting, watching the second hand swing around the clock, until Grandad's head poked around the door.

"Something bad?" he said. "I heard the tone of your voice."

"Van's had an accident. Serious. He's in the Royal. He wants to see me. I'm trying to get hold of Momma, but she's in a meeting."

"Yes, that is bad. Shall I wait at the telephone, and you can go now?"

"Oh. Yes. Thanks. I said I'd be there in five minutes and it's almost that now. Tell her he's in Nightingale."

She gave him the receiver, took a tote bag from the hook, ran up to Van's room, snatched up a few things she thought he might need, stuffed them into the bag, and ran down. Grandad was still waiting at the telephone. He waved reassuringly to her as she went out.

She reached the hospital in a sweat of hurry, panting and with her heart racing, stood in the main lobby to steady herself, and went straight to the ward. The ward nurse was obviously surprised to see that she was nothing like grown up.

"You're Letta?" she said. "There isn't another one?"

"No. We're trying to get hold of my mother . . ."

"It's you he wants. He's a bit delirious. It's something about his motorcycle. I've got to give you the keys. In my office."

Letta followed her. The telephone was ringing. The nurse answered it and began to talk about some other patient, but at the same time took a set of keys from a drawer and passed them over, then made signs about which way Letta should go to find Van. She walked anxiously up the long ward, peering at beds. He was in the farthest left-hand corner, curtained off. She slipped into the narrow space between the bed and the curtains.

He was lying half-propped on his back with his eyes closed. There was a tube going in through his nose, but his face seemed undamaged, though it was a horrible gray beneath the tan. His right arm was splinted and strapped across his chest so that he couldn't move it. There was an intravenous drip going into his other arm, and the blankets were supported clear of his body by some sort of framework, so Letta guessed there must be something badly wrong there too. She touched his hand and he opened his eyes, looked puzzled for a second, saw her, and smiled.

"Hi, Sis," he whispered. "She gave you the keys?"

Letta held them up.

"Grandad's calling Momma at work," she said. "I'm sure she won't be long."

He frowned, then nodded. The tiny movement must have hurt, for he closed his eyes and paused before he spoke.

"Right," he said. "I want to keep her out of this. That's why I asked for you. Listen."

They were talking in Field, and since no other Varinians lived within twenty miles of Winchester there wasn't a chance of anyone who overheard them understanding what they were saying, but even so he lowered his voice still further, so that she had to crane to hear.

"This is complicated," he said. "You've got to get it right first time. Find my bike."

"Where is it?"

"Don't know. Last thing I knew I was bombing down the M3. The cops will know. Say you want to get my stuff out of the panniers before it's stolen. Now, look at the keys. See the one with two notches in the rubber? That's the ignition. Unlock the panniers with the other one. Take everything out . . . hold it . . ."

Once again he closed his eyes. His lips went taut as a spasm of pain came and died away.

"Shall I get someone?" Letta whispered.

His grip closed on her hand. After almost a minute his face relaxed and he let out a sigh.

"I'm okay," he whispered. "Right, you've taken everything out. Close the panniers and lock them. Now take the *ignition* key—got that?—put it into the locks and turn it twice in the wrong direction. You'll hear a click. Unlock the panniers again with the other key. They've got false bottoms. You'll find two packets, one yellow, one black. Take them out. Keep them separate if you can. Don't let anyone see them. Push the false bottoms shut—they'll latch—and lock the panniers. Take the packets home and hide them somewhere. Separate. They're quite safe if they're separate. They're safe anyway, Sis, but you can be dead sure if they're separate. Got all that?"

"I'll do my best."

"Good girl. Now the next thing is to call Hector—number's in my address book in the panniers. Do it from a pay phone. Chances are our phone's tapped. Tell him you're Viv-

ian's sister. Not Van, Vivian. Don't say anything about bikes
or accidents. He'll ask you a question. When you answer, if
you've got the packets okay, get 'yellow' into your answer.
He'll make it easy. But if something's gone wrong, 'red.' Got
that?"

"Yes, but—"

"No time. He'll want a number to call you back. He'll have
to get out to a pay phone, because his line's going to be
tapped too. Have you got a friend you can ask, a neighbor?
Think of someone. And when you give him the number sub-
tract six from it. Right?"

"I suppose so, but—"

"This is for Varina, Sis."

"All right."

"And you're going to do this by yourself. You're not going
to tell anyone—anyone at all—what you're up to?"

Letta looked at him and didn't speak.

"Varina, Sis. Varina," he whispered.

"All right."

"Promise? Bones of St. Joseph?"

"Promise."

She saw him relax. His eyes closed but his mouth fell open.
His breath came in small sighs. She thought he'd fainted until
he spoke again.

"That's a load off my mind," he whispered. "Now you can
go and tell that nurse to give me something to stop it hurting. I had to make as if it wasn't too bad till I'd seen you, or I
might have been too dopey to explain."

Letta found Momma listening to the ward nurse. Without a
word Momma hugged her to her side and went on listening.
Van's life wasn't in danger, but his right foot was badly
crushed and might need to be amputated. That was the worst

thing, but his arm was broken in three places too, and his collarbone, and he'd got several broken ribs, one of which had gone into his lung, so they'd had to drain a lot of blood out of it. Letta didn't interrupt. It wasn't easy with Momma there. She couldn't explain about Van not wanting drugs till he'd seen her, and if she just said he'd started to hurt badly they might think something new was wrong. To her relief Momma thanked the nurse and let go of her.

"Do you mind waiting here, darling?" she said. "I think one at a time's enough."

As soon as she'd gone Letta explained, just saying it was a family problem Van had wanted to tell her about.

"I'm sorry," she finished. "You see, I can't explain, but he doesn't want to bother Momma with it. It isn't really that important, but . . ."

"Don't you worry, dear," said the nurse. "I knew he'd got something on his mind, and as long as he stops fretting about it now it's all the same to me. That's what matters, keeping him quiet, isn't it? Good looker, isn't he, though. Broken a few hearts in his time, I'll be bound."

She almost winked. Obviously she thought the "family" problem must be something to do with Van's love life. Letta managed to smile.

She wanted to be alone, to try to think, so she went slowly out to the waiting area by the main doors and settled into a corner. She was worried sick. There was only one thing she could think of which might be in the packets . . . two of them . . . absolutely safe if they were kept separate . . . he must have been a bit delirious to tell her that much . . . she'd promised on the bones of St. Joseph . . . he was her brother . . . it was for Varina . . .

She hadn't got anywhere when Momma came out and sat beside her, stiff and controlled.

"I knew this was going to happen," she said. "I've had nightmares about it. I've hated that bloody bike from the moment I saw it. Let's hope it's a total loss."

"But he's going to be all right?" said Letta.

"All right? With that foot? Oh, darling! You've seen little boys running? Lumps with legs? Van wasn't like that, ever. When he was only five he ran properly, like a deer, beautiful. . . . Get me some tea, darling. It'll be disgusting, but I can't drive like this."

"Why don't we walk home and come back for the car?"

Momma stared into space. Letta guessed she was remembering what Van had looked like, a small, dark child running like a deer.

"All right," she said suddenly. "Let's do that."

There was a young policeman in the hall, talking to Grandad, loud and slow, because he was bothered by Grandad's accent and had decided he must be stupid. He turned with relief to Momma, who took him into the living room, while Letta went into the kitchen with Grandad and told him about Van's accident. She put an extra mug onto the tray, but by the time she carried it through, the voices had stopped and the policeman had gone.

Momma drank her mug in silence, standing by the window and staring out at the shaggy old rosebushes.

"He could be dead," she said, not turning round. "He was coming down the outside lane when a van pulled out in front of him and forced him into the divider. They don't think he was going desperately fast. The woman in the car behind him

saw it all. He was thrown off his bike and landed half on the
roadway and half on the divider and then the bike came slith-
ering along and went over his legs. She managed to stop just
in time, and there was a doctor in another car which stopped
too. The ambulance was there in twenty minutes."

"I'm sorry" was all Letta could think of to say. "Would you
like some more tea?"

Momma shook her head and went on staring out of the
window. Grandad came across and put his arm around her
shoulders. She didn't seem to notice. She sighed, shook her
head, and tried to laugh.

"God, I wish I hadn't given up smoking," she said. "I bet
there isn't a cigarette in the house. Never mind. They want us
to go and get his stuff from the bloody bike. I don't think I
can bear to look at it."

"I'll come with you," said Letta. "You can just sit in the
car."

"Oh, would you, darling? You don't mind?"

"Of course not. Where's the bike?"

"At a garage in King's Worthy. He must have been almost
home."

"We could get a taxi if—"

"No, I'll be all right. We've got to pick up the car in any
case."

"Are you going to ring Poppa?"

"I can't till—oh, God—at least ten o'clock tonight. He's
on a survey."

"I will call Steff and Mollie if you like," said Grandad.

"Oh, yes, please. And if you could wait by our telephone, in
case . . . in case . . . Oh, I'll call you from the garage."

"Yes, of course," said Grandad. "Oh, my dearest child, I am
grieving for you."

"It's all right. That's what we've got to hang on to. It's all right. He could be dead, and he isn't!"

Momma drove more slowly than usual, but perfectly calmly. They found the garage and knew at once it was the right one because the bike in its unmistakable colors was parked in a side area behind the forecourt next to an old yellow subcompact with its hood crushed. The bike itself looked almost all right, apart from having a smashed head-lamp. Momma stared ahead, trying not to see it.

"Why don't you go and phone Grandad?" said Letta.

"I'm going to. In any case we'll have to go and tell them who we are or they'll think we're stealing."

They found a young man in oily overalls who didn't even ask for identification. Only as they were turning away he said, "Them panniers is locked, you know. You'll be needing the keys."

Momma stared at him, not seeming to understand.

"It's all right," said Letta quickly. "Van gave them to me."

Momma didn't seem to notice anything odd, and started asking about telephones. Letta went around to the bike. She'd brought a suitcase and a duffel bag. Trying to stand so that what she was doing was screened from the road—the van was a help—she unlocked the right-hand pannier. It was scraped and dented but the key turned easily and the lid opened. She took out two plastic bags full of clothes and a pair of sneakers, put them in the suitcase, closed the lid, locked it, swapped the keys, turned the new one twice the wrong way, heard a sharp click from inside, swapped the keys back, and opened the pannier again. What had seemed to be the bottom of it had opened up on a spring, and underneath was a yellow packet about the size of a thick paperback book. She took it out and slipped it into the suitcase beneath the bags of clothes.

She glanced over her shoulder. Momma had still not got back to the car, so she went around to the other pannier, which turned out to be half full of books and papers. She put them into the carrier and did the trick with the keys again. The packet below the false bottom was, as Van had said, black —stiff paper, heavily taped, holding a lumpy padded shape.

She took it out and weighed it in her hand. It felt like a small piece of machinery. Now, as she stood there hesitating, the shock of what she was doing almost overcame her. This wasn't Varina long ago. It wasn't legend. It wasn't a struggle against enemies everyone could see. It was England, now, real. Her whole impulse was to put the packages back, to turn away, have nothing to do with them, let the mess sort itself out without her.

But then what would happen to Van, if anyone found them?

She couldn't think about it now. There wasn't time, and her mind wouldn't work. She tucked the black package down under the books, closed and locked the pannier, and went back to the car, feeling sick and ashamed, as if she were betraying everyone she loved.

LEGEND

THE SHOULDER BLADE OF ST. JOSEPH

There was a man called Paulu, of the clan of Kalaz, being second cousin to the Kas, though his mother was a Bulgar. He came to the Kas and said, "See, Lash the Golden is swaggering around our camp. His grandfather killed my grandfather, who was your own grandfather's brother, by the Iron Gates and threw his body in the river. My grandfather's spirit moans to me in my dreams, asking how can I endure the shame."

The Kas Kalaz said, "That feud is frozen. I have sworn on the shoulder blade of St. Joseph that while Turk abides on the soil of Varina we will do no harm to Lash."

Paulu said, "Not so. That oath was fulfilled many years ago, when we drove the Turks away. Did not Lash himself know this and flee? Have you resworn the oath since he returned?"

"I have not," said the Kas Kalaz.

"So is the feud frozen, or is it not?" said Paulu. "Tell me, and I will abide by your judgment, for you are the Kas."

Then the Kas Kalaz looked at him sideways and said nothing, for he too had heard the spirit of his great-uncle moaning in his dreams.

Then Lash the Golden came to Restaur Vax and said, "The men of Kalaz look at me with bullets in their eyes, though they have taken oath on the shoulder blade of St. Joseph that our feud is frozen."

So Restaur Vax took thought and saw what was in the hearts of the Kas and his clan, and gathered his chieftains and said, "Selim is come, and Varina is in such peril as she has not seen since the days of the Red Serpent.[1] We have no time for feuds or thoughts of feuds. Let us travel then to Riqui and renew our oaths on the shoulder blade of St. Joseph."

But the man Paulu, hearing this, went swiftly by night, journeying by goat paths and the paths of the hunter and found the priest of Riqui at his midnight prayers and crept up behind him and put a dagger to his throat and said, "Do what I say and tell no man, or the manner of your death will be remembered through seven generations."

He made the priest lie in a chest and closed the lid so that he should not see. Then he took the shoulder blade of St. Joseph from its reliquary and replaced it with that of a dog, which he had found by the way as he traveled, and released the priest and threatened him once more.

The priest knew well that some sacrilege had been committed, but said nothing when the chiefs came to Riqui, for he was afraid. Thus it was that the Kas Kalaz and the other chieftains swore their new oath not on the shoulder blade of St. Joseph but on that of a dog.

When it was finished the man Paulu went to the Kas Kalaz and told him what he had done and asked him again, saying, "Tell me, is the feud frozen, or is it not?"

The Kas Kalaz crossed himself, but looked sideways at the man Paulu, and said, "For myself, I do not know. But let no shame fall on my house."

———

1. *Nothing is known about the Red Serpent. This is the only reference to the creature in the surviving literature.*

SEPTEMBER 1990

When they got home Grandad told them that there'd been nothing from the hospital, but Biddie had called to say that her parents were going out to see a film and would Letta like to come and spend the last evening of vacation with her. Once more Letta felt a wave of sick guilt at the way everything seemed to be helping her in her lies and betrayals, but Momma said, "It will do you good, darling. It'll take your mind off things. I can see you're upset. No point in our all sitting around being miserable together. I'll be all right."

So, feeling worse than ever, Letta went and put the suitcase and duffel bag up in Van's room and took the packages up to her own room, where she hid the yellow one behind her paperbacks and the black one at the back of her jeans drawer. On the way down she copied Mr. Orestes' number out of Van's address book. Normally she'd have gone up and said good night to Grandad, but she was sure he'd look at her and see she wasn't just upset about Van, and ask her, so she didn't.

Biddie was watching *EastEnders*.

"I'm not allowed to if Mum and Dad are around," she said. "I feel I'm not normal if I don't give it a go, and . . . What's up?"

"Van's in the hospital. He had an accident on that bike I told you about."

"That's awful. How bad an accident?"

"He's not going to die unless something goes wrong, but he's broken a lot of bones and they might have to cut his foot off. Momma's very upset."

"I bet she is. We could go back up to your place, if—"

"No, it's all right. Besides . . . is there a pay phone near here?"

"Nearest one's at the station."

"Look, don't ask what it's about, but I've got to go out and make a call and then I've got to come back here and wait for someone to call here . . . I'm sorry. It's important. Van asked me, and I promised. Is it all right?"

"I suppose so. You'll have to warn whoever it is they only get three minutes."

"Oh, God, I'd forgotten. I suppose it'll have to do. At least it'll get it over. Thanks. See you soon."

The pay phone in the station was occupied by a girl in a black leather miniskirt with lank black hair and a ghoulish white face who babbled on and on, chain-smoking, while Letta hung around feeling more and more sick and anxious. It must have been at least twenty minutes before the girl stopped. Letta had the money ready and dialed. Mr. Orestes answered at once. Letta knew it was him by the permanent slight whine in his voice.

"I've got a message from Vivian," she said.

"Yes."

"He's in the hospital."

Pause.

"I'm sorry to hear that. I shall send flowers. Do you know his favorite color?"

Letta answered on the spur of the moment. It was something to do with Mr. Orestes' voice. She could hear, as sure as if he'd told her, that he didn't give a damn about Van lying in the hospital in agony with his foot so smashed he'd probably never walk properly again. It didn't matter that Mr. Orestes didn't actually know about that. If he had known he wouldn't have cared. All he cared about was his conspiracy, and the secret messages, and the excitement of what he was planning to do with the packages. Till that moment Letta had been telling herself that though she didn't like it at all, and was badly frightened, at least passing the message on would mean that Mr. Orestes would come and take the packages away, and the whole thing would be out of her hands, out of the house, clear, nothing to do with any of them, even with Van, because it'd obviously be months before he was well enough to do anything much except lie around and get well. . . .

Now, because of Mr. Orestes' voice, she changed her mind and said, "Red."

Another pause.

"You're sure?"

She gulped and said, "Yes."

"Perhaps you had better give me the number so that I can inquire for myself."

Letta had written it down while she was waiting for the ghoul-girl to finish. Half-panicking she read it out.

"Thank you. I will call in a few minutes."

"Wait. I, er . . . there won't be anyone there for about ten minutes."

"Very good. Thank you."

Only as she put the receiver down did it strike her that she ought to have made a mistake over the number. Then he couldn't have called back. She'd have time to think. What could she say now? She couldn't find the bike? No, it mustn't be anything which he could find out in the end was a lie, because then he'd know she'd been lying about the packages. He could find the bike himself somehow. He could ask the man at the garage. He'd known she and Momma had been there, taken things away. The panniers had been locked.

Or she could change her mind again, tell him she'd made a mistake about the colors, after all. He'd just think she was a stupid little girl . . .

Biddie let her in.

"A man just called," she said. "He was asking for Vivian's sister. I said did he mean Letta, because if he did you weren't back, and he said he'd try again, and I said he'd have to wait five minutes because we've got a trick phone. Is that okay?"

"Thanks."

"I thought your brother's name was Van. Is it short for—"

"No. I'm sorry, Biddie. I don't want to involve you, but—"

"Do you want me out of the way while you're talking?"

"Doesn't matter. We'll be talking in Field."

Biddie was frowning at her, really worried.

"I'm sorry," said Letta. "It's all right."

"Is it?"

"No, but I can't tell you. Oh, Biddie!"

"I'm sure it's not your fault. I'll make some sticky sweet cocoa."

Letta waited by the telephone. The red light which showed you couldn't use it was still glowing. After a little while it went out. A few seconds later the phone rang. The moment she answered Mr. Orestes said, "What can you tell me?"

"He was coming down the motorway. A van pulled out and pushed him into the divider. He's got a broken arm and collarbone and ribs, and his foot's smashed."

"My regrets. Where is the motorcycle?"

(No, thought Letta. If that's all he can say about Van I'm not going to tell him I made a mistake. I didn't. I was right.)

"At a garage at King's Worthy," she said. "A policeman told us where it was."

"A policeman? Us?"

"Just a traffic policeman. My mother drove me out. She doesn't know. Look, we haven't got all that time before this phone goes off again. I'm sorry. It was the best I could do."

"Understood. Go on."

"My mother was telephoning when I got Van's stuff out of the panniers. Nobody was watching. I got the false bottoms open okay, but there wasn't anything under them."

"The false bottoms? Explain. There are supposed to be two packets."

"Yes, I know. One yellow and one black. Van said they were in his panniers, under the false bottoms. There's a trick with the key to open them."

"That is where he told you to look?"

"Yes. He told me exactly. All about the keys and so on."

Pause.

"When will you be seeing your brother again?"

"Tomorrow, probably. It depends how ill he is. Look, I really don't want to worry him."

"We are speaking of Varina, my dear. You could surely ask him—"

"Only if I get him alone. And listen, he doesn't remember what happened . . ."

"Nothing?"

"I don't know. He just said he didn't remember about the journey. I don't know how far back."

A longer pause.

"Listen," said Letta. "Time's nearly up. I'm not supposed to be using this phone. My friend's parents will be coming back any moment. Don't call back. I'll try and think of something better, and if I find anything out I'll call you from a pay phone tomorrow."

"And meanwhile, if you could go back to the motorcycle . . ."

The telephone gave its warning buzz.

"I will if I can," gabbled Letta, trying to fill the time without putting her foot in it at this last moment. "But I really don't think—"

The line went dead and the red light glowed. Letta blew out a gust of the spare breath she didn't know she'd been holding. Her heart was pounding so that it almost hurt. It could have been worse, she thought. It could have been much, much worse. She'd told several lies, but provided she stuck to her story there wasn't anything anyone could find out about unless they searched her room. Now all she had to do was get rid of the packages. You couldn't put something like that in a garbage can. And she'd have to think of something to tell Van . . .

Dazedly she made her way into the kitchen. Biddie was pouring hot milk into two mugs. They sat down at the kitchen table. Biddie's parents didn't approve of sugar, and never bought it, but they collected free packets from restaurants and airlines in case they had visitors less high-minded than themselves. Letta slowly tore five open and dribbled the sugar into her mug, then stirred, hypnotizing herself with the brown eddy.

"Did you hear any of that?" she said. "Did I sound as if I was lying?"

"I don't think so—just dead worried."

"You can say that again."

Letta sucked at the cloying cocoa—just what she needed. Good old Biddie.

"Can I tell you?" she said. "I've got to tell someone. I promised Van I wouldn't. . . . Oh, hell!"

"Did you understand what you were promising?"

"Not really. Not what it meant."

"Then it wasn't a promise. Wait. If it's as bad as that, then I'm not going to promise anything. I can't. Don't you see? I'll do my best, but . . . well . . . that's how it is. I'm sorry."

"No, you're right. It's like the daughter of Olla."

"Come again?"

"They used her. She didn't understand. It's one of our stories. Hell. Listen. Suppose somebody told you there were two packages he wanted you to collect, and you've got to do it secretly, and you mustn't tell anyone. They're in a hiding place. Two hiding places, because they've got to be kept separate. They're quite safe like that. They're probably safe if they're together, but they're quite safe if they're separate . . ."

Biddie nodded and stared at the table, doodling a blob of spilled cocoa with her forefinger.

"This somebody isn't a scientist?" she said. "Nothing to do with scientists?"

"No. I'm pretty sure."

"I was trying to think of something else. It's got to be a bomb, though, hasn't it? Explosives in one packet, timer and detonator in the other."

"That's what I thought."

"Bad."

"Yes."

"You'd better tell me. You've pretty well told me, in fact, haven't you?"

"I suppose so."

"Something to do with Varina?"

"Yes."

"I thought that was all bagpipe dancing and poems about mountains."

"It's people. It's people taking my grandmother away, and the body of a girl they thought was my mother, and no one ever seeing them again. Remember, I told you about that."

"I am remembering. It's like the worst kind of nightmare."

So Letta started right back at the festival. Some of it Biddie had heard before, but bits and pieces in no special order. It took a while. Biddie asked a few questions, getting things clear. When Letta had finished she sat thinking.

"If it's a bomb," she said slowly, "then we're not up to this. We've got to pass it on to grown-ups. I ought to tell my parents, if you think you can't tell yours."

"Van made me promise not to. He did it in a way . . . oh, I can't explain."

(How could she? The bones of St. Joseph? Letta didn't really believe that they were his bones, or ever had been, but still they were a kind of password, a proof. If you broke a promise on the bones of St. Joseph it was as if you had stood up and said, "No, I am not a real Varinian. I am only playing at it. But when it comes to the hard test, I'm an outsider, and Potok was a pretty dream.")

Biddie was looking at her, desperately worried.

"If you tell your parents they'll tell the police," said Letta. "Van will go to prison. It would break Momma's heart."

"Yes, I know, but I ought to. I'll have to think. But if you tell yours, I won't. I still ought to, but I'll leave it to your family. And please, Letta, do think yourself about what I said before. He made you promise, didn't he? And you didn't understand what you were promising . . ."

"I did, sort of. He'd told me about the packages first."

"But he made you. He'd sent for you specially. He was hurting badly, waiting just for you, so he could pass the message on and have some painkiller. You couldn't have said no, could you?"

"No. But . . ."

"All right, let's try it like this. This Otto Vasa is bad news?"

"Definitely."

"Not just bad news in himself—bad news for Varina, bad news for your brother?"

"Yes. If you'd seen the way he winked when he came in through the window . . ."

"Okay, let's take that as fixed. Now, he gave your brother the bike. Did it have these secret compartments in it when he gave it to him?"

"I should think so. It looks sort of all one piece."

"So it wasn't just a present. It was so Otto Vasa could use your brother to carry things in secret."

"Right—but listen! He must have had it ready before anyone knew Van was going to be thrown out. I was talking to

Grandad about this. There wouldn't have been time to get it painted up in our colors."

"Let's take that as fixed too. What Otto Vasa wants is bad news for Varina. He gave the bike to your brother to do something he wanted. That has to be bad news for Varina too. Your brother had his accident and had to get you to finish the job off, but it was bad news for Varina so you found a way of not doing it. So far so good."

"Biddie, you're impossible! Nothing's ever as easy as you make it sound!"

"When it's over it can be. When it hasn't happened yet it's tricky. But listen, you've got it right so far, but you can't stop there. Otto Vasa is bad news for Varina. Who is good news for Varina?"

"Oh, lots of people. Grandad's the obvious one, only he's old and tired and they won't let him go back."

"But he'd know some of the others?"

"Yes, of course."

"Well, the best way you can help the good-news people is telling them what the bad-news people are up to. Don't you think?"

"Yes, but—"

"Put it the other way. Suppose you were Grandad and you learned afterward that you—Letta—had been in this trouble and hadn't been to him. How would you—your grandfather you—feel? Sad, wouldn't you? Let down? Cheated? After all those crumpet teas."

(Biddie had been a couple of times since she'd got back. Grandad liked her a lot, in spite of having to speak English.)

"I promised," said Letta, miserable. "He's my brother. It was Momma and Grandad he was mostly talking about when he said not to tell. Oh, God. And the nurse said he mustn't be

worried, and he's going to worry himself sick about not knowing how I got on, and he's going to ask when I see him. And
. . . listen! I bet you the next thing Mr. Orestes will do is try
and come down and see him himself, to find out what happened to the packets!"

"Tonight?"

"What's the time? No, I don't think so. Tomorrow,
though."

Biddie sat in silence again. Letta could almost feel her
thinking things through. *If this, then that, or that, but not that
. . .* A cheeringly ridiculous thought struck her.

"You're too like Jeeves," she said.

"Come again?"

"The great mind turns."

Biddie smiled and put the interruption aside.

"That makes it easier. You've got to stop Mr. Orestes from
seeing Van," she said. "You've got two ways. You could call
him again and say you've made a mistake . . ."

"No."

"Good, because then I think I should have to tell my parents. So you've got to get the hospital to say he isn't well
enough to see anyone."

"He doesn't know which one."

"He can ring around. There's not that many, and he'll try
the Royal first. But the only person, far as I can see, who can
tell the hospital to say Van's not well enough is your mother.
That means you've got to tell her. Now. Tonight."

Letta felt sick again. She couldn't move. Anything she did
would be wrong.

"Do you want me to come with you?" said Biddie.

She meant it, too, though it was after the time she was
allowed out without permission. She'd be in serious trouble,

and she wouldn't be able to explain. She'd already worked all that out, of course, but she'd still have come if Letta had asked.

"I'll be all right," said Letta, standing up. "Thank you, Jeeves."

LEGEND

The Death of Lash the Golden

Now the army of Selim surrounded Potok, and the army of Restaur Vax waited in the hills, and each feared to fight the other where they were. So Restaur Vax called a council of chieftains and said, "I have word from Potok that unless we come to their help they will surrender within the week."

The chieftains said, "Selim has thrice our numbers, and great guns beside. How can we fight him in the valley before the walls of Potok?"

Restaur Vax said, "We will do it thus. We will attack at dawn, from between the Knees of Athur.[1] Selim has outposts on the ridges, and first we will capture those, and our Captain of Artillery will set up her guns there to hinder the gathering of Selim's *bazouks,* and we will be upon them before their great guns are laid ready."

"Still they will be too many," said the chieftains.

"Very like," said Restaur Vax, "and they will drive us off and pursue us, and we will retreat between the Knees of Athur as far as Tresti, where we will have strong positions dug ready, and there we will turn and make a stand. And Lash the Golden will command the rearguard to hold them until we are ready. And we will have our best marksmen hidden along the slopes, and they will fire into the flanks of the *bazouks,* as will the Captain of Artillery, and so the odds will be leveled, and being Varinians fighting for Varina we will surely win. Now, will you be men, or will you see Potok fall?"

So they agreed, and each chieftain chose from his clan the best marksmen, and among those chosen by the Kas Kalaz was the man Paulu. On the Eve of St. Jafur they came quietly down from the mountains and mustered at Tresti, where they prepared positions to turn and fight. Then they stole silently down toward Potok.

Before dawn the Kas Kalaz stormed the eastern ridge and Van Jirri stormed the western ridge and the Captain of Artillery set up her guns and as the sun rose the men of Varina hurled themselves against the encampment around Potok and slaughtered many *bazouks* while the Captain of Artillery hindered the gathering of the rest from around the city. But at last they came, in great numbers, marching to surround the Varinians. Then Restaur Vax gave the order to retreat and withdrew his army between the Knees of Athur while Lash the Golden, commanding the rearguard, hindered the pursuit.

When they were not yet fully in between the ridges Selim, riding with his commanders, looked about him and saw how the land lay and said, "This is a trap. Let us halt and clear the mountainsides before we pursue further."

Then Lash the Golden, seeing they no longer pursued him, halted his men also and said, "These Turks are cowards. See, they outnumber us yet two to one, and still they dare not follow us. Let us encourage them a little."

So saying he strode back toward the Turks and stood on a little mound and mocked them for their cowardice, while they, daring to come no nearer, fired hotly upon him but did not hit, at which he mocked them the more.

Now the man Paulu, lying upon the mountainside and seeing this, said in his heart, "If a bullet were now to strike Lash, who but I would know who fired the shot? Thus the house of Kalaz would not be shamed." So he took good aim and fired and hit Lash below the shoulder blade, and Lash gave a loud shout and fell down.

Thereon the Turks were encouraged, and forgetting Selim's order they charged forward between the Knees of Athur, and the men of Varina met them from the positions they had prepared, and the Captain of Artillery fired her guns into their flanks, and the marksmen shot among them until the barrels of their muskets were too hot to hold, and there was great slaughter. Notwithstanding the battle stood in doubt, for the *bazouks* were so many, until Selim, riding past the mound where Lash lay, saw the body of a man with yellow hair lying facedown. Rejoicing that one of his chief enemies was slain he ordered that the body should be turned over, to be certain that it was indeed Lash.

Now Lash was not dead, but sore wounded and dying. He had fainted with the loss of blood, but being moved he woke and saw the shape of a Turk leaning above him. Then he drew from his bosom a small pistol he carried there always, and quickly fired, and the ball struck Selim in the eye, so that he fell from his horse, and by the time his body touched the ground he and Lash were both dead.[2]

At that the cry went up that Selim was slain, and the Turks lost all their courage and fled, and the Varinians pursued them with great slaughter, until the valley between the Knees of Athur was scarlet with their blood.

When the victory was sure Restaur Vax gave orders that a search be made for the body of Lash the Golden, and it was found, with the body of Selim Pasha dead beside it. So Restaur Vax came and knelt and lifted the body of his companion up by the shoulders and held it to his chest and wept and spoke praise for the hero.[3] But even as he spoke he felt the wound beneath his hand, and thus knew that Lash had been shot from behind.

Still speaking he looked at the gathered chieftains and caught the glance of the Kas Kalaz and saw how his face was troubled, and how he in his turn glanced toward the man Paulu, who looked away. Thus Restaur Vax knew what had been done. Nevertheless he spoke to a finish and laid the body back and rose, hiding his bloodstained hand within his coat, and said no word.

———

1. *The Knees of Athur are two spurs of the mountain with a valley between, level and fertile at first but narrowing to a precipitous defile. The Battle of Tresti took place here in 1826.*
2. *Alexo Lash is known to have died at Tresti. According to Marie McMahon he was commanding the rearguard during the retreat from an unsuccessful attempt to raise the siege of Potok when he was cut off and surrounded, but the group fought on to the last man. The respite they provided may have been sufficient for Restaur Vax to rally his*

forces for the decisive counterattack. The rumor that he was killed by treachery on the part of Kalaz emanates from Lash's own clan.

3. Somewhat surprisingly, though Restaur Vax makes many references, and wrote several complete poems, to other comrades of his in the War of Independence, there is no mention of Alexo Lash.

SEPTEMBER 1990

Momma was in the living room, knitting and watching TV with the sound off. The knitting was a gaudy jersey for Poppa which she'd been making for at least three years because she only got it out when she was seriously bothered about something, and then she started off by unpicking most of what she'd done last time.

"You're early," she said. "More trouble?"

"Yes."

"Is it about Van? You had his keys."

"You didn't say anything."

"I wasn't noticing. I thought about it after you'd gone. Come here, darling. I need someone to hug."

She dropped the knitting and made space on the chair beside her. They did their best to arrange themselves comfortably. There seemed to be a lot of elbows.

"Just like your father," said Momma. "He's all corners too.

Well? No, wait. Before you start, you don't have to tell me it's not your fault. I know that already."

That helped a bit. Letta stared at the screen. It was golf. No one in the family was remotely interested in golf, but you got close-ups of grass, with a little white ball trickling across and popping into a hole, or missing it, which was soothing in a hypnotic sort of way.

"He asked me to get something out of his bike," she said. "He made me promise not to tell anyone about it—he meant especially you or Grandad. It was two things in secret compartments in the panniers. I had to keep them apart, so they were safe. Then I had to ring Mr. Orestes. I had to use a pay phone because he said our line would be tapped and then I had to give Mr. Orestes a separate number to ring back from a pay phone on his end. There was a code. Yellow meant I'd got the things and red meant I hadn't. I felt really bad about it, not telling you. Anyway, they were there. I got them while you were telephoning."

"Let's get this straight. You had to keep them separate, to be sure they were safe?"

"That's right. He said they were probably safe even if I didn't, but—"

"Oh, God! Where are they now?"

"In my room. In two different places."

"All right. Go on."

"Then Biddie had called, which made things easy. I went to the station and called Mr. Orestes from there to give him her number but—I still don't know why I did this—it was something to do with the creepy way he was talking—when he asked a question to give me a chance of saying 'red' or 'yellow' I said 'red.' It wasn't a mistake. I did it on purpose. I told him I hadn't got them."

"Oh, thank heavens!"

"Then when he called me back at Biddie's I said I'd found the bike but there was nothing in the secret compartments and Van was badly smashed up in the hospital and he couldn't remember anything about the journey. That's all. But listen, Momma. I'm pretty sure the next thing he'll do is come down and try and see Van at the hospital to find out what's happened. You've got to stop him. You've got to tell them to say Van's too ill to see anyone. I'm sorry. I'm really sorry."

Momma was breathing slowly and deeply. Her arm around Letta felt like iron.

"I knew there was something wrong about that bike," she muttered.

On the screen it looked as if someone must have won something. He was prancing around punching his fists in the air.

"Can you phone Poppa?" said Letta.

Momma looked at her watch.

"No," she said. "I've left a message for him to call at eleven. You're going to have to move, darling. I should have given your grandfather his pills twenty minutes ago."

"Are you going to tell him?"

Momma thought, then sighed.

"I suppose so," she said. "I don't want to. He's old and he's tired and he's done his work, but there isn't anyone else. I'm out of my depth. Oh, God, I've spent the last twenty years of my life trying to get us all clear of this sort of thing, and now it comes back. I wish . . . Oh, there's no point in wishing. At least your grandfather will have some idea what's going on. It may not be as bad as I think. All right. Will you come? He'll want to ask you things. I suppose we'd better take the bloody packages, too, while we're at it."

They climbed the stairs together. While Letta groped be-

hind her books, Momma stood in the doorway in what seemed
to be a sort of daze, but as Letta crossed to get the other
package out from behind her clothes she strode in, took one of
the plastic bags which held Van's clothes out of the suitcase,
and looked at the print on it.

"Vienna," she said. "He was supposed to be in Wolverhampton."

"It might be from when he came over before."

Momma tipped the bag out. There were some new socks,
still with their wrapping strip around them. The writing was
German. A receipt fluttered to the floor. Momma picked it up
and read the date.

"This Monday," she said. "Come on."

Grandad was sitting up in bed playing his own brand of
solitaire on a tray while he listened on his short-wave radio to
what sounded like a news broadcast in Romanian. He must
have been expecting Momma with his pills, but was clearly
surprised to see Letta.

"Hello, my darlings," he said, then looking at them more
sharply added, "Not bad news from the hospital, I hope."

"No. Well, not from the hospital," said Momma. "But we
need your help. Letta's got something to tell you which I
don't like the sound of at all. Can you stand it? I know it's
late, but we've got to make our minds up tonight . . ."

"Of course."

He looked questioningly at Letta, who told her story again.
It was far easier doing it for him than it had been for Momma.
He held out his hands for the packets when she got to that
part, looked at them briefly, and laid them down on either
side of his bed. When she'd finished he shook his head.

"These people are idiots," he said.

"Van told us he was going to Wolverhampton," said

Momma, "but he seems to have been in Vienna. I don't like my children lying to me. It's some kind of bomb, isn't it?"

"Almost certainly," said Grandad, picking the yellow package up and weighing it in his hands. "Semtex, or something of the kind. If it had been the sort of explosives we used, they would need a far larger amount to do any serious damage. If so, it should be highly stable, and perfectly safe. . . . I have one thing to say, my darlings. These people are conspirators. Because of that they see conspiracies everywhere. They will not automatically assume that Van has betrayed them, or that Letta has lied. They are perfectly capable of believing that the accident was deliberately engineered by some powerful organization, the CIA or the British Secret Services, so that the packages could be abstracted. In fact that is what they would prefer to believe. It will fuel their own myth about themselves, their belief in their importance . . ."

"What on earth do they think they're up to?" said Momma. "This is England, for God's sake! It's got nothing to do with Varina!"

"It's hard to say precisely what they intend," said Grandad. "My best information is that part of Vasa's strategy is to engineer a breakdown in relations between Romania and Bulgaria, and then to stage some kind of incident at Listru next year between the Bulgarian authorities and Varinians who are Romanian citizens attending the festival, thus giving the Romanians an excuse to intervene, and ultimately to annex our southern province into Romania. This would allow a unitary Varinian state to begin to be formed, under the hegemony of Romania. If this is right, it is a crazy strategy. It is inconceivable that the Romanians, with their concern over their Hungarian minority in the north, would let themselves be lured into such a scheme. Vasa has some influence in Bucharest, but there is a limit to what even he can do with bribery and blackmail."

"Anyway, it's got nothing to do with us," said Momma. "What on earth could he gain by blowing anything up here?"

"Publicity, of course. The most likely target is some kind of cultural monument. . . . Ah, there is to be a Bulgarian trade fair in Birmingham in November . . . that is a possibility, for an overt motive, at least. But I think it likely that Vasa and his immediate circle may have another idea in their minds. Suppose such an explosion were to take place. Suppose it were then revealed that my grandson was directly implicated, that the explosives had been stored in the house where I live . . . You follow?"

"Oh, God!" said Momma. "We've got to get them out of here."

"Couldn't you ask your policeman to help?" said Letta.

"Policeman!" said Momma.

"He's not that kind of policeman," said Letta.

"I'm afraid he is," said Grandad. "There are limits to what even a privileged security official would be prepared to hush up, and a plan to commit a terrorist offense on British soil is certainly one of them. Unpleasant though it is, we are trapped by Van's complicity. Minna, you will have to find somewhere to dispose of them. Separately, if possible. Deep."

"All right," said Momma. "I'll think of something . . . oh, yes. Do you remember, Letta—"

"Don't tell us," said Grandad. "The less we know, the fewer lies we have to remember."

"Oh, God," said Momma. "I thought we'd got clear of all this sort of thing. All right."

She spoke in Field, because of Grandad, but it was the same strained, dry voice she'd used to tell Letta what had happened at Lapiri. She put her hands to her face, hiding her eyes, and bowed her head. She paid no attention when Letta moved to her side and put her arm around her to comfort her. Letta glanced at Grandad, but he held up his hand to stop her from speaking. He seemed far away. After a while he reached for his pad and made some notes.

"It seems to me I shall still have to talk to my policeman," he said.

"No! Please!" said Momma. "Van's been punished enough."

"I am partly thinking about Van. We have to shield him from Hector and his friends."

"I'm going to phone the hospital and see if I can get him a private room. And Letta, you must send him a card saying everything's all right."

"That is sensible, but it is a short-term measure. We must persuade these people to leave Van alone indefinitely. Suppose they were led to believe that Van was being followed by the British security services, who then took advantage of the accident to search the motorcycle, and discovered the bomb, and removed it, I think Hector would rapidly retract his patriotism into activities such as bagpipe dancing. He is not the stuff of heroes, you know. I can tell my policeman enough to give him cause to interview Hector, but not enough to incriminate Van. Then, when Van is well enough, he must be given the same version of events . . . Minna, dear, you had better call the hospital before it is too late."

"I suppose so. I haven't given you your pills."

"Letta can do that. Will you take these things now?"

He flicked his hand contemptuously toward the packages.

"I'll put them straight in the car. I must set my alarm. I want to get there when it's just light. Oh, Poppa, please,

please be careful what you say! Letta, you'll have to get your own breakfast. And your poppa's going to call any minute. Oh, what am I going to tell him now?"

The sentences came in gasps, with slow in-drawn breaths between. She sounded at the end of her tether, but then she straightened, moving her head from side to side as if she was easing her neck, and picked up the packages.

"All right," she said, in her normal brisk voice. "I think that's the best we can do. Good night, Poppa. Thank heavens you're here. Don't be too late, Letta, and remember to set your alarm. If you hear mine, just go back to sleep."

She left. Grandad made some more notes while Letta started counting the pills out, thinking as she did so about what had just happened. Something struck her and she looked around. The movement must have caught his eye, because he glanced up inquiringly.

"You said 'partly,' " she said.

He raised his eyebrows.

"You were thinking partly about Van."

"Yes. My darling, this is something I need to talk to you about. I was also thinking partly about Varina. We have an even more dangerous state of affairs than I had realized, but at the same time there is a glimmer of hope. My policeman is in fact a very good friend, and we agree about most things, but he has had difficulty in persuading his masters to take Varina, and especially Otto Vasa, sufficiently seriously. They have other things on their minds. I think I can tell him exactly enough to give him the evidence he needs, so that his masters will then think it worthwhile to put pressure on the government in Bucharest to counter Vasa's activities by allowing me back into the country."

"No!"

Letta had almost shouted the word. Grandad looked at her in surprise. He smiled, nodded, and put his pencil and pad aside.

"You still forbid me to go?" he said.

"No, of course not. I can't forbid you anything. I just don't want you to, that's all."

"You don't remember? Last summer—when was it? Soon after we started reading the Legends, I think—we had almost this conversation, and in the course of it I told you I would not go permanently back to Varina without your permission."

"Unless I could come too, I said."

"I'm afraid there is no question of that."

"I know. . . . Anyway, it doesn't count. We didn't really mean it, did we? It was a sort of game we were playing."

"I meant it."

"Oh . . . still . . . it's not my . . . But anyway, it isn't fair, Grandad! On you, I mean. You aren't well. You're . . . Do you want to go?"

He put the ghost fingers against the real ones and cocked his head to one side.

"I have asked myself that often," he said. "The answer is, I don't know. I should of course prefer to die in Varina—remember that, my darling, if it should happen. That apart, the question is unimportant, trivial. If I have the opportunity and refuse it, what will have been the point of my life? What will have been the point of my bearing the name I bear? You see?"

"No. No, I don't. Whatever happens, you're you. Whatever you're called. There isn't anyone else like you and there never will be. Oh, please . . . I'm not allowed to say that, am I? I'm supposed to say 'If you must go, then you must go.' But I won't. I won't!"

He was looking at her, nodding his head, considering.

"You do forbid me, then?" he said.

"No. It isn't like that. I've told you I can't."

"You could, and if you did I think . . . I think I would stay. Remember that I am not sure that even if I were allowed to go I could achieve anything. I am old. I am tired. It is very likely too late. I am telling you the truth, my darling. I do not know."

He started to take his pills, one at a time, with sips of water between. Letta watched him. His hand quivered as he lifted the glass. A moment ago he had been full of energy, but now he looked as frail as a fallen leaf. What could one old man do?

The window was open and the curtains drawn. The town lights glowed below, and glowed again from the cloud base above. Somebody was having a party a couple of streets down the hill. There were whoops and cheering. The noise reminded Letta of sitting with her back against the sun-warmed wall of ruined St. Valia's, listening the the noise of Potok rejoicing in the festival, and that in turn reminded her of the picture, almost like a vision, she had seen in her mind when she was sitting with Biddie in Richoux, the warplanes screaming between the mountains, the stampeding crowd in the palace square, Parvla falling under their feet . . . It wasn't anything to do with what she wanted, she realized, or with what Grandad himself wanted, for himself. Perhaps he could make the difference. And if he couldn't, then no one could.

"I think you're sort of fixed," she said. "You've got to go if they'll let you, haven't you?"

"I'm afraid so, my darling."

LEGEND

RESTAUR VAX AND THE BISHOP: II

The Princes of the World came to Potok to see Bishop Pango enthroned Prince of Varina, and there was a great feast, and wine flowed from every fountain, and all went late to bed. But Bishop Pango was troubled by a dream and could not sleep, so he rose, and dressed himself as a poor priest and let himself out by a side door, and walked down by the river below St. Valia.

At the water's edge one came walking toward him, leading a great horse, wearing a sword at his belt and bearing a musket on his shoulder.

The Bishop said, "Where do you go, my son, carrying these weapons of war, now that Varina is at peace?"

The man answered, "These are gifts I had from Bishop Pango to fight the Turks. I would return them to him now that the Turks are gone."[1]

By that the Bishop knew that he spoke to Restaur Vax, whom he thought to be far off in Rome. And he was troubled, for under the terms of peace agreed among the Princes of the World, Restaur Vax must not set foot in Varina, for the Turks could then also return and take away his Princedom. Nevertheless, knowing what debt Varina owed to the hero, he, Bishop Pango, knelt by the waterside and asked for a blessing.

Restaur Vax said, "My blessing is on you and all Varina, until the Turks return. See that my horse is well fed, and lodge my gun and my sword among your rafters. But when you have need of me, let my horse be led forth and saddled, and my sword strapped to the pommel. Then fire my gun three times into the air, and I will return."[2]

Then he raised Bishop Pango to his feet and kissed him on both cheeks and put the sword and the musket and the reins into his hands, and vanished.

By this Bishop Pango knew that he had seen only the shadow of the hero, and that Restaur Vax himself was dead, far off in Rome, across the sea. And within a week came a messenger with news that it was so.[3]

━━━━━━

1. *Under the Treaty of Milan, Varina was given full self-government, but remained technically part of the Turkish Empire until 1868, when the suzerainty was transferred to the Austrian Empire. A vizier was appointed by Byzantium to "advise" the Prince-Bishop, but his duties were purely ceremonial.*

2. *Edward Lear, who made a sketching trip through Varina in 1873, records seeing four separate skeletons of Restaur Vax's horse, with the same legend attached to each of them.*

3. *This is perhaps the most popular of all Varinian legends. Nevertheless its chronology is completely mistaken. Pango was enthroned as Prince-Bishop on St. Joseph's Day, 29 August 1828, shortly after*

the Treaty of Milan. He died in 1850. Restaur Vax lived until 1865. His widow brought his body for burial in the family grave at Talosh when the Austrian Empire assumed hegemony of Varina in 1868.

SEPTEMBER 1991

Letta was staring out the window of what used to be Grandad's room, and was now going to be hers. When he'd left for Varina she had come up here once a week to dust and sweep and air, so that if he came back he could move straight in. She'd known in her heart that he wasn't coming back, but it had been a sort of magic, a way of looking after him, as if by pretending that one day he would come back he had to stay alive for it to be true. Even now, when the magic hadn't worked, she was glad that she'd done it.

Almost as soon as the news had come she'd asked Momma, not knowing how to put it without hurting, if she could move up here, and Momma had seemed pleased and said, "Yes, of course. He'd like that."

She'd begun by clearing a lot of Grandad's books into boxes, not anything in Field or Formal, and not the battered old Wordsworths and Walter Scotts he'd used to teach himself English, but the political ones and the ones in languages she couldn't read. She'd worked steadily until the thought came to her that school was starting tomorrow, and that meant it must be exactly a year since she'd sat here talking about whether he had to go back to Varina. A wave of sadness washed through her at the knowledge that she would never see him again, so she stopped sorting and stood by the window, not really crying but seeing the roofs and the treetops mistily.

It was all right, she told herself. He'd said he wanted to die in Varina. She didn't mind that the Romanians had said they couldn't all go out to the funeral. Horrible Otto Vasa was sure to have hijacked it, of course, and even if he hadn't it would still have been a great public thing, a nation mourning its hero. It would all have been about Restaur Vax, not Grandad. Grandad was crumpets oozing with butter. He was a boy who had stared out of a schoolroom window, hating past conditional optatives. He was an outlaw who'd slipped down from the hills by night to hold his almost unknown daughter on his lap. The hero was a sort of shadow. Grandad was the solid, living person who had cast the shadow. He was what mattered.

Someone on the stairs! But there was no one in the house! Then she heard the uneven tread, climb and drag, climb and drag, and her fright changed to a different kind of tension. Things had never been right between her and Van since the accident. For a few days she'd managed to avoid any questions by always visiting him at the same time as Momma, but then there'd come a visit when she'd known at once that something was badly wrong, and he'd practically ordered Momma to go and talk to the nurse about something and as soon as she was out of earshot he'd said, "I've had a card from a chap called Andrei—friend of Otto's. It had a lot of red roses on it. He asked me whether they were the right color. What's up? You sent me this."

He held up her card with its field of yellow daisies. She'd gulped, though she'd known it was bound to happen sooner or later.

"I'm sorry," she'd said. "I didn't want you to worry."

"You lied to me."

"I thought I'd better."

"None of your business, Sis. So what happened?"

"We went out to the garage. Your clothes and books were there okay, but there was nothing in the secret compartments."

"You're sure?"

"Yes."

"I don't see it. How on earth could that have happened? I hadn't taken my eyes off the machine. I'd slept with it, even . . ."

"I suppose somebody could have been following you and seen the accident."

He'd thought about it, and nodded.

"You told Hector red, I suppose," he'd said. "I haven't had a squeak out of him, you know. . . . Well, don't lie to me again, Sis. It's not up to you to decide what's good for me, see?"

"I'm sorry," she'd said, miserably, feeling the new lie inside her, like vomit she had to keep down. The feeling was still there now, after a whole year. There seemed to be no way she could tell him, and she wouldn't get rid of it until she had. She wiped her eyes, turned, and waited till he put his head around the door.

"Moving in?" he said with a sharp smile.

"Do you mind? Momma said it was okay. In fact she said it was a good idea."

He nodded and limped across to look at the half-empty bookshelves.

"No," he said, harshly. "It's all yours. I'm not stepping into the old boy's shoes."

He turned and looked at her with the same hard, angry smile.

"Aren't you going to ask me where I've been?" he said.

She hadn't been meaning to. When Van had simply disappeared, in the middle of a physiotherapy course for his foot, they'd all guessed that he was trying to get to Grandad's funeral, whether the Romanians let him or not. He couldn't have done it alone. He'd have had to ask Otto Vasa for help, and if it wasn't for Otto Vasa, Grandad might very well still be alive. While half of what used to be Yugoslavia boiled into war close by, Grandad had gone back to Varina to try to prevent the same thing happening there, but Otto Vasa kept on stirring things up. Grandad was tired, and old, and his doctors kept telling him to rest, but he hadn't been able to. And then, twelve days ago, the man Grandad used to call his policeman had rung Momma in the evening to say that Grandad was dead. That was all he knew.

Whatever Van thought about politics, he must have known what Momma and the rest of the family would feel about his having anything to do with Otto Vasa. Now he was pretty well forcing Letta to talk about it.

"Varina, I suppose," she said. "Or didn't they let you in? Or did they throw you out again?"

"Not exactly. They didn't let me in, but I went. They didn't throw me out, but I left. Do you want to know?"

"Do you want to tell me?"

He lowered himself into Grandad's chair, leaning on his stick and moving with care. She could see his foot must be quite a bit worse than it had been when he'd left.

"Not much," he said, "but I'd better. You're the right person. Okay. When those bastards in Bucharest told us we couldn't attend the old boy's funeral—not even his own daughter, for God's sake!—I said the hell with them—I'm going. I called Otto's office in Vienna and talked to someone called Andrei and said they'd got to get me through to Potok, somehow. Andrei's a slimy little turd. He's spent the whole of the last year doing his best to see I didn't have any contact with Otto, and of course he tried to put me off, but I told him I was coming anyway, and when I got to Vienna he was all smiles and couldn't do enough for me. He said there was no question of the Romanians giving me a visa and they'd have to smuggle me in."

"That sounds pretty romantic."

"Just what I thought, but it wasn't, it was just uncomfortable. We went in one of Otto's cars, a big Merc. There were four of us, the driver, Andrei, a grinning thug called Jagu, and me. When we got to a border, we just hoisted up the backseat cushion and I curled up in a special compartment underneath. It had an odd smell, mechanical, but not automobile mechanical. It took me a bit of time to place it, and then I remembered. Light oil and graphite. Know what that means, Sis?"

"No."

"Guns. . . . You don't look surprised."

"Not really. Were you?"

"No. Look, Sis—I've got something to explain. You remember those packages I asked you to look for in my bike after my accident, only they weren't there?"

Letta didn't hesitate. She looked him in the eyes and said, "They were there, actually. I gave them to Grandad. They were a bomb, weren't they?"

He stared at her. The knuckles of the hand which was holding his stick went white.

"I did it for Varina," she said.

"So did we all," he snapped. "God! If I'd known . . . So you lied to me twice, Sis?"

"I'm afraid so."

She waited, watching him think the thing through. He shook his head and shrugged.

"Leaves a nasty taste, doesn't it?" he said.

"Yes."

"Well, it's turned out all right, somehow. Maybe I shouldn't have asked you in the first place. Let's call it quits. Where were we? Yes, it was about that. These people, Andrei and the others, they've got a way of cornering you. They sort of nudge you into a position where you're doing things you're not at all sure you want to, only there doesn't seem any way out unless you're going to make things worse for something you really care about. That was what happened then. I didn't like it at all. And all the way while we were heading south in the Merc I began to feel more and more that the same sort of thing was happening again. There was something up between Andrei and Jagu, a joke they knew about and I didn't. And my foot was hurting—I'd had to do a lot more tramping around on my way out than it's used to, and Jagu kept offering to carry me, as if I were a baby. Not much fun.

"Anyway we finished up jolting along over what weren't much more than mule tracks to reach Otto's place without actually going through Potok. He's managed to install himself in the Prince-Bishop's summer palace. It's up in the hills, a couple of miles south of Potok. The Communist bosses had had it as a perk, so it's been looked after. In fact it's pretty luxurious. Otto was there, very friendly as always, and very sympathetic about my foot. He said he was planning a big rally in honor of Grandad the evening before the funeral, and he wanted me to speak about the old boy, as a representative of the family, and I'd got to keep under cover till then in case somebody spotted me and I got thrown out. I didn't like that at all. Two whole days. I've got friends in Potok I wanted to see. I wanted to know what was going on, what people really thought. I didn't get a chance to object because at that point he was called away and sent a message back saying he wouldn't be around till the evening.

"There must have been some sort of a crisis on, because everyone was scurrying about, only that grinning oaf Jagu stuck to me like a limpet until, mainly to get rid of him, I said I was tired and my foot was hurting and I was going to go and lie down. He said okay, and took me up to my room and told me to stay there, and then, do you know what the bastard did? He went out and locked the door! That was the final straw. I wouldn't have taken it from Otto, and I certainly wasn't going to from a jerk like Jagu.

"It was a pretty stupid thing to do anyway, because it wasn't that sort of lock. I mean, it was to keep people out, not in. It was just screwed to the inside of the door, and the bolt went into a bracket which was screwed on too. All I had to do was unscrew the bracket with my penknife. By that time the bustle had died down. I'd heard several cars leaving.

"I wasn't running away. There was no way I could have made it into Potok without transport. I just wanted to show myself, and them, that I wasn't going to be treated like that. I was thirsty, so I decided to find myself a drink and headed for the kitchens. There seemed to be no one around. I didn't like the smell of the tap water and I was looking for something else when a couple of maids appeared. They'd heard my stick on the stone floor, they said. Anyway, they knew who I was from seeing me at Otto's rallies when I'd been there before and they rushed over and started sobbing about Grandad, and what a fine man he'd been, and how much the country was going to miss him, and how frightened everyone was about what might happen without him."

"Really? In Otto Vasa's house? They were saying that?"

"They were just a couple of serving maids hired from the town. They weren't Otto's people. But yes, I was surprised too. One of them said she had two sisters in the western province, and she knew all about what was happening up in Croatia, and she was scared stiff that it might start happening where her sisters were if the Serbs were given the slightest excuse to start ethnic cleansing around there.

"Then they looked at each other and I could see they were frightened at what they'd been saying and they changed the subject and talked about last year's festival. One of them said I'd met her cousin then, and—you know how everyone in Potok is related to everyone else and they all seem to know each other?—it turned out the cousin was one of the people I wanted to see, so I asked her to give him my love and say I hoped to see him after the rally, but could he keep quiet about me being there till then.

"Then we heard a car come back. It was a false alarm, actually, but they were obviously scared of losing their jobs if they were found talking to me, and my foot had begun to act up again, so they found me some mineral water and I went back to my room and screwed the door shut and took a couple of codeine and lay down, and—you know, this is very odd, but almost for the first time since I'd got to Vienna I began to feel happy about what I was doing. I felt in control of my life again. I lay on my bed, thinking about the two girls, and how ordinary and real they had seemed, and how much more they mattered to me than creeps like Andrei and Jagu. And then I managed to have a nap.

"Well, not much else happened that day. Otto came back and about half a dozen of us had supper together and he was full of his big, vague ideas about Varina claiming its proper place in the world—he asked if I wanted to be UN representative, and it wasn't a joke. And he talked quite a bit about what a mistake it had been, giving in to the Bulgarians over the Listru festival, but of course my grandfather had been a sick man by then. In the old days, when he'd had real fire in his belly, etcetera, etcetera . . . And all the while I could feel the others watching me to see how I took it. Ah, well . . .

"Next morning, I'd asked to have breakfast in my room to rest my foot, and the girl who brought my tray up was one of the two I'd talked to the day before, the one with the cousin, remember? I could see she was pretty nervous. She put her finger to her lips and put the tray on the bed and just lifted the corner of the cloth and pointed, so I nodded to show I'd understood, and thanked her as if I'd never seen her before, and let her go. Want to guess what was under the cloth?"

"I don't know. A key? No, a message from your friends."

"Right. And . . . ?"

"Give up."

"Grandad's last letter."

"No! What did he say? Where is it?"

"Come to that in a moment. I'm telling you all this because the letter was for you."

"Oh! Give it to me! Now! Please!"

"I'm afraid I haven't got it. Not my fault. You'll see why. Let me go on. The message was from a chap called Riccu, not the girl's cousin, but *his* cousin, a teacher at the university, very bright, full of ideas, a really good guy. I hadn't known him that well, but I'd met him a few times last year, because he'd been very interested in what Otto was up to, very keen, but now he started off bluntly by saying he'd been working as Grandad's secretary for the last year. In fact he'd been with him when he died. Riccu was at his desk when he heard a thud from next door and he'd gone in and found Grandad on the floor. He was conscious, and he tried to say something, but then he closed his eyes and he was dead. The first thing Riccu did after he'd called for help was to take all the important papers off Grandad's desk, including the letter he was writing to you, and hide them, because he knew what was going to happen as soon as the news got out. And it did. A gang of Otto's people swept in and took over, and seized all the papers they could find and they were actually trying to get Grandad's body out of the house when some of Riccu's group showed up and there was pretty well a pitched battle and only then did the police start taking notice—Riccu says they are never around when Otto's people want to make trouble. They calmed things down and took the body off to the morgue. There was a bit more—obviously Riccu had been scrawling in a hurry, but the chief thing was that he begged me not to commit myself till I'd had the chance to talk to somebody who wasn't on Otto's side.

"I wasn't as shaken as you'd think. Ever since the accident I've been brooding about what happened last year, and how I got myself into the position I did, and more and more I'd come to think I was being *used*. And I'd hardly heard from them, as if they didn't give a damn once I was laid up with my foot and couldn't be any use to them. I wouldn't have gone to Otto now if I could have thought of any other way of getting in to Varina. What's more, I'd already done what Riccu wanted, talked to somebody who wasn't on Otto's side —those two girls in the kitchen."

"My friend Parvla says the same. She was thrilled when Grandad came back, and she started talking about him and Otto Vasa working together, and then she started to go off Vasa, and now she's frightened. She was praying for Grandad every night. I haven't heard from her since he died."

"Right. Well, then I read Grandad's letter to you. It started off saying he was going to have to wait for someone to carry it out of the country because he thought it likely that anything he mailed from Romania would get opened and read. And then he said some of what you'd expect, you know, thanking you for yours and saying he was a bit tired, and he was missing you, even more than he missed crumpets and marmalade. Then he said things had been going fairly well for him here and it shouldn't be long now before he could stop being so careful about just seeming to be a moderating influence and letting Otto carry on much as he wanted, because he'd at last got evidence that Otto was working hand in glove with the old Ceauşescu gang in Bucharest, and the main question now was how or when he could use it."

"Wow!"

"He didn't say a lot about that, actually. He went back to chat. He'd paid a visit to his father's farm, and he was hoping to get out to Lapiri for a funeral, Minna somebody . . ."

"Minna Vari."

"That's right."

"She was Momma's foster mother. You've got to tell her. That's important. What else?"

"Nothing. That was where he'd got to when he died."

Letta burst into tears. They rushed up into her head, filling her face and streaming down her cheeks. She turned to the window, seeing only a foggy rectangle of light, groped for the sill, and leaned there, sobbing. Vaguely she was aware of Van hobbling to her side and putting his arm around her, but he didn't try to say anything, just let her cry the fit out until she was able to master it, shake herself, drag her sleeve across her eyes, and say, trying to make a joke of it, "You better have a good reason why you haven't got my letter."

"I have, Sis," he murmured. "I think you'll understand. Tell me when you're ready."

"I'm all right. Go on."

He went back to the chair but waited while she found some tissues and mopped herself up.

"Well, then," he said, "I wrote a note for Riccu saying I was glad to hear from him and I wanted to talk to him and I'd be careful, but I didn't put it under the cloth, which was just as well, because Jagu showed up before my tray was taken away. He said Otto wanted to see me. Otto was all smiles. We got into one of his cars and he took me down to his office in Potok, and gave me the speech he wanted me to make at the rally. He said I'd better learn it by heart, so that I could make it look as if I were making it up as I went along.

"I said okay, but as I'd come all this way to represent the family I'd like to be able to put in something personal about Grandad, and what he'd meant to me and my brother and sister, and he said that was all right provided I kept it short. I said I would, and I'd finish that part by saying that of course Varina was Grandad's real family, and that would get me into the speech he'd given me. Then I asked him how Grandad had died, as if I didn't know, and he told me he'd been ill for a while, and hadn't been doing very much, and had passed away in his sleep, and it had all been very serene. 'A good death for a hero,' he said. He went all gruff, as if there were a lump in his throat. That was what finally made my mind up. About whether to trust him or Riccu, I mean."

"Didn't you want to strangle him?"

"Pretty well, but I managed not to let him see. In fact, in a funny sort of way, I'd begun to enjoy myself. He thought he was using me, the way he'd done from the start, but actually now I was using him. So I wrote a harmless little bit about us all going to meet Grandad at the airport when the Communists let him out, and then I settled down to learn that bloody speech. It was pure rant about Varina's inalienable rights, and how our enemies were still trying to take them from us, but the spirit of Restaur Vax and Lash the Golden, etcetera, etcetera. You know Otto likes people to think he's some kind of reincarnation of Lash?

"That took the rest of the day. We sat in the office, and then we drove around, and Otto got out and saw people while I sat in the car with the blinds drawn, learning my lines. Then we went back to the the summer palace and I ran through the speech with him. I really hammed it up, and he was pleased as Punch. I couldn't stand another supper with his gang of creeps, so I said my foot was hurting and I'd better go to bed. I slept in next morning too, and hung around getting more and more nervous most of the afternoon until a car arrived to take me to the rally.

"It was in the meadows below St. Valia, where the camp had been for the festival. They had a stage up, and a sound system, and they smuggled me in through the ruins with Jagu to keep an eye on me so that I kept out of sight till the time came for my big moment. Jagu was on top of the world. He said it was the biggest rally they'd had for months. There might be a few troublemakers around, but I'd know who were our people by their yellow sashes. They had a band, and marching, and then a pathetic woman talking about what the Serbs had done to the village where she'd been living in Croatia . . ."

"Was that true?"

"I should think so. There've been quite a few refugees from the north, I gathered later—I'll come to that. Anyway the chairman figure who was introducing the speakers cut her short and said that was the sort of thing Varina had got to expect if we didn't take our destiny into our own hands, and everyone cheered—at least it sounded like everyone from where I was, but it was probably pretty well orchestrated because at that point Otto strode on and whipped up the cheering like mad and stood there saluting and triumphant for several minutes—I could see him sort of haloed from behind—and then got them quiet and began to speak.

"He started off quietly, saying that the future of Varina was in the balance, but first they must honor the past, and the hero Restaur Vax, who had given his life for his country. He talked a bit about Grandad's doings in the war—rather good and honest-sounding—and then he said that the oppressors of Varina had attempted to deny the family of Restaur Vax their natural, God-given right to attend the funeral, but that he, Otto Vasa, had refused to accept that and had arranged for one member of the family to be there, whatever the oppressors might decree.

"Then Jagu gave me a push and I climbed up onto the platform and Otto came over and shook my hand and slapped

me on the back and led me up to the microphone. There was a
lot of cheering which went on quite a while, and I had time to
get used to the lights.

"It was a huge crowd, I don't know—twenty thousand? A
lot of them were wearing yellow sashes, especially at the front,
but quite a few weren't, and after a while I realized that at
least half of those weren't cheering either. I made signs to
them to quiet down, and in the end they did. Otto had gone
back to his seat but I could see him out of the corner of my
eye. As soon as they'd let me I started in on the part I'd
written for him about meeting Grandad at the airport. I saw
Otto relax and begin saying something to the fellow on his
right.

"You remember that part finished with me saying how
much Grandad had meant to the family? Well, instead of
going on about Varina being his real family I said I'd got
Grandad's last letter with me, to my sister, and I'd read it to
them to show what sort of a man he was. I saw Otto sit up
with a jerk, and frown, but I pretended not to notice. I
skipped the part about not trusting the Romanian mail and
started in on the marmalade and the crumpets, and he relaxed
and went on muttering to the chap next door to him. So I
don't think he was listening when I got to what Grandad said
about what was going on in Varina.

"That was when everything changed. It's difficult to explain. Everybody had gone very quiet. You'd have said it was
reasonably quiet before, between the cheering, but there were
coughs and murmurs and so on, the sort of background noise
you get with any big crowd, but the sound system meant the
speakers could be heard without yelling, so it had been quiet
enough. Now it was dead quiet. I could hear the river. Every

single person in the whole crowd was listening with all their attention to what I was saying.

"In fact Otto took a moment or two to catch on. I saw him jump up and make a signal and I grabbed the mike and carried on. I'd learned this part by heart because I'd known they'd never let me get away with it so it didn't matter when somebody snatched the letter out of my hand. There were several of them, trying to wrestle the mike away from me and somebody got an armlock around my throat but I got it all out, the whole part about Otto working with the old Ceaușescu gang, before some bastard stamped on my foot and I yelled and collapsed—God, it hurt!

"In fact I don't know what happened next but I must have managed to crawl to the front of the platform because people were trying to grab me from below and I was fighting them off, and then I heard them yelling that they were friends— there was a colossal racket going on and my foot was still screaming at me—and I let them help me down, and then I must have fainted.

"When I came to I was being jostled about but people seemed to be holding me up and trying to support me and there was this hullabaloo going on, so I couldn't hear what anyone was saying. I realized they were trying to push their way out through the crowd, but then someone pointed back over our shoulders and we swung around to look and there was Otto, up on the platform in the spotlights, absolutely purple with rage and yelling, though no one could hear him —he'd completely lost it—and all the while his hands were tearing something into smaller and smaller shreds and scattering them onto the stage. I don't think he realized what he was doing, but it must have been Grandad's letter. That's why I haven't got it. I'm sorry."

"It's all right. It was worth it. Go on."

"Oh, well, it was chaos, fights going on everywhere between the yellow sashes and the others, and yells and boos and whistles and catcalls, and the yellow sashes trying to get organized cheering going and being drowned out. The people I was with went struggling on till we were right at the edge of the crowd, and they made a space for me and took off my shoe and somebody fetched water from the river and they bathed my foot, which helped a bit—it was swelling up like a balloon —and by the time they'd done that things had quieted down a bit, and Otto had got control of himself, but he made the mistake of trying to carry on with his rally.

"It was a disaster, from his point of view. They never let him get a word out. The more he tried to rant and bully them into silence, the louder they catcalled. He'd got the microphone and the sound system, but they drowned him out. Then they started chanting Grandad's name. *Vax! Vax! Restaur Vax!* Over and over and over. They destroyed him. You know, they destroyed him with Grandad's name! What's the joke?"

"What you just said. I hope he was watching. Tell you later. Go on."

"We saw one extraordinary thing. You know there'd been fighting? There was a gang of yellow-sash thugs over to our left, and now we realized they were fighting among themselves. Some of them had taken their yellow sashes off and were trying to make the others do the same. And then all the lights went out and the sound system went off—it was pretty well dark by now—we decided afterward that Vasa's people must have done that as a way of getting him out of the jam he was in. There was still a lot of yelling and shoving and fighting, but the people I was with found a stretcher and carried me back into Potok, to one of their apartments, and went out to find doctor or a nurse who could do something about my foot.

"Next thing, Riccu turned up. He said the police were looking for me. His group had friends in the police, and there was a rumor going around about someone being arrested at the rally, a foreigner. Riccu thought they meant me. It would have been something Otto had laid on, to stir things up still further, arresting Restaur Vax's grandson on the eve of the funeral . . ."

"He sort of did that with Grandad, didn't he? Last year? Pretending he was being beaten up in prison when he was on his way back to England, really."

"I remember. In fact I asked him about that, and he just grinned and said it was politics. I'm afraid I thought it was okay at the time."

"What happened next?"

"Oh, a jolly old doctor showed up, who'd actually known Grandad before the war. He couldn't do much, but he gave me some aspirin, and then about a dozen of us sat around talking all night. I couldn't have gone to sleep anyway. My foot was throbbing like a jungle drum, but even so I was a lot happier than I'd felt for ages. Riccu said he'd known I'd got his message and Grandad's letter because the kitchen maid had told him, and he'd guessed I hadn't let on because she'd not got into trouble. They'd gone along to the rally, he and his friends who'd been helping Grandad, to heckle a bit and try and let people know that not everyone was wild about Otto, but there weren't a lot of them. Most of the non–yellow-sashes had been more or less neutral, ordinary Varinians, who'd gone along—I don't know—to try and find out what they thought, I suppose. You see, Otto hadn't just been keeping me under wraps to prevent me from being seen. As well as

that he didn't want me to find out that what Grandad had
said in his letter was true. He'd been immensely popular a
year ago. He could have done anything he liked with Varina
then, almost. But then things started getting worse and worse
in Croatia, and his own people threw their weight around
trying to frighten the opposition off the streets, and rumors
began to spread about Otto's friends in Bucharest, so people
stopped being so keen on him. They still desperately want a
free Varina, just as you and I do and Grandad did, but not
with Otto Vasa in charge. And not his way. Not his sort of
Varina. The rally was a last throw, an effort to whip up a great
frenzy of enthusiasm, and use that to hijack Grandad's funeral
and give himself a fresh start. But it didn't work. Grandad
fixed him, after all, despite being dead."

"You and Grandad."

"I suppose so."

He was sitting on Grandad's chair with his foot up on the
stool which Letta used to use for toasting crumpets. It was
obviously still hurting. He must have had a lot of pain from it
while he was away. His face was drawn, and lined. He looked
ten years older than he had before the accident, and for the
first time Letta could see that what Minna Alaya had said
about his being the spitting image of Grandad might be true.

"Is that all?" she said. "I'm sorry, I didn't mean that, but
what about the funeral, and how did you get away, and what's
happening now? Is it going to be all right?"

"God knows," he said. "Anything could happen. All you
can say is it's better than it might have been, because people
have seen through Otto, at least for the moment. But they're
still pretty discontented, not just about independence. Prices
keep shooting up, and there's a lot of racketeering and corrup-
tion, and deep distrust of the Romanian and Bulgarian gov-

ernments, and fear of the Serbs. . . . I think all you can say is we aren't going out of our way to pick quarrels with anyone, and that's what Otto was trying to set up. But if somebody chooses to pick a quarrel with us, well, I think we'll fight. It'll be pretty well hopeless if we have to do it on our own, but we'll do it. It's nothing like over yet, Sis.

"I went to the funeral. I couldn't risk trying to get into the cathedral, so I stood in the crowd in St. Joseph's Square. A lot of people recognized me. They kept coming up and shaking my hand. The service was relayed from the cathedral. There wasn't any trouble. It was very respectful. Moving, I suppose. A lot of people were crying, men as well as women. After the service they drove the hearse around the square, very slowly, while people crowded to touch it, and then they halted in front of the palace while the mayor made an oration from the balcony. It was supposed to have been Otto, but he'd cried off. The poor old mayor didn't make much of an oration, in fact he had trouble getting the words out, he was so choked.

"That took pretty well all morning, and then they drove out to Talosh to bury him in the family grave, and absolutely anybody who had a car or could hitch a lift drove out after them to watch. I went with nine other people in the old doctor's car. We couldn't get near the church because of the jam—the road's just one track—and I wasn't up to walking the last half-mile. It was very hot and still. The grapes were just getting ripe in the vineyards. There were hundreds—oh, I don't know, maybe thousands—of us out there among the scrub and the boulders in that sweltering sun watching those tiny figures down in the graveyard. Far too far off to hear anything. Grasshoppers and cicadas buzzing away. I don't believe anybody moved a muscle or said a word all the time they were by the grave.

"Then the bigwigs left and the men began filling in the earth and we all went down and filed past the grave in silence. My friends took turns carrying me, but they put me down at the entrance and I hobbled past on my own. We'd all picked up a handful of earth or a few pebbles on the hillside, and as we went past the grave we added it to the mound. I felt that everybody in all Varina was with us, moving quietly past and saying thank you."

"I wish I'd been there."

"You were, Sis. You were."

Neither of them spoke for a while. Letta was crying, but somehow not with grief. Van left her alone, not trying to help or comfort her till she was ready.

Downstairs the front door slammed. A moment later Momma's voice called up, "Van! Van! Is he back? Where are you?"

"Left my knapsack in the hall," he said. "I'll be back."

"I want to know how you got out. And everything else."

"Okay. I'll be back."

He eased himself onto his feet and limped to the door, but turned with his hand on the handle.

"Must be teatime," he said. "Let's have a memorial banquet. Got any crumpets?"

Next morning, because it was first day of the term, Letta left early. The postman was coming up the steps as she opened the front door.

"One for you," he said. "Fancy stamp, too."

It was from Parvla. Letta opened it as she walked up the hill. Several sheets of the slanting, dutifully looped handwriting. (Parvla thought Letta's neat italic very odd and tricky to read.) A photograph, a bit out of focus, gaudy colors, flowers, brown patches, a white cross with writing on it, nothing making sense. Of course not, she'd got it upside down.

She turned it and it became a mound, a grave, dug out of sun-parched soil among yellow tussocks of grass which she could hardly see because all the space around was covered with wreaths and sheaves of gladioli, carnations, and gaudy daisy-shaped things. The photograph must have been taken the day after Van had been there because the flowers were already shriveling from the heat. The cross was not on the mound but a bit to one side. It didn't look official, and Van hadn't mentioned it. Somebody had nailed two bits of wood together, driven the upright into the ground, and written three words on the crosspiece, one middling, one short, and one long. Because the focus was slightly blurred Letta wouldn't have been able to read them if she hadn't known what they must be.

Restaur Vax. Anastrondaitu.

Why that? What did it mean? Somebody wishing Grandad had been forgotten? Surely not, unless . . . yes, perhaps, for his sake at least, that he'd been left in peace, to die in peace, far away in Winchester. That's how Momma would have read it, anyway.

Or perhaps it wasn't about Grandad at all, but about his name, and the other Restaur Vax, and everything that went with them, the whole marvelous, bitter, deceitful past. That? Only last night there'd been a program about Croatia, smashed towns, refugees, lives that had lost their meanings, all because of things that had been said and done long, long ago. And not just Croatia. All around the world the same. If only this, or that, or that, had not been remembered!

Did she think so too, Letta, in safe England, walking up the hill to start a new term at the same old school? No past at all? No memories? No Field, no Formal, no dancing the *sundilla*? No Legends, no "Stream at Urya," no songs about boastful shepherds, no *dumbris,* not even the word itself on Grandad's grave?

No. Somehow it still had to be worth it. You can't have everybody the same. That was what Ceaușescu had wanted, wasn't it? So somehow it had to be worth it.

But *anastrondaitu.*

It pierced her to the heart.

CHRONOLOGY OF VARINA

500–700 A.D.	(?) Veterans of Varingian Guard settle on Danube, near Iron Gates.
893	Valia, daughter of Khan Kalasko, converts to Christianity rather than marry a heathen, then suffers martyrdom for her choice. Appears in a waking vision to her father, who in remorse orders all Varinians to convert.
1054	Great Schism between Catholic and Orthodox Churches. Separate Church of Varina proclaimed.
1408	Battle of Tarnaki. Death of Count Axur. Conquest of Varina by Turks. Varina divided into three provinces and eight pashaliks.

1620–1750	Phanariote oppression. Abolition of Old Varinian language.
1738–1777	Selim rules as Pasha of Virnu.
1766	Birth of Stephan Pango, later Archbishop Supreme of Varina.
1785	Birth of Alexo Lash (Lash the Golden).
1792	Birth of Restaur Vax.
1818	Bishop Pango enthroned as Bishop Supreme.
1819	Riqui Incident. Start of War of Independence.
1822	Destruction of Monastery of St. Valia. Exile of Bishop Pango.
1823/24	Winter Campaign of Restaur Vax in western province.
May 1, 1824	Independent Republic of Varina established. Restaur Vax declared President.
June 15, 1824	Restaur Vax marries Mariu Kori.
September 1824	Turkish armies invade Varina.
September 1825	Turkish armies besiege Potok.
March 1, 1826	Battle of Tresti. Death of Alexo Lash. Republic of Varina reestablished.
October 1828	Milan conference. Central Powers guarantee independence of Prince-bishopric of Varina under Turkish hegemony. Exile of Restaur Vax.
1850	Death of Prince-Bishop Pango.

1852	Massacre of Jews in St. Joseph's Square.
1865	Death of Restaur Vax in Rome.
1868	Suzerainty of Varina transferred to Austria. Body of Restaur Vax brought to Talosh for burial.
1912	"Balkan Wars" against Turks. Secret agreement between Serbia, Bulgaria, and Romania for future division of Varina.
1914–18	World War I.
1918	Allies agree to division of Varina as inducement to bring Romania into war on Allied side.
1919	Hague Conference. Varina divided. Minor uprisings suppressed by new ruling powers.
1939	Outbreak of World War II.
1941	Germans invade Yugoslavia, including western province of Varina. Varinian Resistance formed under leadership of Restaur Vax II. Northern and southern provinces join Resistance. German garrisons installed in Potok and Listru.
1945	Germans leave. Independent Republic of Varina declared. Restaur Vax II elected Prime Minister. Leads delegation to plead Varinian cause with Allies. Arrested by Russians and sent to Siberia. Remainder of delegation executed. Varina redivided between

Romania, Yugoslavia, and Bulgaria, all
under Communist rule.

1963   Restaur Vax II transferred as prisoner,
to Bulgaria.

1976   Restaur Vax II released and goes into
exile in Britain.

Family of Restaur Vax II

1908   RV born.

1935   Marries Parvla Kanors.

1937   Daughter, Minna, born.

1945   Parvla Vax arrested. Never seen again.

1953   Minna Vax marries Petru Ozolins.

1955   Grandson, Stephan Ozolins, born.

1957   Grandson, Van Ozolins, born.

1960   Ozolins family goes into exile in Britain.

1975   Stephan Ozolins marries Margaret (Mollie) Smith-
Bingham.

1976   Great-grandson, Nigel Ozolins, and granddaughter,
Letta Ozolins, born.

1987   Great-granddaughter, Donna Ozolins, born.

PETER DICKINSON

is the author of many books for both adults and young readers and has won numerous awards, including the Carnegie Medal (twice), the *Guardian* Award, and the Whitbread Award (also twice). His novel *Eva* was a *Boston Globe–Horn Book* Fiction Honor Book. *Eva* was also selected as an American Library Association Best Book for Young Adults, as were his novels *AK* and *A Bone from a Dry Sea.* Born in Zambia and educated at Eton and King's College, Cambridge, he has four children and lives in Hampshire with his second wife.